OVERLOAD

Other Books by E. R. Paskey

The Guardians:
Bad Faith
Portal Woes
Treason's Edge
Freedom's Children

Ink Realm Duology
Lady Ink

Finder Series
Head Case
Magna
Old Wounds

Stand-Alone Novels
The Other Side of the Horizon
Galaxy's Way
In Plain Sight

E.R. PASKEY

OVERLOAD

FINDER SERIES BOOK 4

For my husband, Timethy.

CHAPTER 1

Every table in the noodle shop was full. Finder Vince Grable didn't think they ever had a slow day here.

A buzz of conversation filled the eatery, broken only by the occasional burst of laughter. Soft, unobtrusive music played in the background. Wait staff in black trousers, white shirts, and black vests darted here and there through the dim circles of golden light cast by round golden lamps that hung above every booth and table. Most carried trays laden with plates and bowls of delicious food.

Vince leaned back against the slick royal purple material that covered the seats in every booth, though on his seat it was wearing thin in a few places, and inhaled deeply. The familiar tangy smells of garlic, peppers and soy sauce met him, with a mouthwatering undertone of cooking meat—real and plant-based. His stomach gave an appreciative rumble.

As far as he was concerned, Pho's Noodle Shop on Level 5 in Zone 4 was one of the best places to eat on Zyga Space Station. He wished Mr. Pho, the owner, could expand and open a restaurant in

Zone 5 so he could eat there more often. As it was, he could only occasionally make the trek to Zone 4.

Reaching for his glass of ice water, Vince took a measured sip and swallowed. The cold liquid burned a trail down to his stomach while he looked around the noodle shop. It had been a month or two since he'd last been able to get away and come here for dinner. First because business had been non-existent and he'd not been able to afford it, and then because business had picked up and he was so busy he almost couldn't keep up with his new caseload.

Nothing much had changed in his absence. Pho's Noodle Shop was as comfortingly the same as it ever had been, catering to the inhabitants of Zone 4 as well as the spacers and tourists who flooded in and out of Zone 4's many docking bays.

Even in the dim lighting, as Vince glanced around, he guessed that approximately half of the patrons were either spacers or tourists. The tourists were usually easy to spot; they tended to dress differently than your average Zyga Station inhabitant. As far out of the way as the Cartha system was, news of fashion trends usually arrived faster than the actual ability to imitate them.

The spacers, too, were relatively easy to pick out. Some of that was also their attire—boots and special thermal clothing that helped keep them warm—but it was more an attitude. There was just something about them that screamed that they'd spent serious time traveling through the cold, lonely vacuum of space.

And then there were the gamers.

Vince spotted a few of them amid the tourists and spacers, but most of the gamers were citizens of Zyga Station. They were ensconced in the corners of their booths, eating mechanically while immersed in worlds that took them far, far away from their present surroundings. Some were bent over handheld devices, while others wore special headsets with sleek visors and earpieces.

As far as Vince knew, immersive gaming was a thing across the galaxy, but it seemed more prevalent on Zyga Station. Maybe it was the fact that the space station had been built alongside a massive mining operation and young people didn't have much hope here of improving their lives. Vince wasn't sure.

What he *did* know was that the bulk of his business came from locating gamers who'd lost themselves to reality, dropped off the grid and vanished. Sometimes family members were the ones who hired him, and sometimes people the gamers had robbed in their quest to continue their addiction.

His stomach rumbled again, making him glance hopefully in the direction of the kitchen. He was so ready to eat dinner.

There *were* perks to the massive pickup in his business. He'd gotten a new assistant out of it. Bella Escovedo, as her shiny new identcard proclaimed her, was currently manning the office in case any prospective clients dropped by in-person.

Vince would have brought her along to have dinner as well—he considered it one of his life's goals to introduce people to Pho's Noodle Shop whenever possible—but Bella didn't need to eat any-more. She only tasted things.

One of the downsides to being a human consciousness stuck inside an android body.

Vince cast a glance down at his comlink, which lay on the shiny black lacquered tabletop at his elbow, but it was silent and still. Bella hadn't texted him for any reason—and neither had any-one else. He breathed a sigh of relief and settled back comfortably into the stiff purple cushion of his booth. It was after regular busi-ness hours, and nobody needed him for anything.

Looked like he'd get to enjoy his dinner in peace after all.

Catching movement out of the corner of his eye, Vince glanced sideways in time to see a solemn-faced young man in the noodle shop's black and white uniform expertly come to a halt beside his table with a tray balanced on one hand.

"Pho's Beef Special and dumplings?" he asked in a low, deep voice.

"That would be me." Vince's stomach rumbled again as the familiar, delicious smell of his favorite dish met his nose. His mouth started watering in anticipation.

Most of the meat available on the Station was plant-based, but you could get real meat from animals—provided you could pay for it. This particular meal was a special treat because it contained real beef.

The waiter unloaded the tray, placing a gleaming white plate filled with steaming noodles, thin strips of marinated beef, and colorful vegetables covered in tangy sauce in front of Vince. He then placed two smaller ancillary dishes around the main plate. One held more sauce, while the other held a mound of steamed dumplings.

"Thanks." Vince looked up with a smile, already reaching for his chopsticks.

"Enjoy." With a curt nod, the young man tucked his tray under his arm and vanished into the dim alley between Vince's table and the next, which held a young couple who only had eyes for each other.

Closing his eyes and bowing his head in a brief prayer, Vince then dug into his meal. His first bite was heaven. The beef—it had been months since he'd last eaten any—almost melted in his mouth. Combined with Pho's signature sauce, it tasted *exactly* the way he'd been dreaming of for weeks.

He spared a thought for Bella as he took another bite. It really was a shame she couldn't enjoy this too. Though she assured him she was fine with tasting things and had no real desire to eat, he could see the look in her eyes every once in a while. She missed eating.

Even if she didn't need to anymore.

Vince was reaching for a dumpling when someone abruptly slid into the other side of the booth across the table from him. He froze with the dumpling in his chopsticks, looking across the table with surprise.

His waiter had joined him. The tall, solemn young man folded his hands on the table and fixed Vince with a dark-eyed stare. "You are Vince Grable, the Finder, right?"

"I am."

"Thought so." The young man's fingers tightened, his dark brown skin lightening around the knuckles with the strain. "I'd like to hire you to find my little brother." He paused. "And when you find him, I'm going to kill him for what he's done to us."

CHAPTER 2

HALF A DOZEN THOUGHTS RACED THROUGH VINCE'S mind. Chief among them was a mournful thought that at this rate, his expensive dinner was going to be stone cold before he got to enjoy it. Silently, he set the dumpling down on his plate and studied the man sitting across the table from him.

He pegged the waiter to be in his early twenties, with a slim build and a look in his dark brown eyes that said he'd seen far too much of the darker side of Zyga Station than he should have at his age. He had a round face, a shock of curly black hair, and his dark brown skin was a few shades lighter than Vince's own. The way he'd handled the tray told Vince that he'd probably worked here for a while, though the Finder wasn't sure he ever remembered seeing him before.

The young man also looked dead serious.

Vince lifted an eyebrow in polite surprise. "You want to kill your brother?"

The waiter nodded.

"You *do* realize that's against the law, don't you?"

"I don't care." The young man's hands clenched even tighter. "You don't know what he's done."

After the many years he'd spent working on Zyga Station, Vince could imagine, but he tactfully refrained from commenting. Instead, he shook his head slightly. "I don't find people so that my clients can kill them."

Put them in jail, perhaps, or send them to treatment facilities, but not arrange things so they'd end up dead.

At least as far as he knew.

A look of frustration crossed the waiter's face; his mouth pursed and his eyes flashed. "I don't—I'm not—" He huffed out a breath, pent-up anger suddenly gleaming through the cracks in his solemn facade like a glimpse into a vat of molten metal at a refinery.

Vince recognized that anger. It was the anger of someone who'd had all they could take from someone they loved and didn't know where else to turn. He drew in a breath, let it out slowly, and made his decision.

"You mind if I eat?" He nodded down to his plate, which was still steaming faintly. "While it's hot?"

The waiter blinked at him, his thoughts temporarily derailed. "No. I—uh—" He shook his head, shifting uneasily in his seat. "I'm on break."

Vince nodded and deliberately relaxed back into his seat, trying to put the younger man at ease. He picked up his dumpling again. "Why don't you tell me what happened?"

His waiter eyed him, and then he inclined his head in a sharp nod. "My name is Corwin Antwerp. I'm training to become an electrical engineer, but I've worked part-time here—" he waved a hand to indicate the noodle shop, "—for three years to help my momma pay bills and keep our apartment."

The dumpling tasted just as good as he'd anticipated. Vince chewed happily, even as he listened to Corwin's story.

"It's been me, Momma, and my brother Dent ever since Dad died." Corwin shook his head. "He worked for the Corps, got killed in some freak accident. I was seven."

That, too, was not an uncommon tale on Zyga Space Station. Zyga Mining Corporation—the Corps—as everyone called it, was the largest employer in the Cartha system.

"Anyway," Corwin shrugged, as if to dismiss the memories, "it's just been us three since then. Dent's two years older than me, with what Momma's always called a boatload of potential." A shade of bitterness colored his otherwise flat tone.

Swallowing a bite of noodles and vegetables, Vince reached for his water again. "I'm guessing you don't think he's used any of this potential?"

"It's not just me." Corwin's dark eyes flashed. "Ask anybody—they'll all tell you that Dent's never amounted to anything. He wanted to, when we were kids, but in high school he'd rather play games than do his work." He slashed an impatient hand through the air. "*That* isn't the problem—every kid would rather play games than study. The problem is that he never grew out of it."

Vince used his chopsticks to take another dumpling and dip it into the sauce. "What did your momma want him to do? Work for the Corps?"

"Heck, no. She didn't want him anywhere near the Corps. He's good with machines—she wanted him to get a job with the shipyard. Good money, if you know what you're doing."

That wasn't surprising either. Vince swallowed the last of his dumpling and nodded to Corwin. "Who are you training with?"

"Roda Enterprise." Corwin jerked his head in the general direction of the docking bays five levels below them. "I want to help keep the docks running."

Roda Enterprise. Vince didn't let a flicker of anything show on his face; he had far too many years of experience. But he did wonder...

"That's how I heard about you, in case you're curious." Corwin lifted one corner of his mouth in a grim smile that went nowhere near his eyes. "The business with little Gemma Roda's kidnapping and all a while back. I'm good with faces." He jerked his chin toward Vince. "Remembered yours."

"That would make sense." Vince stabbed a slice of carrot with the tip of one of his chopsticks, a little tension stealing into his large frame.

The second-largest employer on Zyga Station, Roda Enterprises belonged to Terrell and Jewel Roda. A few weeks earlier, their only child, a five year-old little girl named Gemma, had been kidnapped and Jewel had hired Vince to find her. Vince had succeeded, but in the process he'd also found evidence that linked Terrell Roda to an old freighter and her crew that had vanished a decade earlier after stumbling across one of the largest unknown asteroid clusters in the Cartha system. Roda Enterprises had then claimed that asteroid cluster.

The court case was still in preliminary stages; it would no doubt last for months. Roda Enterprises was still functioning as usual, but their stock had taken a severe hit. A ripple of uncertainty and anxiety had swept out across Zyga Station. If the CEO was found guilty of murder and the entire asteroid cluster Terrell Roda had built his company—and his fortune—on turned out to rightfully belong to the *Juggernaut*'s crew, where did that leave all of Roda Enterprise's employees?

It was an intended—and unforeseen—consequence to Vince's side quest for justice.

"Anyway," Corwin waved his hand again, sweeping Roda Enterprises out of the way, "the past few years, my brother's just gotten deeper into trouble. If it was just the fact that he couldn't stay off his game for ten minutes straight, it'd be one thing, but..." His mouth tightened. "He started gambling too."

A wave of sympathy coursed through Vince, stealing some of his enjoyment of the bite of beef he'd just taken. "It happens," he said after he swallowed. "More often than people like to admit."

What followed was the usual list of complaints. Having used up all of his own money and then some, Dent had charmed more money out of their mother. When she finally put her foot down, he resorted to creative ways of stealing it instead.

But the final straw? The final straw was the loan he'd taken out against their tiny apartment—a loan he'd forged in their mother's name and that had interest payments nearly as high as their actual monthly rent.

Corwin and his mother had only found out about it the same day the first interest payment was due—coincidentally the day Dent packed up his belongings and vanished.

"He's never gonna change," Corwin said dully. His hands, still resting on the table, were clenched into fists again. "He's never gonna to do anything to pay all that money back. And as long as he's alive, he'll keep finding ways to screw us over."

"So that's why you want to kill him?" Vince leaned back against his seat again. "So he can't take anything else from you?"

"He's killing Momma," Corwin said softly, but with a hard, implacable core of steel in his voice. "I can't stand by and watch that." He shook his head. "Not if I can do something about it."

Vince nodded thoughtfully. His gaze traveled past Corwin and the circle of soft light that enveloped their table to scan the rest of the noodle shop. Some of it was habit; even if he wasn't consciously looking for anything, his subconscious tracked everything.

After a few seconds, he looked back at Corwin. "It won't work, you know."

"What?" Corwin's forehead scrunched in confusion. "Finding him?"

"You killing him."

Vince had already anticipated the stubborn, mulish way Corwin set his jaw. Through gritted teeth, the younger man ground out, "Why not?"

"Because even if you got away with it—which you might," the Finder added, raising a hand, "although the odds are heavily against you— you'd have to live with that the rest of your life." He paused, then said gently, "You'd have to either tell your momma what you'd done, or else damn her to spend the rest of her life mourning one of her children and wondering what really happened to him."

The Finder looked the younger man dead in the eye. "Are you prepared to live with either of those choices?"

CHAPTER 3

For a long moment, Corwin stared back at him, silent and unmoving. His eyes, however… In his dark eyes, Vince saw the battle raging within. Whatever Dent's sins, Corwin loved his brother. He also loved their mother.

All at once, something broke inside Corwin. The stiffness in his shoulders collapsed as he slumped forward and put his hands on his head. His elbows thumped on the table's black lacquered surface. In that moment, he looked like what he was—a scared, grieved young man who'd been carrying the weight of the galaxy around on his shoulders for far too long.

"What do I do?" His voice emerged from his throat in a choked whisper. "He can't—I can't—"

Vince pushed his half-finished plate aside and leaned forward to rest a fatherly hand on his shoulder. "Corwin, you're a good son. And a good brother." He paused to let that sink in. "I know how hurt and angry you are. I see it all the time."

He paused again, a wry smile tilting the corner of his mouth. "And believe it or not, you're not the first prospective client who's wanted me to find someone so they could take them out."

A weak chuckle escaped Corwin. He raised his head, and Vince saw that his dark eyes were wet with unshed tears. "I don't know what to do, Finder." He sat up, clearly trying to pull himself back together. "Are you saying you won't help me? You won't find him?"

"No." Vince shook his head. "That's not what I'm saying at all." He waited until the young man looked at him again. "What I'm saying is that there's another way." He allowed himself another wry smile. "A way that won't end up with him dead, you in prison for murder, and your momma losing both her sons."

A spark of hope flared to life in Corwin's eyes, though he immediately buried it, as though afraid to let it show lest he be disappointed. "Like what?"

"Like—"

"Corwin," said a stern voice.

Vince and Corwin both glanced to the side, where a short, slight figure had materialized just outside the circle of soft, golden light cast by the lamp hanging over the table. The man moved a little closer, revealing himself to be none other than Mr. Pho himself, the restaurant's owner.

He gave Corwin a sharp look before fixing his black, steely gaze on Vince. "Is everything all right here, Finder?" He gestured to Corwin. "He's not bothering you, is he?"

So Mr. Pho knew who he was as well, beyond the casual recognition of an occasional customer. Vince filed that tidbit of information away for future reference, even as he shook his head. "Not at all. Mr. Antwerp here said he was on break and we were just having a conversation."

"I see." Mr. Pho's gaze traveled back to Corwin and lingered, as though he had the vague notion that something was going on and he wasn't quite sure whether Vince was covering for his employee or not.

Corwin glanced at his wrist before looking up at his boss. "Two minutes, Mr. Pho, and I'll be back at work."

Mr. Pho seemed to make his mind up all at once. Nodding once to Corwin, he then addressed Vince. "Please enjoy."

"I am, thank you." Vince motioned to his plate. "I always enjoy my meals here."

Mr. Pho bowed slightly and then vanished into the dim shadows between tables.

"I've gotta get back to work." Disappointment clung to Corwin's voice. He shook his head slightly. "Don't know why the old man got antsy. Been one of his best workers for three years." He slid out of the booth, looking unhappy.

Vince understood. They hadn't gotten to finish their conversation. He picked up his comlink, held it up for the young man to see. "I'll give you my comm frequency. Call me this evening and tell me the rest of your story. I meant it when I said there's another way. Or you're welcome to come by the office if you want." He shrugged. "Just thought I'd save you the trip."

Corwin produced his comlink from his pocket and they exchanged comm frequencies. "I'll call you." The young man glanced over his shoulder, as though checking on Mr. Pho's whereabouts. "I get off at nine."

"That'll be fine." Vince motioned to his table. "When you get a chance, I'd like a pot of tea, please."

"Sure thing."

Snapping back into work mode, Corwin strode away from the table into the restaurant's interior, leaving Vince to consume the rest of his meal in peace. A few minutes later, the young man returned with a tray bearing a teapot, tea cup, and an assortment of sweeteners, which he placed in the center of the table before vanishing again.

Vince poured himself a cup of green tea and then polished off the rest of his dinner in thoughtful silence, letting the gentle ambient music and the buzz of dozens of different conversations eddy around him. He did want to hear the rest of Corwin's story, though he knew he could probably fill in the missing blanks himself.

As he'd told the young man, this wasn't the first time he'd heard a story like this. It happened all the time on Zyga Station. All the time. Way more often than the media ever bothered to report.

People tried to escape their drab, dismal lives…and wound up trapped in addictions that dragged them to even lower depths than they'd been when they started. Ruined lives and shattered families abounded.

Vince had seen that same pain and grief in Corwin reflected in dozens of clients over the years. And, just like his other clients, he didn't want to see Corwin make a mistake that would haunt him the rest of his life—in more ways than one.

Idly, he wondered exactly who Dent owed. That would have an impact on how he, Vince, handled this particular case.

A faint flicker of amusement curled through him. *Look at you,* he thought. *Not even officially on the case and you're already thinking about the best angle of approach.*

Shaking his head at himself, Vince used his last dumpling to soak up the last delightful bit of sauce on his plate. He chewed slowly, savoring the dumpling, and then reached for his tea. When his cup was empty, he tapped the narrow blue rectangle in the center of the table. It was glowing slightly, but brightened at his touch.

A holographic checkout panel sprang to life above his empty dishes, showing him the balance owed for his meal. Vince pulled a credit chip from his wallet, which he kept inside the breast pocket of his favorite brown leather jacket, and inserted it into the holograph. He paid, adding a tip for Corwin, and then rose from the table.

As he wound his way through the restaurant, which was still as full as it had been when he'd first arrived, the Finder reflected that it was still early enough that he had time to drop by the Docking Bay and visit a friend who worked there. He had plenty of time to get back to his office before Corwin's shift ended.

He wasn't expecting to be waylaid just before he reached the noodle shop's exit.

CHAPTER 4

"FINDER!"

Vince turned at the sound of his name, spoken in a sharp whisper. Surprise flashed through him at the sight of Mr. Pho's short, slight figure. The noodle shop's owner stood near the front exit, as though he'd caught sight of Vince coming and had been waiting for him. His back was straight and his face expressionless, but his steely black eyes were alight with worry.

"Mr. Pho." Vince inclined his head in a nod. "What can I do for you?"

"I need to speak with you a moment." Pho glanced to the left and the right before beckoning Vince to follow him. He strode right out through the door into the boulevard corridor beyond.

Bemused, Vince followed.

This early in the night-cycle, the broad corridor that ran through this Level of Zone 4 was filled with a steady stream of pedestrian traffic and silver transport pods. The hum of dozens of different conversations in multiple languages provided a steady backdrop of sound, and underneath this lay the faint, ever-present comforting hum of Zyga Space Station itself. The glowpanels in the overhead far above had dimmed slightly, signaling that evening had begun, which made the flashing neon colors of the signs belonging to the shops and eateries scattered up and down this portion of the corridor stand out even more.

Mr. Pho did not stop until he was a good three meters away from the entrance to his noodle shop, near a little recess that separated his eatery from the entrance to a stretch of offices that formed the next section of this side of the corridor.

Drawing himself up to his full height, which was a good foot and a half shorter than Vince's own, he turned to face Vince. "I know what Corwin wants to hire you to do." He shook his head earnestly. "You can't do it, Finder. You mustn't do it." He waved a sharp hand through the air. "That boy has been through a lot, but he's not a killer. He's emotional, and he hasn't thought through the consequences. This—"

"I agree."

"—will absolutely devastate his mother and destroy his life and—" Mr. Pho stopped suddenly, realizing too late that Vince had spoken. He blinked at the Finder. "What?"

"I said I agree." It was Vince's turn to shake his head. "He's not a killer. Besides," he gave Mr. Pho a wry look, the kind of look that said the noodle shop owner should know better, "I don't find people just so they can be murdered."

Mr. Pho had the grace to look abashed. He stared up at Vince, wringing his hands together. "I just don't want to see Corwin throw his life away on his—" he pronounced several words in his own language, "—brother. He has too much potential."

"And he's one of the best workers you have," Vince added with a small smile.

"Exactly." Mr. Pho didn't even blink. "I'll hate to lose him someday when he graduates his training, but I want him to do well. He's got potential."

"Mr. Antwerp and I had not quite finished our conversation when you arrived," Vince said mildly, "but I was about to tell him that I believe he has another option. A *legal* option," he added, when the concerned, borderline alarmed expression on Mr. Pho's face did not alter.

The noodle shop owner seized on that word, however, with all the fervor and relief of a man in an environmental suit catching a rescue line when he was on the verge of drifting out into wild space and being lost forever. "Legal." He took a deep breath, his dark eyes shining. "You're sure?"

Vince nodded, his gaze flicking sideways as a group of teenage boys passed a little too close for comfort, one of them bumping him in the process. He caught the hand that attempted to delve into his pocket, his strong fingers closing around the boy's wrist.

"That's a bad habit," he said softly, raising an eyebrow at the teenager, a lean boy of fifteen or sixteen, with light brown skin, messy dark hair, and a smirk that had morphed into an alarmed grimace. "The kind of habit that could get you into a lot of trouble down the line."

The boy's eyes flicked in the direction of his gang of friends, but they were already several meters away. They hadn't realized yet that he'd gotten caught. "S-sorry," he stammered. "Won't happen again."

Vince doubted that, but he nodded once and released the teenager's wrist. In a flash, the boy melted back into the flow of traffic streaming up and down the corridor.

The Finder then turned back to Mr. Pho. As though the interruption had never occurred, he said, "I'm sure. Although I can't make any promises regarding what happens to his brother—depends on just what kind of trouble he's gotten himself into."

The noodle shop owner flicked his fingers through the air, as if to say he'd expected that. "Good." He took a breath, let it out in one quick huff. "Good. You've relieved my mind, Finder."

He looked up at Vince, his expression almost-but-not-quite apologetic. "Thought I knew your standards, but…you know how it is." He raised and lowered his shoulders in a quick shrug.

"I understand."

With a sharp nod, Mr. Pho started to move past Vince, intending to head back into his restaurant.

"Wait," Vince said suddenly.

The shorter man stopped and shifted to face him again. His expression had returned to its usual impenetrable calm.

"What can you tell me about Corwin Antwerp's family?"

Mr. Pho blinked once, twice, and then shook his head. "Not much. He's worked for me for three years. In that time, I have met his mother once or twice when she came here for dinner. She is a lovely lady. His brother has come in a couple of times—usually to beg for money. The last time he was here, he made enough of a scene that I told Corwin I would call Station Authority if he ever darkened my door again. Other than that?" He raised one shoulder in a shrug. "I know nothing."

"Thank you." It wasn't particularly helpful; Vince had the distinct sense that the noodle shop owner could have elaborated a bit further. Still, it at least confirmed the basic details of Corwin's story. He nodded to Mr. Pho. "Dinner was delicious, as always."

A hint of a genuine smile broke across the other man's smooth face. "I am glad to hear it." He offered Vince a short bow. "Please come back."

"Oh, I will."

They parted ways, Mr. Pho hurrying back to tend to his restaurant, and Vince turning his steps in the direction of the main elevator bank a number of blocks away. He chose to walk instead of hailing a transport pod. His half-formed notion of visiting his friend at the Docking Bay could wait for now; he needed to get back to the office and do a little research before he heard from his would-be client.

In his experience, it was always good to know as much about a client as you could in case there were any…surprises.

Not that Vince expected strange things from Corwin Antwerp. It was just a habit that had saved his skin a few times—and he was partial to his skin.

CHAPTER 5

Seen from space, Zyga Space Station resembled a giant wheel floating against the backdrop of the star-studded vacuum on one side, and the gas giant Cartha on the other. A glassy Rim formed the Station's outermost ring. It connected to five spoke-like Zones, which housed living quarters, the Station's small manufacturing base, an Agricultural Department responsible for growing most of the Station's food, and ports for the never-ending flow of space traffic.

A giant orb known as the Core formed the heart of the space station. It housed the Station's engine, life-support systems, and other important machinery, as well as more living quarters. Fifty meters out from the point at which Zone met the Core, a smaller ring called the Hub formed a second connection between the Zones.

The Hub was Vince's current destination. From there, he would travel back to Zone 5, where his office and the tiny apartment he called home were located.

At this time of the evening, there was a short queue of people waiting in front of the massive synthglass elevator bank that stood in the center of Zone 4, providing access to every Level. Each Zone had its own elevator bank, and there were elevator banks in the Core as well. In the Core, elevator transport from Level to Level was free, but out in the Zones, it had to be paid for.

As Vince swiped a credit chip and pushed through the turnstile to join the queue of people waiting for an elevator cab, he reflected that someday someone ought to investigate what Zyga Transport Authority was doing with all the money they made. There was no way it was all going back into the Station's infrastructure.

Though the bulk of the Core was by far the worst-maintained part of Zyga Station, there were signs of disrepair in the lower levels of each Zone. Small things, like patches of rust on bulkheads, or the occasional elevator cab that had a little hitch in what should have been a velvety smooth ride.

They were the kind of things you got used to seeing on a daily basis and didn't think much of—until you went someplace like the Rim or the upper levels of a Zone. Then the stark difference stood out in all its shiny, gleaming glory.

Again, Vince thought to himself, *that's human nature. The people at the top get the best of everything, while everybody else gets to content themselves with the leftovers.*

When the elevator cab disgorged him and a handful of other Station residents on Level 22, Vince marched down to the Hub and hurried along the walkway to the entrance to Zone 5 with quick, distracted steps. On his trip to the noodle shop, he had taken a moment to appreciate the spectacular view of space from the synthglass viewports that ran along both sides of the Hub's bulkheads, as well as the colorful red, blue, gold, and green mosaic patterns that formed the walkways.

Now, however, his thoughts were turned inward, contemplating Corwin Antwerp and his family.

Eventually, Vince reached Zone 5's elevator bank and rode it up to Level 7. He then hailed a transport pod and rode it back to his office. He could have walked—perhaps should have walked, after that scrumptious dinner he'd just consumed—but he was anxious to get back to the office and do a little digging before Corwin called him. (Or showed up in person. That was a distinct possibility, especially given how serious the young man seemed about hiring Vince.)

Transport pods were sometimes hit and miss when it came to general cleanliness. Zyga Transport had standards, but those standards didn't always account for patrons with overactive body odor or too much perfume or cologne. When Vince climbed inside his silvery pod, he sniffed the air tentatively as he settled down on the dark green cushion. To his relief, the air smelled only of faint traces of cleaning agents and that general mechanical smell that seemed to permeate every transport pod.

He gave the pod's onboard AI the location of his office and settled back as the pod expertly whisked him through wide corridors across Level 7. Along the way, he texted Bella to let her know he was on his way back. His new assistant didn't mind staying after normal business hours, but Vince was trying to encourage her to branch out socially a little.

He fully acknowledged that was hard for a woman who now occupied an android body—particularly when androids were currently illegal aboard Zyga Space Station

After a few moments, the pod slowed to a halt in front of his office. A small sign hung over his door. *Vince Grable, Finder.* Vince paid for his ride with a swipe of a credit chip and disembarked. The pod immediately pulled away and vanished up the boulevard in search of another fare.

The tangy smell of soy sauce and garlic from an eatery a few blocks along the boulevard drifted through the cool air, but he was still too comfortably full from dinner to appreciate any more food. It did, however, bring the almost ever-present tickle in the back of his throat to life. Zyga Station's airscrubbers did a good job of filtering odors and particulate matter from the Station's air, but Vince had discovered almost since the moment he'd arrived that whatever remained still bothered him.

Thank God for the ability to purchase and install private airscrubbers. He couldn't wait to get back in his office and breathe cleaner air.

Vince strode briskly up to his office door, casting a quick—but thorough—glance around, assessing his surroundings. The wide window that ran along the front of his office was dark, but that didn't mean anything. It was one-way synthglass he'd installed expressly to avoid prying eyes.

People streamed up and down the sidewalks on both sides of the wide corridor. Some were returning from work, others heading to work, and still others out for a bit of shopping or to eat. The Finder glimpsed a few familiar faces—individuals who traveled this same route this time every day—but nothing suspicious jumped out at him.

Not that he was expecting trouble. He just liked to keep a healthy awareness of his surroundings.

Unlocking the heavy metal door of his office with a touch of his hand and a keycode, Vince stepped inside. He took in everything with a glance—the office was empty, save for his assistant—and then nodded to Bella, who sat behind her jade green desk by the door.

"Hey, Boss." Bella greeted him with a smile. "How was your dinner?" Tall and willowy, with long, glossy black hair, she was easily one of the most beautiful women Vince had ever seen. She had pale skin and dark, almond-shaped eyes set in a heart-shaped face.

In another life, she'd been a cleaning lady. Now, her consciousness trapped in an android body, she had a new identity and worked as Vince's assistant.

The loss of her old life—and the circumstances surrounding it—still grieved her, but Vince thought Bella was coping tolerably well. The fact that she no longer had a grocery bill meant she was able to put more into her clothing budget—and it showed. Today, his assistant wore black slacks over high-heeled black ankle boots and a soft, sapphire-blue sweater that draped in all the right places.

Vince had been concerned about those boots that morning—when he'd first met Bella, she'd tripped over her own feet and fallen flat on her face. At the time, she'd been so unused to her new body that her klutziness practically knew no bounds, but in the weeks and months since then, she'd gained a fair amount of control. As far as he knew, she hadn't tripped once all day.

"Dinner was excellent, albeit a little interrupted." Vince tapped the doorpanel to shut the door behind him and then locked it. He forewent his usual security protocols—the way his goatee was tingling right now, he had a strong feeling that Corwin Antwerp would be dropping by later.

"Interrupted?" Bella's forehead crinkled in a frown, then smoothed in comprehension. "You picked up another client?"

"Maybe." Vince headed across the office to the jade green sideboard that ran along one of the pearly gray walls. A drink maker and a small basket holding an assortment of his favorite teas sat there, waiting for him. Made from recycled material, the sideboard matched both Bella's desk and his desk, which sat in front of the window. (Although he'd never quite worked out why they had to be jade green—Zyga's admittedly small manufacturing base had the capability to make other colors.)

Next to the sideboard was the door to the office's tiny hygiene unit. On the wall perpendicular to it, sat a comfortable brown couch with a little glass stand next to it that held an aloe plant. The discreetly hidden door that led up to Vince's apartment above the office stood beside it.

On the wall perpendicular to Vince's desk stood his filing cabinet, also jade green. (At least it went well with his beige carpet.) The furniture had been cheap, however, which partly explained how he'd ended up with it all. You didn't have much of a budget when you were just starting out as a Finder.

And in the years since he first arrived on Zyga Station, he'd had good seasons and bad seasons, but none good enough for him to justify going out and buying brand-new replacement furniture. Everything did its job; he just had a lot of jade green.

True, his business had been going gangbusters the past couple of months, but that was something new. An aberration… and Vince didn't trust aberrations. Just because he was up to his ears in work and he'd made more money since taking Bella on as an assistant than he had in…well…forever…didn't mean that the fountain would continue.

After all, he'd practically been flat broke that first night Bella knocked on his door.

No, Vince thought as he brewed himself a cup of jasmine tea, *best to keep expense low and bank all that money for a rainy day.*

That was the life of a freelancer. Feast or famine—there was never any in-between.

CHAPTER 6

CARRYING HIS STEAMING TEA OVER TO HIS desk, Vince settled down into his comfortable office chair and brought his computer terminal to life with the touch of a finger. He glanced over at Bella. "Day's over—you're more than welcome to go home." He smiled lopsidedly. "Not paying more overtime tonight."

"What, leave before this mysterious 'maybe' client shows up?" Bella raised her eyebrows at him. "Not a chance."

"Bella..." Vince set his tea down on his desk. "As much as I appreciate your work ethic, there *is* more to life than work."

"Is that the rule you live by?"

She had him there. Vince put on a stern expression. "This—" he motioned to his office, "—is my life. I'm married to it." It was his turn to raise his eyebrows. "You're not."

Bella rolled her eyes, a little too dramatically, and slumped back in her own chair. "What am I supposed to do?" She shook her head, sending strands of glossy black hair flying. "I can't contact any of my old friends because they all think I'm dead or something, and I can't go back to any of the places I used to spend time—on-Station or on the ComNet." Her full red lips twisted into a bitter smile. "You're the only friend I have, Boss." Her slim shoulders rose and fell in an eloquent shrug. "I don't know what else to do."

Vince blinked at her, taken aback. When he'd considered her situation the past few weeks, it had seemed so simple. She just needed to get out and find some things she enjoyed, and meet people in the process.

Now, however, the full scope of her problem began to dawn on him like the first radiant glimpse of the sun peeking around the gas giant Cartha. How *did* you make friends as an adult? What had *he* done?

To give himself time to think, Vince reached for his tea and took a sip. He regretted that immediately—it was too hot. Restraining a wince at the flare of pain in his scalded mouth, he set the tea back down on his desk.

How did people usually make friends after they moved someplace else? Coworkers? Neighbors?

"To be honest," he said, "I'm probably not the best person to ask." It was his turn to shrug. "I don't exactly have what most people would consider a normal social life."

"I've noticed." Bella's voice was very dry.

"But, again, that's because of work." Vince waved a hand in her direction. "It doesn't have to be like that for you." He leaned forward, his expression earnest. "There's gotta be something you enjoy doing—or would enjoy trying—where you could meet people."

His assistant considered him for a long moment, her lips pursed. "Maybe." She glanced away. "I don't know. And I guess part of it is I just—" she waved a hand to indicate herself; her fingernails were long and silver, "—want to make sure I have control before I spend a lot of time around people."

Vince inhaled sharply. She didn't want anybody to figure out she was anything other than fully human. He nodded. "I can understand that." He offered her a small, gentle smile. "I just don't want to see you waste your second chance at life."

Bella looked at him, her eyes widening, before grief flooded her features. If she'd been back in her old body, she'd probably have started crying. But this android body, as far as they could tell, didn't shed tears. Instead, she only nodded and ducked her head.

"So you're going home?" Vince eyed her over his desk, reaching for his tea again.

"Not a chance." Bella flashed him a wicked grin. "Told you, I want to hear about this client."

"He may not show up in person," Vince cautioned. "He's in Zone 4—there's an excellent chance he'll just call."

Bella spun a lazy half-circle in her chair. "Then you can tell me about him." She folded her long, graceful arms behind her head. "Either way, you're stuck with me, Boss."

This was a losing battle if Vince had ever seen one. Shaking his head, he turned back to his computer terminal. The light smell of his jasmine tea filled the air, calming him, and being back in his office with its extra-scrubbed air had already worked its magic on his breathing. The tickle in the back of his throat was gone.

While he searched for more information on Corwin Antwerp and his family, Vince gave Bella a quick run-down of his evening. His assistant was just as intrigued as he was.

"I wonder if his brother owes money to one of the Families." Bella tapped her cheek with a long, silver fingernail.

"If he does," Vince said grimly, "he picked the wrong place to hide."

The Bok Family and Oswari Family controlled the Core, which was roughly split into two territories. They had an uneasy truce, but both Families' influence snaked through the rest of Zyga Station.

Bella nodded. "So you think it's more likely Dent owes money to a two-credit subsidiary?"

"He probably ranks a little higher than two credits, but yes." Vince's goatee was tingling. "That's my gut assessment based on what little I know so far."

Bella nodded again, her expression going distant.

Vince wondered if she was thinking about her cousin Cara. Cara had gotten too deeply involved in a game and ended up owing money to the wrong people. She'd tried to settle her debt by selling Bella to the head of the Bok Family's eldest son—which had resulted in Bella ending up in an android body. Cara herself was probably dead now.

The hair prickled on the back of Vince's neck; he pushed the memories of that night away. He didn't want to think about any of that, especially right now.

Half an hour later, Vince had little enough to show for his time. As far as living a law-abiding life was concerned, Corwin and his mother, Tisha, were quite boring. Their online footprint was small and cut-and-dry. Corwin had left out a few minor details, such as the fact that his mother had spent a year or two working as a hostess at an exclusive restaurant on Zone 4's Level 2 before her husband had died, but the rest of it seemed to check out.

Dent, on the other hand…

Vince whistled under his breath. Corwin's older brother had a *large* online footprint. It wasn't difficult for the Finder to trace the path Dent's life had taken since high school—all he had to do was follow the wreckage and complaints. And that was before he even read through Station Authority's full record on Dent.

Just as Vince had told Corwin, it was a familiar story. The Finder rubbed a hand over his face, ending with smoothing his goatee. A familiar sad, tragic story featuring a young person who'd ended up throwing his life away. There was a chance Dent could recover—but he had to *want* to recover. He had to be willing to work for it.

And, given the fact that Dent had just up and disappeared rather than own up to his sins, Vince doubted he was interested in recovery.

The door chimed softly, drawing both his and Bella's attention.

Bella sat bolt-upright in her chair, looking excited. "He came!"

Despite the fact that he didn't want her to waste her life, Vince couldn't deny that a part of him was warmed by Bella's enthusiasm for the Finding business. Over the months since he'd hired her, he'd discovered it was really…nice…to work with someone who enjoyed his work as much as she seemed to.

Vince reached for the small panel in the corner of his desk that triggered a pop-up holographic vid feed from the cam mounted above his door. "It could be someone else."

Bella just shot him a look that said, *Are you kidding me?*

He needn't have bothered.

It *was* Corwin. The young man had changed into street clothes—a bright red jacket over light-wash jeans and a white shirt—but there was no mistaking that serious round face.

Rising from his seat, Vince went to answer the door.

CHAPTER 7

IN THE DIM LIGHT FROM THE GLOWPANELS in the corridor's overhead, Corwin looked much older and more tired than he had any right to be at his age. He nodded as Vince motioned for him to enter the office and hurried across the threshold with quick strides. He glanced around out of mild interest—and Vince knew the exact second he spotted Bella.

The young man just sort of froze. There for a second, he didn't even seem to be breathing. He just stared at Bella, his eyes wide.

For her part, Bella didn't let it faze her. Arching a dark eyebrow at him from her seat behind her desk, she extended a slim, pale hand. "You must be Corwin. I'm Bella Escovedo, Finder Grable's assistant."

Corwin shook her hand automatically and then seemed to snap back to himself. Clearing his throat, he said gruffly, "Nice to meet you, Ms. Escovedo."

Vince shut and locked the office door before waving Corwin toward the brown chairs that sat in front of his jade green desk. "Please, have a seat."

"Can I take your jacket?" Bella asked.

Corwin's dark eyes traveled from Vince to Bella and back. "Uh, no. That's okay. I'm good."

"Cup of tea?" Vince jerked a thumb toward the sideboard and the drink maker as he crossed the office and rounded Corwin to get to the other side of his desk. "I'm afraid I don't have any coffee at the moment."

He'd contemplated keeping some on hand for prospective clients, but just hadn't had the time to get to it yet.

"No, thanks." Corwin wrinkled his nose. "Never could get into that stuff. My mom loves tea, but…" He shrugged and shook his head, as if to say he didn't understand tea drinkers at all, but he still loved his mother.

Vince noticed the way the young man's gaze flicked briefly to Bella again and hid a smile. Instead, he seated himself behind his desk and looked across at Corwin. "Why are you here, Mr. Antwerp?"

A flicker of irritation flashed through the younger man's dark brown eyes, giving him a little boost of energy. He straightened in his chair. "You *know* why I'm here. I want to finish our conversation." He wet his lips. "You said—before Mr. Pho showed up at your table, you said there was another way."

Vince nodded slowly. The boy *was* serious about exploring other options, then. "Yes, I did."

"Well, I'd like to hear what it is." Corwin sat back in his chair, but the tension cording his muscles belied his show of nonchalance. His gaze traveled sideways to Bella again.

"I've filled Ms. Escovedo in on the basics." Vince waved a hand toward Bella, who nodded solemnly, though one corner of her mouth was twitching like she was trying to repress a smile. The Finder didn't expect Corwin to put up a fuss about confidentiality, and he was right.

The young man just shrugged, a little impatiently. Apparently, he was at the point where he didn't care whether or not anybody else knew he had plans to kill his brother. (Vince rather thought some of that might have been subconscious relief that another option existed.)

He eyed Corwin for several heartbeats, letting the relative silence of his office seep into the space between them. Giving him a call tonight alone would have proved the young man was serious, but the fact that he'd actually traveled to Vince's office in Zone 5 after he got off work spoke far louder than anything else.

At precisely the right moment, Vince said, "Your other option is to hire to me to find your brother and turn him in to Station Authority. They'll prosecute him and deal with the gambling obligations. He'll probably end up on a prison work crew—" Zyga Station had an agreement worked out with the Zyga Mining Corporation to handle prisoners— "but it's better than being dead."

Provided we can keep whoever he owes money from offing him out of spite, Vince thought, but he kept that to himself.

For a long moment, Corwin sat motionless as he digested this. In the background, Vince's airscrubber kicked on, but the young man didn't even blink.

Finally, he dragged in a breath and shook his head. "I thought about that. Stars." He tipped his head back to stare up at the overhead, before dropping his chin to shoot an almost accusing glare at Vince. "Sure, that's the easy way out—"

Easy way out? Vince had to use his long years of experience to hide his incredulity at this statement. There was nothing *easy* about tracking somebody down who didn't want to be found and hauling them all the way to a Station Authority precinct to face justice.

"—but what about my mom's apartment? That option gonna fix the lien and the payments that are due *now*?" Deep, old anger, and resentment simmered in Corwin's dark eyes.

"Legally, once fraud is proved, the debt will be—"

"The hell it will!" In the blink of an eye, Corwin had shoved his chair back and was on his feet.

At her desk, Bella jumped in fright. The thud of her knee banging into the side of her desk went unnoticed as Corwin slammed both palms flat on Vince's desk and glared down at the Finder.

"You think those sharks are gonna care about who really owes 'em?" His chest heaved and his dark eyes blazed. "You think they won't come after my mom and me to pay 'em back?"

Vince didn't move, though his pulse jumped a little. Corwin wasn't the first client—would-be or otherwise—who had practically charged across his desk in the heat of the moment.

Probably wouldn't be the last, either, he reflected wryly.

"Mr. Antwerp, please sit down." Vince kept his voice calm and reasonable as he nodded to Bella. "You're scaring my assistant."

A muscle in Corwin's dark jaw twitched. He swallowed, his nostrils flaring, and his gaze darted to Bella for a second. She was staring at him, wide-eyed, one hand pressed to her ample chest. Visibly gritting his teeth, the young man collapsed back into his chair.

"Thank you." Vince stroked his chin; his goatee was tingling again. Something else was going on here—something beyond Corwin's concern for his mother and their wellbeing—but he didn't yet have a clue as to what it was.

Deliberately, he leaned back in his chair and raised an eyebrow at the younger man. He wasn't frightened of Corwin and his anger; he'd seen it too many times over the years. "Would you like me to continue?"

That muscle in Corwin's jaw jumped again. Some of the anger had bled from his eyes, leaving wariness in its wake. "There's more?"

"Of course there's more." Vince made a dismissive gesture with one hand. "Having your brother arrested once found might sound like the easy way out, but I assure you, it's a good deal more complicated." He allowed one corner of his mouth to lift in a wry smile. "As you pointed out, there's the matter of his debtors to consider."

Wariness slowly changed to guarded hope. "You've got a plan for that?"

Vince inclined his head in a slow nod. "I've been a Finder for more than ten years. This—" he indicated the space separating them across his desk, "—may be a crisis for you, but it's nothing new to me." He paused to see how Corwin handled that matter-of-fact statement, but the younger man took it like a champ. "How we handle your brother's debtors depends on how closely connected to a Family they are."

He didn't think he imagined the look of fear that flashed over Corwin's face. It was gone almost immediately, but Vince had seen it—and cold certainty settled in his gut. Whatever else was going on in this situation, it either had something to do with a Family or else Corwin *believed* that it did.

If Vince had been a different man, he might have chosen this moment to mention that he'd actually met the head of the Bok Family—and lived to tell about it. But that didn't seem important right now, and, really, it was sheer providence that he and Bella hadn't joined the ranks of those who simply…disappeared…on Zyga Station.

Instead, Vince reached for his datapad. "All right. Give me everything you've got on your brother."

Corwin sat up a little straighter, his fingers unconsciously gripping the arms of his chair. "You'll take the case?"

Vince regarded him for a few seconds before nodding. "If you're sure you want to hire—"

"I do." Corwin glanced at Bella before looking back at Vince. "It might take me a while to pay your full bill, but—"

"I'm sure you will." Vince gave another dismissive wave. Judging from the kid's work ethic at Pho's Noodle Shop, he wasn't worried about whether or not Corwin would make good on paying up or not.

"Thank you, Finder."

Vince didn't think he was imagining the sheer relief that flooded Corwin's face and voice either. He nodded to his datapad before drilling Corwin with a stern look. "When I say everything, I mean *everything.*"

CHAPTER 8

When Corwin finally left over an hour later, Vince had a plethora of facts and other bits of information about the Antwerps' life over the years. The bulk of it specifically delineated Dent's habits over the past few years, but there were other interesting family intersections. The holo unfolding before the Finder's eyes was so similar to those he'd seen before that it was tempting to draw the same conclusions, but—his goatee was still tingling.

Something about this case was different. Vince had no idea what that might be, but he trusted his intuition. Eventually, with more digging, he'd figure out what it was.

Bella departed not long after Corwin, with a cheerful wave and a reminder to Vince that he really ought to get some rest.

Coming from a woman who no longer needed such mundane things as sleep, Vince found this highly ironic, but he appreciated the concern. He'd been on his own so long it had taken him a while to get accustomed to having someone around who cared about his wellbeing. His new assistant simultaneously reminded him of his mother and a well-meaning sister, wrapped in a package that could have easily graced the holo ads for the latest fashions from outside the Cartha system.

He *was* tired, though. It had been a long day, and he hadn't intended to be up quite this late. But, clients were clients and cases were cases. Work was work—and after the dearth of work he'd lived through a few months ago, he'd take everything he could get.

Well, Vince amended, forcing himself to rise from his comfortable office chair and make his way across the beige carpet to the discreetly hidden door that led up to the small apartment above his office, perhaps some moderation was in order. He'd be of no use to any of his clients if he ran himself so ragged he couldn't think.

In a Finder's line of work, brain power was everything.

With a press of his finger on the door panel, the door to the stairs slid open and a soft light snapped on to illuminate his steps. Vince ascended wearily. The door at the top of the stairs slid open just as he reached it.

"Lights, low."

Soft, golden light flooded his apartment from several glow-panels in the overhead and a lamp on a tiny end table. His apartment was small, which was fine, because it wasn't like he needed a lot of space. A tiny kitchenette and dining nook, his bedroom, a hygiene unit, and a little living area big enough for an end table, a couch, and a recliner comprised the whole of it. Vince considered himself blessed to have this much space plus his office—he'd seen smaller apartments on Zyga Station.

The relative lack of large spaces was one of the peculiarities of the space station—or rather, her architects. Zyga Station had been constructed in space and there were really no limitations on how big it could have been, except for her architects' imagination and how much the Zyga Mining Corporation had been willing to pay for it.

That, as it turned out, was not as much as they *could* have paid. The result, of course, was that living aboard the space station mirrored life practically everywhere else in the galaxy. Those who could afford to pay for extra space got it, while those who couldn't afford it lived squeezed in with their neighbors.

The faintest hint of vanilla from a tiny diffuser next to the lamp on the table in the corner of the living area met Vince's' nose as he crossed to the kitchenette to get himself a little snack before he hit the rack. The air aboard the station often had a metallic undertone—when it wasn't full of lingering traces of various body and cooking odors, perfumes, etc. Vince had gotten used to most of it, but he was still sometimes a little sensitive. And though Zyga Station's airscrubbers were frighteningly efficient, he'd learned the hard way over the years that it was best for him to have his own private airscrubbers in his work and living space.

The occasional gentle scent diffused through his apartment didn't hurt either.

After snagging a slice of cheddar cheese and a couple of crackers, Vince made his way into his bedroom to gather some clean clothes. A moment later, snack consumed and clothes in hand, he exited his room and stepped into the hygiene unit.

Usually, he'd stand there for a little while, letting his daily shower water ration wash over him and pound away the stress—and accumulated particulate matter, depending on where he'd been—of the day. Tonight, however, he was just too tired to linger.

Clean and refreshed, Vince padded back into his bedroom and climbed into his bed with a grateful sigh. His bed was perhaps his one concession to materialism—it was full-size, even though it meant he had very little room for his nightstand and dresser, or even to walk around the bed. He'd saved up for a good mattress too; a good night's rest was important.

"Lights, off. Fan, on."

The round little glowpanel in the center of the room's overhead obediently shut off, plunging his bedroom into blessed darkness. At the same time, a little fan on his dresser switched on and began to gently rotate back and forth, stirring the air and providing soothing background noise. His windows were opaque; he'd never bothered with curtains.

Bella thought that was strange, but Vince didn't care. He was the only person who lived here, and he'd never seen the need to pay for window dressing. Either the synthglass windows were in clear mode to allow him to see out, or they were opaque. And given that he spent most of his waking hours either in the office or out trekking across Zyga Station…well…it didn't really matter, did it?

Nestling down into his soft gray blankets, Vince closed his eyes and took a few deep breaths, deliberately emptying his mind of everything except sleep. He had no pressing matters to engage his mind tonight; all he needed to do right now was rest.

He was out before he'd taken more than four breaths.

Bzzz.

Bzzz.

Bzzz.

There was a giant honey bee hovering in front of him. It was angry—very angry—and as Vince looked down at his hands, he suddenly realized why. He held a large jar of honey—and the bee knew it. The lid was off, revealing the thick, dark gold liquid within.

The bee wanted the honey back.

But it couldn't have the honey back. Vince clutched the jar to his chest, taking a tentative step backward. He'd already *paid* for this honey.

The buzzing grew more insistent as the bee zipped up to him. Its alien-looking black eyes stared right at him, its antennae waving a little as it beat its wings furiously in the air.

"I need this honey," Vince tried to tell it. "It helps my throat." He backed up another few steps; the bee followed. "And I *paid* for it."

The bee buzzed angrily, bobbing up and down in the air. Apparently, this wasn't a good enough answer. Suddenly, it charged forward and—

Vince bolted upright with a start, his heart pounding and his fingers clutching a handful of his blankets. A little disoriented, he stared around his pitch-black room with wide eyes. The dream shattered, shards of it already melting away into nothingness, but the buzzing continued.

The buzzing. The sound resolved itself into something familiar. He passed a hand over his face. Not a bee, but his comlink.

A glance at the floating green numbers in the corner of the room told him it was just past five o'clock in the morning cycle. Who could be calling him now?

The Finder reached over to the nightstand for his comlink, his fingers locating it easily even in the dark. One glance at the display told him the comm frequency wasn't anyone he knew. He could ignore the call—probably *should* ignore the call; it was most likely spam—but the way his goatee suddenly bristled told him that would be a bad idea.

"Hello?" His voice emerged gruff and gravelly from sleep.

A woman's terrified, tear-filled voice met his ear. "Finder Grable?"

"This is he."

She immediately launched into a hysterical stream of words. Vince only caught a few of them: 'my son', 'Station Authority', and 'brother'.

The bristling in his goatee grew more pronounced; he unconsciously stroked his chin, his eyes narrowing. He had a horrible suspicion he knew who this woman was. "Hold on, ma'am. Slow down, please. I can't understand you."

It took a second for his words to penetrate. When they did, the woman broke off with a sob.

"Let's start over," Vince said gently. "Who are you?"

"I'm Tisha Antwerp." She took a great, gulping breath. "Corwin's my son and—and Station Authority just took him away. He told me to call you—they wouldn't let him—let him call anybody." Her voice broke on a sob.

A heavy weight settled in the pit of Vince's stomach. "Why did they arrest him, Mrs. Antwerp?"

He suspected he already knew the answer.

"They think he—they said he—" Mrs. Antwerp's voice cut off, as though she'd pressed a hand to her mouth to muffle another sob. A second later, she said through a voice thick with tears, "They're saying that he's murdered his brother."

CHAPTER 9

His brother. Vince sat back against his headboard, his mind reeling. Was she saying what it sounded like she was saying? Dent Antwerp was dead and Station Authority had already found his body *and* connected him to Corwin?

Vince frowned, scrubbing a hand over his face. That was awfully fast work, given how Station Authority usually operated when it came to Zyga Station citizens who didn't have much in the way of money or prestige.

"His brother?" he asked gruffly.

"My eldest son—Dent." Mrs. Antwerp choked on a sob. "They want me—want me to come to—" another sob, "—identify his body." She sobbed again. "Oh, my boys, my boys!"

And Corwin had told his mother to call *him*.

A stone settled in the pit of Vince's stomach. Any desire to return to sleep fell away as he threw back his covers and jumped out of bed. "Mrs. Antwerp, I need you to listen to me. Where are you?"

"At—at home. We were—we were asleep when Station Authority came." Mrs. Antwerp drew in a great, gasping breath. "I thought at—at first they were—somebody else."

I'm sure you did, Vince thought grimly. With Dent's creditors out to be paid, he could only imagine what Corwin and his mother had felt when they'd been awakened by all that ruckus.

"Lights, on."

The glowpanel in the ceiling snapped on. Wincing against the golden light flooding the room, Vince crossed to his tiny closet and rummaged around for clothes. "Stay right where you are. I'm coming to you. Don't open the door for anybody else."

"You're coming to me?" A ray of hope—albeit confused hope—pierced her bewildered panic and grief.

"Yes, ma'am." Vince shifted the comlink to his other ear as he started pulling on a pair of pants. "I don't know if your son Corwin told you or not, but he hired me last night to find Dent."

"He did?" More confusion, mixed with a hiccupping sob. "But—"

"Mrs. Antwerp." Vince gentled his voice. "If your son Dent is dead, I am truly sorry for your loss. That said, I don't think Corwin is responsible."

On the other end, Mrs. Antwerp drew in a ragged breath that ended in a sob. She swallowed it, however, to ask, "You—you don't?"

Vince paused for a nanosecond to consider that question. It wasn't something to answer lightly. He drew in a breath and let it out. His goatee tingled.

He'd looked that boy right in the eyes not six hours earlier. And while he'd seen the anger and hurt and the rage, he'd also seen the hope when he, Vince, had offered an alternative.

"No, ma'am," he said finally, "I don't think he did it."

His mouth twisted into a grimace. Granted, there was another possibility—and this would most definitely be one that Station Authority latched onto. It was possible Corwin had run into his brother on his way home—and Dent had run his mouth off, resulting in an impromptu fight between the brothers that left him dead.

Even so…even so…Vince rubbed his chin fiercely before shoving his feet into his boots and grabbing his favorite brown leather jacket from its hanger in the closet. Then he strode briskly out into his apartment and straight for the door leading down to his office. He rarely actually used his apartment's front door.

"Give me your location, please. I'll be there as fast as I can."

To her credit, Mrs. Antwerp didn't hesitate.

Once he had their location fixed in his mind, Vince repeated his earlier instructions. "Don't call anybody, don't open the door for anybody, and don't go anywhere. I'm on my way."

"Thank—thank you." She was starting to sound dazed; shock was setting in. She ended the transmission without another word.

Under different circumstances, Vince would have suggested Corwin's mother call someone—a good neighbor, or a close friend—to sit with her. But this time…his goatee bristled at the very thought. This time was different. He had that same murky sense that something else was going on, that something much, much larger was lurking at the edges of the holo frame.

Dent Antwerp—by all accounts a nobody and not worth the effort it would take to shove him out of an airlock—was dead and Station Authority had already arrested Corwin.

Vince couldn't wait to hear the particulars of how this had gone down.

A moment later, he had retrieved a tiny snub-nosed laser pistol and a pocket holster from the safe hidden in his office floor, exited his office and locked the door behind him. He then flagged a transport pod to take him to the synthglass elevator bank and sat back against the seat's royal green cushion, barely registering the faint smell of cheap cologne.

The Finder shook his head slightly. He hadn't expected this twist.

At this early hour in the morning cycle, there wasn't much traffic yet. Traveling down to Level 22 and crossing the Hub to return to Zone 4 took very little time. Vince then hailed another transport pod to take him to the synthglass elevator bank that stood in the center of Zone 4 just like the one in Zone 5. Once he stepped out of the elevator cab on Level 16, he caught another transport pod to take him halfway across the Level to the quadrant where Corwin and his mother lived.

Despite their many similarities, each of Zyga Space Stations Zones had a few unique peculiarities. Vince didn't know if the space station's architects had intended things to be that way, or if the Zones had simply developed those peculiar differences over time. Zone 4, being the Zone that handled all incoming and outgoing space traffic, had a specific theme that ran through its Levels, no matter how poor and otherwise unimportant some of them might be. Flags, silhouettes of ships, and all manner of colorful fabrics and paintings that resembled fabrics adorned the bulkheads along the corridors and compartments.

For all that many parts of the actual docking bays were gray and greasy, the rest of Zone 4 exhibited an exotic, colorful air that boasted of its proximity to people from all over the galaxy.

A particularly vibrant depiction of gold and green flag of the Wyndel system caught Vince's eye as his transport pod carried him past a block of apartments. He shook his head. It was ironic, really, when you took into consideration the fact that the vast majority of the Station's inhabitants had been born here, would never get any farther than the mines (if they left the Station at all), and would eventually die here.

The thought of death brought Vince's mind full circle back to Corwin and his brother. He drummed his fingers against the royal green cushion beside his leg, willing the pod to move faster. He knew it wouldn't; unless you were Station Authority and happened to know the emergency override code, all of Zyga Transport's pods adhered strictly to set speed limits throughout the Station.

Briefly, Vince wished he'd taken the time to make himself a cup of tea before he left. He could have finished it all before he reached Mrs. Antwerp. He promptly pushed that thought aside; time had been of the essence. He'd known that, with a deep, inexplicable certainty he felt all the way down in his bones.

He *had* to get to Mrs. Antwerp first. Even if he had absolutely no idea who else might be heading for her.

...especially since he had no idea who else might be heading for her.

As the transport pod neared the Antwerps' apartment complex, Vince tensed. Every nerve in his body started to hum, ready for action. With any luck, he wouldn't encounter any trouble between here and Mrs. Antwerp's door.

The weight of the little snub-nose laser pistol in his pocket holster seemed suddenly much heavier. Vince had never been able to satisfactorily explain it to his friend in Zone 5's Station Authority, Sergeant Anita Rychek, but there were times he knew he should carry a weapon and times he knew he shouldn't. Rychek couldn't understand that—in her experience, if a weapon was worth carrying one day, it was worth carrying every day. And while Vince agreed in principle...he couldn't agree in practice.

There were times and occasions in his line of work when being armed would have exacerbated certain situations. For example, when he and his best Core informant, a young gamer named Rav, had set up a sting operation a while back that resulted in Vince having to rescue Rav from a secret lab in the bowels of the Core's Authorized-Access-Only levels, he'd walked into that lab unarmed. Taking his pistol along would only have resulted in him losing it.

This, however, was not one of those occasions.

As his transport pod glided to a halt in front of the apartment complex, Vince put a reassuring hand into his pocket. His fingers grazed the textured surface of the pistol grip. Whatever happened in the next five minutes, he was ready.

The Finder paid his fare with a credit chip and then exited the transport pod. As soon as the door slid shut behind him, the pod was gone, floating serenely back the way they'd come. Vince glanced up and down the broad corridor as he hastened toward the entrance to the apartment complex, his sharp gaze searching for anything out of the ordinary.

Movement across the corridor from a narrow access corridor caught his eye.

The access corridor jutted down between another apartment complex and a block of compartments that held a laundromat, a couple of small businesses, and two eateries. As Vince watched, two figures in dark, unobtrusive clothes detached themselves from it. They headed across the broad corridor toward him with loping, purposeful strides.

Vince didn't hesitate. Marching toward the entrance to the apartment complex like he belonged there, he let himself in and made a beeline for the elevator. Those men *might* be here for a completely different reason but...

...the way his goatee was bristling said it was unlikely.

CHAPTER 10

The Antwerps' apartment complex was one of the most basic aboard Zyga Station, being merely a collection of apartments stacked on top of each other with corridors running through them and short elevators attaching each level. In terms of security, there was none. Anyone could walk in here, just like Vince had done.

The small, narrow gray lobby smelled of old vegetables and garlic and was devoid of furniture or anything else, save for a bank of two elevators and another door that led to the stairs. Both elevators opened as Vince neared it, and a crowd of sleepy-looking men and women in the navy blue uniforms of the Docking Bay piled out. He skirted past them to step into the elevator on the left.

Just as the doors closed, he glimpsed the two strange men trying to push their way through the crowd of workers. His goatee continued to bristle; Vince rubbed it briskly as he hit the button for Level 5. (This apartment complex was too basic for voice-controlled elevators as well, which was a shame.)

The air in this elevator was full of cologne, perfume, and various other hygienic scents. Vince hadn't taken more than two breaths before the back of his throat began to itch. Shaking his head, he cleared his throat a couple of times and swallowed heavily.

The itching abated, but it was still there, like an ever-present tingle. That would have to do.

The elevator door opened on Level 5 and Vince forgot about his scratchy throat. Hurrying out of the cab, he glanced left and right along the pale gray door-lined corridor. At one end, a man in a cheap suit had just stepped out of his apartment, balancing a lidded coffee cup in one hand. The other end was empty.

Mrs. Antwerp lived in apartment 511, which lay to the right. Vince headed that direction, keeping his ears peeled for the sound of the elevator. He was almost positive those men were on their way up here too.

His pulse quickened as he caught sight of a door labeled 511 in dark gray stenciling. In seconds, he was pressing the comm button on the door panel.

"Hello?" Mrs. Antwerp answered, albeit in a rather choked and teary voice.

"It's Finder Grable." Vince resisted the urge to look over his shoulder. "May I come in, Mrs. Antwerp?"

A click was all the warning Vince had before the door slid aside to reveal a short, slight woman with a halo of curly black hair illuminated by a bright light from inside her apartment. She wore a flowing brown and orange patterned dress, and clutched a bright gold shawl edged with orange around her thin shoulders. Her dark eyes—red-rimmed and swollen from tears—focused on him out of a thin face that looked like an older female version of her son, Corwin.

"Finder Grable?" she asked tentatively.

Vince nodded. "May I come in?"

In answer, Corwin's mother silently stepped aside.

Just as Vince crossed the threshold, he heard the elevator down the corridor ding. A tinge of satisfaction curled through him. He'd beaten them here.

…but that didn't mean they were completely safe.

Tapping the panel beside the door to close it, he pressed the lock button. Once he'd heard the door click, he turned to Mrs. Antwerp, who was regarding him with dull curiosity. She looked like she'd had a good cry during the time it had taken him to reach her.

She also looked like one good blast of air could knock her clean over.

Quickly, Vince took stock of his surroundings. They stood in the main living area, which had the same pearlescent gray bulkheads that could be found practically everywhere else throughout each Zone, but Mrs. Antwerp had done her best to brighten things up. The couch was covered with a cheerful blue, red, yellow, and white patterned fabric and several prints of abstract art, also in vivid, bold colors, hung on the bulkheads. Another chair stood in the corner, with a small brown coffee table in front of it. A doorway led into a small kitchen with a bar that opened on the living area, and three other doors led off to what Vince guessed were the hygiene unit and two bedrooms.

He focused on Mrs. Antwerp. Inclining his head, he said gently, "My condolences." Then he gestured toward the kitchen. "Corwin tells me you love tea. I'm a tea drinker myself. You look like you could use a cup."

Mrs. Antwerp had to swallow twice before she could form audible words. "But—Station Authority—my—my son." Fresh tears pooled in her dark eyes again.

"It's barely six o'clock in the morning," Vince said firmly. "They can wait long enough for you to have a cup of tea to steady your nerves. Besides," he added with a small smile, "you know how it is with Station Authority. Most of them don't even start work until at least eight."

Under different circumstances, that might have coaxed a smile out of Mrs. Antwerp. As it was, Corwin's mother drew in a sudden breath, like she was swallowing a sob, and then nodded. Clutching her gold shawl a little tighter around her shoulders, she allowed Vince to lead her into the kitchen and settle her at the small dark brown table pushed up against one wall.

Though tiny, the kitchen was clean and tidy. It had a pale green tiled floor and Mrs. Antwerp had affixed an emerald green vine pattern around the top of the pearl-gray bulkhead near the overhead. It had all the usual accoutrements—refrigerator, short counter with a small sink, a few cabinets, and a small cooking range.

Corwin's mother pointed out where she kept mugs and tea and Vince moved efficiently about her little kitchen, fixing them both a cup. She had a good selection, including a black tea that was excellent for starting one's morning off on the right foot, but Vince chose a blend better suited for calming nerves.

He kept an ear peeled for any sound that those two men had arrived at her door, but there was nothing. He wasn't sure if that was a good thing or not.

As he carried two steaming crimson mugs to the table, Mrs. Antwerp nodded to the cupboard on the other side of the tiny sink. "I keep a bottle of honey there if you'd like some." She lifted one thin shoulder in a modest shrug, though her eyes were still hollow and wet with tears. "From Zone 3, you know. Better than sugar, I think."

Warmth spread through the Finder. Smiling, Vince handed one of the mugs to Corwin's mother before setting the other down in front of the empty chair. "I know exactly what you mean."

Retrieving the honey from its aforementioned spot and producing two spoons from a drawer, Vince handed honey and spoon to Mrs. Antwerp and waited for her to doctor her tea. When she was finished, he added a small dollop of honey to his own tea, stirred, and took a tentative sip. "Excellent tea," he said approvingly, once he'd swallowed. "Thank you."

"Corwin never could understand why I like it." Mrs. Antwerp curled her fingers gingerly around her hot mug, letting the warmth seep into her skin. "Never saw the point of drinking water that'd had leaves in it." She looked down at the steaming golden brown surface of her tea. "Of course, he drinks coffee, and that's just ground up beans in water…" She trailed off, as though deciding the rest of the explanation was superfluous.

It was, of course. Vince had made that same observation himself a time or two. Taking another careful sip, he nodded to Mrs. Antwerp. "Drink your tea. It'll make you feel better. In the meantime, I'm going to make a call."

Despite the numb, heavy weight of combined grief and shock that had descended on her, a spark of energy seemed to momentarily innervate Corwin's mother. She looked at him, her expression halfway between fear and hope.

Vince just gave her a small, encouraging smile as he extracted his comlink from the inner breast pocket of his brown leather jacket and started to cross the kitchen. "Which precinct did they tell you to report to? The one on Level 6 or one further down?"

The precinct depended greatly on where Dent's body had been found—Station Authority maintained a headquarters precinct in each Zone but had otherwise split the Zones into sections with smaller precincts every six levels. Given Dent's predilections, there was no telling where he'd been when he got himself killed.

Mrs. Antwerp shook her head, pointing a silent finger up toward the overhead.

Up? Vince's footsteps faltered, but he covered his surprise smoothly. "They want to see you at headquarters on Level 1?"

Mrs. Antwerp nodded.

That was…extremely unusual. Vince blinked once, twice, as he processed this information. He then glanced down at his comlink display, his goatee prickling. Well, at least now he knew which precinct to focus on.

Thanks to more than ten years as a Finder, he knew a number of officers from Station Authority precincts in each Zone across the whole of Zyga Station. Sergeant Rychek, he knew the best, but he was on friendly enough terms with others. Scrolling through his Zone 4 Station Authority contacts, Vince settled on Detective Belzi, in Precinct 1's Homicide department.

If Dent Antwerp had indeed been murdered, Belzi would know about it.

CHAPTER 11

DESPITE THE EARLY HOUR, THE DETECTIVE ANSWERED on the second ring. "Belzi." He had a gruff, no-nonsense voice that sounded like it should be coming from a giant of a man, but in reality, Belzi was half a head shorter than Vince and a good deal skinnier.

"Morning, Detective. Finder Grable."

"Right. Been a while." Belzi paused, thinking. "Not since the Ling Ling case?"

Vince nodded, even though the other man couldn't see him. "That's correct."

"Pretty early for you to be calling. What's on your mind?"

"Frankly, Detective, I'm calling to find out if a client of mine has indeed been arrested on suspicion of murder."

Across the kitchen, Mrs. Antwerp flinched.

"A client of yours? Murder?"

Vince's goatee bristled again. He knew that tone. That was the voice Belzi used when he was playing dumb.

"Yeah." He glanced over at Corwin's mother to make sure she was still drinking her tea. "My client was arrested about an hour ago for the murder of his brother, and his mother was told she had to come up to headquarters to identify the body. Wanted to make sure it was a legit operation."

That was the other thought that had occurred to him—that this was an elaborate hoax perpetrated by Dent's creditors to terrify the Antwerps into paying up.

A brief pause greeted this. "What would give you reason to think it wasn't?"

It was Vince's turn to pause, his gaze darting to Mrs. Antwerp again. He lowered his voice slightly. "Let's just say the vic had a large gambling problem and owes money to the wrong people."

He didn't have to say any more. Belzi knew what that meant as well as any other Station Authority officer who actually worked the Station's corridors.

"Vic's name?" the detective asked finally.

"Dent Antwerp."

"Client's name?"

"Corwin Antwerp."

Belzi made a soft hissing noise. "So it *is* true."

Something twisted in Vince's gut. He raised a hand to rub his chin; his goatee was still prickling fiercely. "What's true?"

It was Belzi's turn to lower his voice. "That the kid is your client."

"He's there?" Vince kept his voice controlled and level.

"Yeah. Uniforms brought him in a little while ago. Don't know much about it—not my case. Belongs to Commosky," he added, before Vince could ask. "Kid was making a big deal about being your client and kept asking to call you."

A flicker of anger curled through Vince, bright and blazing. "And Commosky obviously wouldn't let him."

"No. And I don't know why." Belzi sounded apologetic. Then his voice turned a shade suspicious. "How do you know, anyway?"

"Kid's mother called me," Vince said grimly. "Look, Belzi, I appreciate your info. Can you tell me one more thing?"

"Depends on what it is."

"Did Commosky put a detail on the Antwerps' apartment?"

"A detail? Why?"

In a few words, Vince explained about the two men who had followed him into the apartment complex.

Belzi hesitated again. "It's not my case. Don't know exactly what's going on."

"Understood."

That was all right—Vince hadn't really expected Belzi to know. He *was*, however, counting on the strong likelihood that some inkling of this conversation would get back to the other detective.

Station Authority tended to work that way, no matter how much they liked to present themselves as a shining example of law-abiding morality.

Vince had a sudden flash of inspiration. He wouldn't *ask* Belzi to relay a message—detectives tended to be touchy about that sort of thing—but there was a way to get the information across and give Belzi the chance to get info out of Commosky on whatever else the detective might need at a later date.

Casually, he said, "Thanks for your help, Detective. I'll be escorting Mrs. Antwerp to Precinct 1 shortly to ID her son's body."

"Sure thing, Grable."

Ending the transmission, Vince turned his full attention back to Corwin's mother. She sat motionless at the table, staring down into the depths of her tea as though it held all the answers to every question ever asked about life, the universe, and everything. Her eyes were dry now, but still red-rimmed and heavy with the combined weight of shock and grief.

Since nobody had attempted to break down the door yet, Vince concluded that the two men he'd seen must have orders to hang around and observe only—at least for the moment. What happened when he emerged from the apartment with Mrs. Antwerp in tow would be a different story.

As far as he was concerned, it was still even money as to whether or not they were Commosky's men or belonged to Dent's creditors.

Approaching the table, Vince gently cleared his throat. Jolting slightly, Mrs. Antwerp came out of her deep reverie, her eyes snapping up to meet his. She didn't speak.

The Finder nodded to her tea. "How are we coming?"

Blankly, Mrs. Antwerp looked down at her tea. "Half-finished. I—" Her fingers tightened convulsively on the mug's red surface "I—was thinking back to when the boys were little. Before their father died." Grief flattened her lips into a thin line as she shook her head. "None of this would have ever happened if he was still here with us."

That was unlikely, Vince wanted to say, but he didn't argue with her. The last thing they needed right now was a debate over the merits of the space lane not taken.

"If you feel like it, finish up and we'll go to the precinct." Vince picked up his own now-much cooler mug and took a healthy swallow. Though colder than he would have preferred, the tea tasted wonderful and it felt good sliding down his throat. He caught Corwin's mother's eye and held her gaze. "It's going to be all right."

Ordinarily, he tried to avoid using that phrase when talking to clients—or relatives of clients. But this morning, with the way his goatee was bristling and facing the helpless, hopeless grief in this woman's eyes…Vince couldn't help himself.

One certainty rose to the forefront of his mind and he clung to it as thought it was the last bastion of sense left in the galaxy: Corwin Antwerp did not kill his brother.

As of yet, he knew nothing else about the situation, but he knew that—and for him, that was enough.

It didn't take long for Mrs. Antwerp to ready herself to leave. Moving like a shadowy wraith, she silently deposited both their tea mugs in the sink and left the kitchen. A moment later, she returned carrying a small brown leather purse, still clutching the orange and gold shawl around her thin shoulders.

She had the grim, resigned look of a woman who knew she was marching off to certain doom and couldn't see any way to avoid it.

Vince motioned for her to unlock the door and then step aside, just in case those men were lingering in the corridor outside. One hand sliding into his pocket to grip his pistol, he eased over to the door and cast a quick glance down both ends of the corridor.

Nothing.

That was…surprising…but he didn't let his guard down. The men could have deposited a tiny cam somewhere along here to keep an eye on Mrs. Antwerp's door. They could be loitering in the seldom-used stairwell.

Or they could be hanging out in the lobby below.

All of these possibilities flashed through Vince's mind as he stood in the doorway. He and Mrs. Antwerp didn't have much of a choice when it came to leaving. If somebody had men stationed in the lobby, he was willing to bet they had somebody stationed at the apartment complex's back entrance as well.

Nevertheless, he extended a hand to Mrs. Antwerp. "All clear."

She joined him in the corridor and allowed him to shepherd her down to the elevator, though the Finder wasn't so sure it was as much by choice as it was simply the fact that she was numb right now. Along the way, the elevator stopped and picked up passengers from three other floors. Vince positioned himself at a slight angle beside and in front of Mrs. Antwerp, though he kept his body language neutral and non-threatening.

When the elevator stopped on the lobby, he placed a gentle hand on Mrs. Antwerp's back as he said softly, "Keep up."

They moved out in the center of the clump of passengers as they all streamed through the lobby and spilled out into the broad corridor beyond. Vince made no obvious show of looking around, but he caught movement in his peripheral vision. One of the men who'd followed him into the apartment complex had just peeled away from the bulkhead he'd been casually leaning up against.

That was curious.

Well, Vince thought grimly, *we'll find out soon enough if they're Commosky's men or not.*

Raising a hand in the air, he flagged a passing transport pod and bundled Mrs. Antwerp inside. "Elevator bank," he told the pod's AI curtly.

They might be tailed, but there wasn't much he could do about that at the moment. At this time of the morning cycle, there was enough traffic in the corridor that it would be difficult to determine if another transport pod *was* following them.

Besides, he didn't *know* exactly who those men worked for—and if he and Mrs. Antwerp *did* run into any trouble before they reached the Station Authority Precinct, he knew just who to call.

Vince narrowed his eyes at the round window in the door beside him. He'd find out the real truth soon enough.

CHAPTER 12

For the duration of the ride to the elevator bank, Corwin's mother sat silent and ashen-faced. One hand clutched her orange and gold shawl at her breast; the other clutched her brown purse in her lap. She stared out the transport pod's other round window, her expression a million miles away.

Vince took this opportunity to update Bella. It was still too early for his assistant to be at work—she didn't usually start until 8 AM—but he thought it prudent to give her a heads-up on the current situation before anything changed. This situation felt like he was teetering on the edge of a ride from one of the holoparks, about to drop down a precipice along a track full of unexpected twists and turns.

Bella answered immediately. "Hey, Boss. Everything going good?"

"So far." He gave her a quick rundown. When he was finished, he said, "When you get to the office, lock it down. Take calls, but I don't want you letting anybody in until I get back."

"You think somebody connected with this case might decide to come here?"

That was another thing he liked about Bella. She was sharp.

"It's a possibility."

"Got it, Boss."

"Anything on the Station's newsfeeds about this yet?"

"Not as far as I've seen." Bella's voice took on an apologetic note. "It's not exactly the sort of case you'd expect to make the news, right?"

Vince made a noise of agreement. So far, so good, then. Under normal circumstances, Dent's death wouldn't even be a blip on any of the Station's media feeds. Unfortunate, sure, but that was just life on Zyga Space Station.

You were either important, or you weren't.

And the vast majority of Zyga Station's population—Vince and Bella included—just weren't that important.

Which was yet another reason Vince took his job as a Finder seriously.

Vince glanced out the window again as he felt the transport pod begin to slow. They'd arrived at the elevator bank. "Thanks, Bella. I'll keep you posted."

"Likewise, Boss."

Ending the transmission, Vince shoved his comlink into his breast pocket. The transport pod stopped in front of the turnstile and he paid their fare before helping Mrs. Antwerp out of the pod. At the turnstile, he swiped the same credit chip twice and they hurried through to join a long—but fast-moving—queue of people waiting for elevator cabs.

A discreet glance over his shoulder netted him no familiar faces. Wasn't proof-positive they hadn't been followed here, but it was an encouraging sign.

The chatter of dozens of different conversations washed over them as the queue moved toward an elevator cab. Though Vince kept a sharp eye out, no one paid them any attention. Mrs. Antwerp's orange shawl stood out against a cluster of Docking Bay workers in their navy blue overalls on one side of them, but blended in just fine against the array of colors worn by a clump of students, office workers, and restaurant workers on the other.

As always, Vince glanced up at the synthglass elevator shaft as he and Corwin's mother neared it. The shaft narrowed and dwindled to a pin prick as it stretched far above their heads, elevator cabs zipping up and down along its length like people-filled synthglass beads. He almost fancied he could glimpse the top, all the way up on Level 1. It had been a while since he'd had reason to visit this Zone's uppermost level.

In another moment, Vince and Mrs. Antwerp had stepped into an elevator cab with a handful of other people and were rapidly ascending to the next level, where they stopped to disgorge a few passengers and pick up another couple. The ride up to Level 1 took a little longer, due to all of the traffic, but soon enough the elevator cab came to a gentle stop.

Vince glanced around. Only four other passengers had made it all the way up here. One was a young man in a neat—albeit mid-price range—navy pinstriped suit; probably a receptionist. Another was a stern-faced middle-aged woman who looked like she could be an accountant. Vince had no idea if she was or not, but that was the occupation that came to mind.

The last two passengers were a pair of well-dressed women in expensive clothes and even more expensive high-heeled shoes who had both gotten on at Level 3 and spent the entire ride holding a private conversation about the personal foibles of one of their employers. Vince guessed they must work at one of the major businesses that had ritzy offices on Level 1, though it wasn't entirely clear from their conversation what either one of them actually did.

The two colleagues exited the elevator first, followed by the older woman and the receptionist. Mrs. Antwerp moved to exit as though pulled by an invisible string, and Vince flanked her. Once they had passed through the turnstile and left the elevator bank behind, Vince offered her his arm.

The smooth, dark skin of her face was even more bloodless than it had been at her apartment, and she moved as though a sudden gust of air could knock her right over. Her grip on his arm, however, was tight.

Just like in every other Zone on Zyga Station, Zone 4's Level 1 had been constructed with an eye to beauty. The space travel theme so prevalent in the lower levels of the Zone carried through here as well. Swirls of bright color ran through the white-marbled deck, leading to various planetary crests embedded into the floor. Here and there, miniature models—some real and some holographic— of the freighters and mining vessels that had made Zyga Mining Corps so wealthy stood among little park-like clumps of potted trees and metal benches.

Blocks of buildings with three and four levels stretched out around them, and far above their heads, a synthglass ceiling was all that separated them from the black, star-studded vacuum of space beyond. Glowposts shone with muted captured sunlight at regular intervals, and a series of glowpanels ran along the entire edge of the synthglass ceiling to provide Level 1 with plenty of light.

Here and there a few people could be seen walking to work, but for the most part, people on Level 1 preferred to travel in the shiny transport pods gliding up and down the avenues laid out between the blocks of buildings and compartments.

Vince had never quite understood that. If he worked up here, he'd walk and have the chance to appreciate the view of open space above them. Life everywhere else in aboard Zyga Station meant living in enclosed spaces. People up here had access to a different view.

But, he supposed it was just proof that human beings could get used to anything—even a spectacular view.

Glancing down at Mrs. Antwerp, the Finder noted that her gaze was fixed straight ahead, and not on any of the beauty that surrounded them. "Have you ever been to the Precinct up here before?"

"Once." Mrs. Antwerp's voice emerged in a barely audible whisper. "After my husband died."

Vince nodded slowly. So she was unlikely to remember how to get there. That was all right—he knew the way.

Raising a hand in the air, he flagged another transport pod. At this point, saving time was more important than saving a few credits. He could expense it later, if it came to that.

A faint, clean scent greeted them as he and Mrs. Antwerp climbed inside. That was one thing Vince appreciated about traveling on Levels 1 and 2—transport pods up here were a lot cleaner than the ones on lower levels. He settled back against the royal blue cushion for the ride, but Mrs. Antwerp still sat as straight as though she had a synthsteel rod running the length of her spine.

Within moments, the pod slowed to a halt in front of a construct as impressive as any other Station headquarters throughout Zyga Space Station. Level 1's Station Authority Precinct stood five stories tall, with a series of marble steps and tall, slender pillars leading up to the grand front entrance. From the outside, it had the illusion of broad windows, but Vince knew on the inside the windows were heavily reinforced to prevent anyone from attempting to break through them and escape.

Mrs. Antwerp's gaze fixed on the precinct as Vince helped her out of the pod and her dark face grew a little more bloodless. Her fingers were cold.

Vince wished there was something he could say to ease her mind, but the situation seemed even bleaker now that they were actually standing at the precinct's doors. He paid their fare and then walked Mrs. Antwerp up to the synthglass double doors.

Time to face the inevitable.

CHAPTER 13

ONE OF THE LARGE DOUBLE DOORS OPENED automatically for them, and Vince and Mrs. Antwerp stepped into a lobby that wouldn't have been out of place in one of the grand hotels near the Docking Bay for important—or just plain wealthy—visitors to Zyga Space Station. Unlike most of the precincts scattered throughout the rest of each Zone, Station Authority Headquarters on Level 1 was as ritzy as everything else up here.

A globe-like chandelier hung from the center of the ceiling, casting soft, piped golden sunlight over the interior. It made the pale marble floor seem to glow, save for the crimson Station Authority emblem embedded in the center of the floor beneath it. Traces of a faintly aquatic air freshener tinged the air.

A handful of comfortable chairs in muted beige, a matching couch, and a small dark wood coffee table were arranged off to one side of the lobby, beside a set of doors that led to a couple of small hygiene units. A pinched-looking older woman in a brown dress and a muted blue headscarf wrapped around her graying hair occupied one of the chairs, clutching a sheaf of papers. The rest of the seats were empty.

At the back of the lobby stood an ornate—but heavily reinforced—door that provided access to the rest of the building. Beside it stood a security booth that held two rather sleepy-looking Station Authority officers. One of them sat slumped back in his chair with the brim of his blood-red hat pulled down over his eyes, while the other was engrossed in his comlink display. Vince wasn't sure if they were the shift that had just started, or if they were waiting for their shift to end so they could go home.

The bulk of the Finder's attention, however, was on the broad reception desk that occupied the other side of the lobby. It was long enough for three people to sit at comfortably, though at the moment, only two of the stations were occupied. Vince led Mrs. Antwerp over to this desk, their shoes making soft slapping sounds against the marble floor.

The first receptionist, a young man with a shaved head beneath his regulation gray hat and a neatly-trimmed dark beard, glanced up as they approached. He looked them both up and down and then said in a flat voice, "Good morning. How may I help you?"

"This is Mrs. Antwerp." Vince motioned to Corwin's mother. "Detective Commosky is expecting her. You have her son, Corwin Antwerp, in custody."

The receptionist's gaze dropped to his datapad for a second and his fingers flew over the holographic keyboard. "And you are?"

"Finder Vince Grable." Vince produced his license from his wallet.

Dark eyes flicked back up to study Vince. "And you are involved in this affair how?"

Vince allowed himself a small, grim smile. "Her son is my client. I believe he's been asking for me."

"One moment." The young man tapped the comm he wore in his ear and his gaze slid past Vince and Mrs. Antwerp as he said, "Homicide. Detective Commosky."

A second later, he lifted his chin, his gaze flicking back across the reception desk again. "Detective, I have a Mrs. Antwerp and a Finder Grable down here to see you." A pause. "I see. Yes, sir." He tapped his comlink again and looked at Mrs. Antwerp. "You may proceed to the security booth. An officer will be down in a moment to escort you up."

"Thank you," Mrs. Antwerp said in a low, barely audible voice. She and Vince both turned away, prepared to cross the lobby, but the receptionist's sharp voice arrested their footsteps.

"Not you, Finder. You're to stay here."

Vince glanced over his shoulder, his dark eyes narrowing. So, that was how Commosky was going to play it now, was it? He shifted to face the reception desk, though he kept his expression and voice pleasant. "I'm afraid that's out of the question. Either I go with Mrs. Antwerp, or Commosky's going to have to come down here to talk to her."

A trace of a sneer curled one corner of the young man's upper lip. "And I'm afraid you don't have that kind of authority, *Finder.*" He spoke Vince's title like it was something unpleasant he'd just scraped off the bottom of his shoe.

Beside him, his colleague shifted in her chair, a little uncomfortably, though the expression on her pale face was just as snooty.

Vince glanced down at Corwin's mother. "Mrs. Antwerp?" He hated to put this kind of pressure on her, but they didn't have time for Commosky's nonsense.

Fortunately, something of that synthsteel rod that had been keeping her spine straight this whole journey remained. Mrs. Antwerp's fingers tightened their grip on her shawl, but she leveled a look at the receptionist like he was a schoolboy she'd just caught doing something he shouldn't have been doing. Her voice was only slightly shaky as she said, "Finder Grable is here because I want him here and my son asked for him. If he can't go with me, then I'm not going up."

Without waiting for an answer, she turned on her heel and marched over to the waiting area, where the pinched-faced woman was watching them out of the corner of her eye. With regal grace, Mrs. Antwerp seated herself on one end of the couch and folded her hands in her lap to hide the way they were trembling.

Vince offered the receptionist a 'what-can-you-do?' shrug and followed. He was pleased to note that the man only gaped after them for a couple of seconds before he contacted Commosky again. The resulting conversation was exchanged in tones too low to travel across the lobby, but that was all right.

Either Commosky would have to let them both up, or else he'd have to come down. It was a win-win, regardless. Even he wouldn't actually dare to have Vince thrown out.

Vince hesitated only a second as he settled down on the other end of the couch. Probably.

Besides, it wasn't like Vince didn't have information to contribute. If nothing else, he could at least corroborate Corwin's story about the earlier parts of his evening.

Vince stilled again, a chilly thought flitting across his mind. Provided, of course, Corwin had told Commosky the truth and hadn't lied to the detective for some unknown, half-baked reason.

Beside him, only the barest rise and fall of Mrs. Antwerp's orange-shawl-covered shoulders indicated she was even breathing. Her hands had stilled their worried wringing and twisting in her lap. She was staring dully at the marbled floor, her thoughts clearly a billion miles away.

Across the small waiting area, the woman with the headscarf shot them periodic curious glances. Catching her eye, Vince gave her a salutary nod. The woman immediately snapped her gaze away.

They didn't have to wait long for Commosky to make up his mind. Two minutes later, the door at the back of the lobby opened and a young officer marched out, headed straight for Vince and Mrs. Antwerp.

"Mrs. Antwerp? Finder Grable?" He came to a halt two meters from them. His crimson uniform jacket and gray pants had been pressed to within a centimeter of their lives, and his black boots were so shiny Vince thought he could see his reflection in them. "You're to come with me."

"Glad to hear it," Vince said.

The officer didn't wait for them to get to their feet, but turned and marched back toward the interior door and the security booth.

Ah, the indomitable arrogance of youth. Vince resisted the urge to shake his head. If he were that officer, he didn't believe he'd put his back to anyone—security booth or no security booth.

When they reached the security booth, the officer breezed right past, clearly expecting them to follow. Mrs. Antwerp did follow, but Vince paused. Much as he'd love to, he couldn't waltz past without mentioning he was carrying a pistol. The booth's weapons scanner would pick it up and he'd cause more of a ruckus than he preferred at the moment. Unlike other places on Zyga Station, the only people allowed to carry weapons in Station Authority precincts were Station Authority officers.

Clearing his throat, Vince caught the attention of the bored-looking officer on duty. In low, pleasant tones, he said, "I'm a licensed Finder and I'd like to register a weapon before I head past." He nodded to the door beyond.

The officer immediately straightened in his seat, his bored expression turning to one of interest. "License and weapon."

Beyond them, the young officer realized what was happening and stopped short, turning to face Vince with something like incredulity. Mrs. Antwerp dutifully stopped as well, her dark eyes traveling back and forth between Vince and the officer.

Vince produced his license and then pulled his pistol from its holster in his pants pocket. He laid it gently in the clear synthplast box the officer held out for him, closed the lid, and pressed his thumb into the lock panel without being prompted. He'd done this before; he knew the drill.

The officer presented him with a bright orange receipt chip. "You'll get this back on your way out."

"Thank you." With a pleasant nod, Vince moved beyond the security booth.

The young officer gave him a haughty look as he approached. "You could have said something."

"Isn't it your job to ask?" Vince raised a curious eyebrow at him.

The young officer just frowned and leaned toward the door panel for a retinal scan. The door slid open and he marched through. "This way."

Mrs. Antwerp glanced up at Vince; he gave her a small, encouraging smile. Then they followed the officer through the door.

CHAPTER 14

A NETWORK OF GLEAMING CORRIDORS AND OFFICES LAY behind the door to the lobby. The scent of that aquatic air freshener was a little stronger here. Everything was done in shades of white, synthglass, and shiny metal—just like in all the rest of the Station Authority headquarter precincts Vince had ever visited. He suspected the Station's architects had been so enamored of this design that they'd just decided to replicate it in each Zone.

No one spoke as the young officer led them through a series of corridors to the elevator that would take them up to Homicide on the third floor. The officer wasn't in the mood to talk to civilians, Mrs. Antwerp seemed to have temporarily become mute, and Vince himself was just taking everything in. There was a time to attempt to extract information out of a Station Authority officer via a little idle chitchat and a time to refrain. This was one of the latter times.

Particularly given this young man's attitude. Vince wanted to ask if Commosky would talk to them in the bullpen or shove them into an interrogation room, but he doubted he'd get the satisfaction of an answer.

At any rate, this was Detective Commosky they were talking about. Vince's credits were on an interrogation room.

He wasn't wrong.

When the elevator doors opened, the young officer marched them past a small reception desk and the entrance to the bullpen to a corridor lined with reinforced doors. Opening the second door on the left, marked Interrogation Room D, he waved an impatient hand for them to enter.

Vince glanced inside. The white-walled room was empty, save for the standard-issue table and chairs and the long, one-way observation mirror that took up the entire side wall. "Where's Commosky?"

"*Detective* Commosky," the young officer said frostily, "will be with you as soon as he is able."

In other words, they were stuck waiting until the detective deigned to grace them with his presence. Vince leveled a cool look at the officer. "Tell the detective I'm sending him a bill if he keeps us waiting too long."

The young officer's dark eyes narrowed, as though he was about to retort, but a sideways glance at Mrs. Antwerp's bloodless face made him change his mind. Without so much as a curt nod, he shut the door, locking them in.

"You might as well make yourself comfortable." Vince pulled out a chair for Mrs. Antwerp, nodding for her to have a seat. "We could be here a while."

Corwin's mother didn't budge. She looked at Vince with those large, dark eyes, and spoke for the first time since they'd emerged from the elevator on Level 1. "He said it was urgent."

"Oh, I'm sure he did." Vince allowed himself a grim smile. "One of those things Station Authority officers tell mere mortals like you and me to make sure we get here on time." He pulled out a chair for himself and folded himself into it, stretching out his long legs beneath the table. "Once we're here, of course, time becomes relative."

"That," said a deep voice from the door, which had just slid open again, "is not entirely true."

Vince and Mrs. Antwerp both glanced over in time to watch a short, stocky man with broad shoulders breeze into the interrogation room. Despite the early hour, he had the look of a man who'd been up and about his business for half the day. Detective Ron Commosky wore his uniform with a casual air that said any minute he'd be rolling up his sleeves, regs or no regs. He was dark-haired, but clean-shaven, with keen black eyes set in a square-jawed swarthy tan face.

"Mrs. Antwerp." He nodded to Corwin's mother as the door slid shut behind him. His dark gaze flicked to Vince. "Finder."

"Detective," Vince returned, in the same dry tone.

Commosky looked at Mrs. Antwerp again. "Thank you for coming in. I'm sorry to have to ask you this, but I need you to come down to the morgue with me and identify the—identify your son's body."

A little more of the color bled from Mrs. Antwerp's dark cheeks, but she nodded jerkily and rose to her feet.

Vince started to rise as well, but Commosky held up a hand. "Not you, I'm afraid." He shot Vince a small smile that didn't reach his eyes, his tone indicating Vince should consider himself fortunate to be sitting in this room at all.

Mrs. Antwerp made a small squeak of protest as this registered, her red-rimmed eyes widening in alarm. Vince smiled at her, trying to reassure her. "It'll be all right, Mrs. Antwerp. I'll be right here when you get back." He glanced at Commosky, as though daring him to argue.

All the detective said was, "We'll be back shortly."

He ushered Mrs. Antwerp through the door and they were gone.

CHAPTER 15

Twenty minutes later, Vince was beginning to wonder if Detective Commosky had lied to him. He sat quietly at the interrogation table, too experienced to fidget and let anyone monitoring him know just how agitated and frustrated he felt. Instead, he tried to distract himself by catching the latest headlines from Zyga Station's various media sources.

Nothing of interest had happened, other than the courts had set a date for Terrell Roda's trial. That was good news—the families of the crew whose disappearance a decade earlier Roda had almost certainly had a hand in arranging deserved justice. Vince had made that discovery while hunting down the people responsible for kidnapping Roda's little girl several months earlier. There was a possibility he, Vince, might have to testify at some point, but it wouldn't be for a long time.

Briefly, he wondered how Roda's wife, Jewel, and daughter were handling everything. It was unfortunate that reuniting their family might ultimately result in them being torn apart again, but the truth was the truth. It couldn't be buried forever.

It was so quiet in the interrogation room that Vince could hear both his own heartbeat and the smooth electric buzzing of the bright glowpanel in the overhead. He rested a hand on the cold white metal table, letting that faint buzz wash over him. It was soothing, reminding him of being in the lower levels, where the faint hum of the Station's engine was just barely audible—a reminder that as long as it was there, they'd all keep on living.

Against the backdrop of all this stillness, the sound of the door sliding open seemed inordinately loud. Vince straightened automatically, his gaze darting to the door in time to see Commosky usher Mrs. Antwerp inside. Corwin's mother looked like she'd been crying; there were freshly dried tear tracks on her thin cheeks.

Something heavy settled in Vince's chest. Any doubt he'd had that there might have been a mistake was now gone. It *was* Dent's body downstairs in the morgue.

Charitably, Commosky pulled out a chair for Mrs. Antwerp beside Vince. The legs squeaked a little as he dragged them across the floor. "Again, Mrs. Antwerp, I'm sorry you had to go through that. We have to be sure, you see."

He didn't look at Vince, but he didn't need to. The Finder knew this statement was more for him than it was for her. There was less sympathy in his deep tones than there should have been.

Mrs. Antwerp just nodded as she sat down, her face downcast and her lips pressed into a tight line. She didn't look at Vince either.

That was all right—he had all the confirmation he needed. The only trouble was how to start Commosky talking without irritating him by asking too nosy an opening question.

Fortunately, the detective settled that all by himself. Pulling out the lone chair across from them, he popped a datachip into a little slot near the edge of the table. Then he addressed Vince. "Now that I've had time to consider, Finder, I'm glad you're here. Saves me the trouble of having to hunt you down."

"Happy to oblige," Vince said dryly. "Are you going to let me talk to my client?"

"We'll see. Depends on a few things." Commosky turned his attention to Mrs. Antwerp. "I need a statement from you, ma'am, and then I'll have one of my people get you something to drink while I talk to the Finder here." He tipped his head toward Vince.

In all honesty, Vince was a little surprised Commosky didn't temporarily boot him from the interrogation room for this process, but he was starting to get the faintest glimmer of the reason why. The way his goatee had begun prickling again bolstered this conviction.

Commosky questioned Mrs. Antwerp carefully, going back and forth over the timeline of the past twenty-four hours, as well as jumping back and forth between various points over the preceding three or four months. Corwin's mother answered everything in the same dull, borderline teary voice. No, she didn't know where Dent went or where he liked to hang out inside his virtual game worlds. No, she hadn't realized how bad things had gotten until it was too late.

No, she didn't think her younger son had killed his brother.

At last, Commosky nodded and tapped the tiny comlink embedded in the collar of his uniform. "Morbeta, Room 4-D."

A moment later, the door opened to reveal a tiny woman in a crimson and gray uniform. She had a pale, pointy face, overly large brown eyes, and mouse-brown hair pulled back in a tight bun. "Yes, Detective?"

"Escort Mrs. Antwerp to the waiting area and get her a cup of coffee or something." Commosky waved a hand. "Whatever she wants."

"Yes, sir."

As though moving through a dream, Mrs. Antwerp rose from her seat and joined the tiny Station Authority officer out in the corridor. Vince followed her with his eyes, but Mrs. Antwerp didn't look back at him until the door was sliding shut. He saw mingled desperation and hope in her gaze.

With Corwin's mother gone, the atmosphere in the interrogation room shifted. Commosky leaned back in his chair, master and commander of all he surveyed, and regarded Vince through narrowed eyes. "What are we going to do about you, Finder?"

"You could take my statement." Vince offered him a cool, polite smile. "As I've told you, Corwin Antwerp is a client of mine."

"I suppose we could start with that."

Strangely, the detective didn't seem to be in any kind of hurry…which only reinforced the growing feeling Vince had that something else was going on here.

The two of them proceeded through the statement routine. Vince left nothing out—except his own opinions—and Commosky only asked for clarification on a couple of points.

When the Finder finished, Commosky grunted softly. "We'll verify that with the noodle shop owner, but I'm sure your timeline is accurate." He grunted again. "That's one point in your favor—you don't usually stretch the truth." He let the rest of that sentence hang between them.

Unless it suits your purposes.

That was neither here nor there—and Vince wasn't about to waste time on veiled, unspoken accusations. He leaned forward, nodding in the direction of the datachip the detective had inserted into the table and had yet to utilize. "I have a few questions of my own, Detective. Such as, where did you find Dent Antwerp's body, and why are you so sure his brother killed him?"

CHAPTER 16

THE AIR IN THE INTERROGATION ROOM GREW tense as the two men locked gazes. Commosky seemed to be holding an internal debate with himself, weighing how much to tell Vince. At last, he shrugged and reached over to tap the panel embedded in the table beside the chip reader. "Found him down on Level 6, in a maintenance corridor not far from his family's apartment."

Level 6. Vince had been expecting Dent's body to have turned up in the Core. He had to admit that didn't look good for Corwin, but raised an eyebrow in polite surprise. "Then why is his body sitting in Station Authority headquarters' morgue instead of the one in your Level 6 precinct?"

Commosky's stony expression didn't change, but something flickered in his dark eyes. "You *would* notice that."

"Anybody with two brain cells to rub together would notice that." Vince lifted one shoulder in a dismissive shrug. "Everyone on Zyga Station knows that common, two-credit gambling addicts who wind up dead don't usually rate attention from Station Authority headquarters." He offered Commosky a wry smile, which the detective did not return.

Still eying Vince, Commosky leaned back in his chair and folded his arms across his chest. A crease formed in the center of his forehead as he frowned, clearly thinking hard.

Vince wanted to tell him not to hurt himself, but kept his mouth shut. He could have gotten away with making a crack like that with Sergeant Rychek back in Zone 5. Commosky, however… If the man had a sense of humor, he kept it buried so deep in the depths of his soul that it couldn't escape.

Finally, Commosky unbent enough to speak. He tapped the panel on the table again, turning the recorder off, and drilled Vince with a hard look. "What I'm about to tell you, Finder, is part of an ongoing classified investigation. If you breach my confidence or otherwise break confidentiality in any way, I'll have your license before you can blink and you'll be on the next prison transport to the mines."

His tone was so calm and even that the detective could have been relaying something as mundane and trivial as the number of ingoing and outgoing visitors to Zyga Station on any given day instead of issuing threats.

"I understand." Vince inclined his head in a polite nod. His goatee was still bristling; he had to resist the urge to rub it.

"Ordinarily, you'd be one of the last people I'd trust with information of this sort, but…" Commosky turned one hand palm up, a small, supercilious smile tugging at one corner of his mouth. "In this case, you have a vested interest, and I think you might actually be useful."

Vince raised an eyebrow again. "As opposed to all those times we've met before when I've been so unhelpful?"

Commosky's black eyes narrowed, glittering with suppressed irritation. "Do you want to hear more or not?"

"Do you want *my* help or not?" Vince countered. It was his turn to hold a hand out palm up. "If so, no need to be an ass, Commosky. Believe it or not, I'm on the side of justice. If I can help, I will."

The detective's eyes narrowed further, as though he had plenty he could say about *that*, but he chose to hold it back. Instead, he took a quick, measured breath and reached out to tap the panel in the table. "This is the crime scene."

A crisp three-dimensional holograph immediately sprang to life. Dent Antwerp lay slumped over on his side in the dimly-lit maintenance corridor, his body half-propped up against the gray bulkhead. He'd been beaten—badly—and bore little resemblance to the images Vince had studied the night before. Something twisted in the Finder's chest. He could only imagine how hard it must have been for Mrs. Antwerp to see her son like that.

"Cause of death?" He glanced at Commosky.

In lieu of answering, Commosky tapped the panel. The holograph changed to a view from another angle—giving Vince a great view of the side of Dent's head, which had been caved in from repeated blows.

Vince felt cold. Someone had been very, very angry with this young man.

"He also had a punctured lung from several broken ribs, but the head injury is what killed him." The detective shook his head slightly. "Poor sap didn't have a chance to put up much of a fight."

Vince looked from the holograph to Commosky. "And you think his brother did this?"

"Corwin Antwerp was angry enough." It was the detective's turn to lift a shoulder in a brief shrug. "We've got proof of that."

"You also have both of our accounts of last night. He hired me to—"

"I know the spiel." Commosky cut him off, a tinge of impatience in his brisk voice. "You don't have to go through it again."

Vince narrowed his eyes, but refrained from retorting. Instead, he turned his attention to the crime scene holograph again. The detective flicked through a few more holos for him, but Vince didn't see anything more of interest. He sat back in his uncomfortably hard chair, his mind racing, trying to fit all these new pieces of information together into a cohesive whole.

"Time of death?" he asked at last.

Commosky hesitated just a fraction. "Somewhere between midnight and four AM."

This time, Vince didn't resist the urge to rub his bristling chin. As he did, he lifted an eyebrow at Commosky. "I'll remind you, Detective, that Mr. Antwerp didn't leave my office until after midnight."

"And I'll remind *you*, Finder, that his brother's body was found not far from their home. But…" Commosky paused again and then shrugged. "What the hell. For what it's worth, I agree with you. I don't think Corwin killed him."

For a second, Vince didn't think he'd heard the detective correctly. He squinted at Commosky across the table. "Come again?"

"You heard me." Commosky folded his beefy arms across his chest. "I don't think the kid's guilty."

Several of the pieces to this puzzle clicked into place inside Vince's mind, while the rest collapsed into a disorganized jumble. His gut had been right—there *was* a reason Dent's body was sitting in Station Authority headquarters' morgue.

He nodded in the general direction of the corridor and the waiting area beside the bullpen. "Then why did you arrest Corwin? Why are you putting his mother through the double hell of thinking one of her sons beat the other to death?"

Commosky smiled. It was not a pleasant expression. "Oh, there's plenty of physical evidence to implicate Corwin. Hairs, fibers—I've got my men searching the Antwerps' apartment while Mrs. Antwerp is here. I'm sure they'll find bloody clothes."

"But yet you don't think Corwin's guilty." Vince nodded slowly. There was only one reason Commosky could look at the evidence and think that—he knew who had really killed Dent Antwerp.

Or at least *thought* he knew.

It was Vince's turn to fold his arms across his chest. "Dent was working for you, wasn't he?" It wasn't a question. "And the wrong people found out and killed him for it."

CHAPTER 17

Commosky didn't answer for a long moment. He just looked at Vince, his expression stony again. The barely audible hum from the bright glowpanel in the ceiling seeped into the silence that fell over the interrogation room.

At last, the detective stirred in his seat. A muscle in his jaw twitched as he swallowed. "This," he said grudgingly, "is why I'm bringing you in on this case, Finder. You grasp things quicker than most."

Vince just waited, arms still folded across his chest.

"Yes, Antwerp was working for us." Commosky suddenly pinched the bridge of his nose, as though he'd just developed a headache. "We recruited him a few weeks ago."

"So you knew about the lien he'd put on his mother's apartment?"

"Oh, yes." Commosky waved a hand. "We knew. In fact, that was part of our strategy for—well—" he made a sour face, as though he'd just bitten into something terrible. "Have to start all over now."

He grimaced. "If that's even possible now that they know we're on to them."

A cold ball of disgust solidified in the pit of Vince's stomach. Looking at Commosky across the table, he saw a man who, while frustrated with the disruption in his plans, didn't seem all that concerned with the permanent disruption to the Antwerps' lives. And now the detective wanted his help, as though it was some big favor he was granting the Finder.

"What, exactly, is it that you think I can do for you?" Vince settled back in his chair, deliberately keeping his body language open.

A small, almost tired smile curled one corner of Commosky's mouth. He shook his head slightly, reaching for his cup of coffee. "I know what you're thinking, Finder. "

"I doubt it."

"No, give me some credit." The detective eyed him over the lid of his cup. "You're thinking that I think it doesn't matter if Antwerp lived or died—the kid was going to bite it eventually, so why not use him?" His dark eyes sharpened. "You're thinking that if it weren't for the fact that he was working for us, I wouldn't care who popped him. And you're thinking he might have lived a little longer."

That was…eerily prescient. Vince allowed himself a slight raise of his eyebrows. "Not bad, Detective. You just forgot one thing."

"Oh?"

"The fact that Corwin Antwerp is innocent."

Commosky waved his free hand. "And, naturally, you think it's shameful that we're booking him on murder charges when we know he didn't do it."

That was precisely Vince's thought, but he wasn't about to confirm it. This entire conversation was proving to be a little surreal for his liking.

"Just remember we're after bigger space monsters, Grable."

"Oh, you've made that very clear, Commosky." This time, Vince did fold his arms across his chest as he leveled the other man with a hard look. "What you *haven't* made clear yet is exactly what you need from me."

He expected Commosky to make a face at his phrasing, or perhaps make some snide remark.

To his surprise, the shorter man just smiled again. "You're a smart man, Grable. I'd have thought that was obvious." He leaned forward a little, turning one hand palm up. "I need you to investigate the places and people I can't. You're not a cop—there are certain doors open to you that somebody like me just can't walk through."

Vince held the detective's gaze for a moment, his goatee still bristling. He'd anticipated Commosky intended something along these lines, but he'd wanted to make the detective actually come out and say it instead of dancing around the subject.

Finally, he shrugged. "I'm going to need a lot more background info before I go wandering around Zyga Station poking my nose into things."

Commosky's eyes glittered. "Hence the warning about breaking confidentiality regarding an ongoing classified investigation."

"You've made that quite clear, Detective." Vince shifted position in his hard chair. "Now do us both a favor and get on with it. We're wasting time."

For a split-second, the Finder saw a flash of resentful anger cross Commosky's face, but the detective mastered himself.

"Fine," he said curtly. "I'll read you in as far as I'm able. This is what we know…"

It was closing in on lunchtime before Vince made it back to the office. Once Commosky finished with him, the detective had given Vince permission to escort Mrs. Antwerp home. Corwin's mother had barely said a word the entire trip; she continued to move like a woman trapped in a nightmare. Only when they reached her apartment door on Level 6 did she rouse enough to thank Vince and to entreat him again to save Corwin.

However angry her youngest might have been with his brother, she still didn't believe he'd killed him.

Vince wished he could have told her even a fraction of what Commosky had relayed to him, but he'd merely nodded solemnly and informed her he would do his level best.

Once Mrs. Antwerp was safely inside her apartment (empty—Vince had checked), Vince turned his steps toward Zone 5. On the way, he sent a simple encrypted message to his best informant in the Core, asking to meet that afternoon. The only stop he made after returning to Zone 5 was at a café near his office, where he picked up a container of chunky vegetable beef soup and some fresh-baked bread.

Despite the plethora of thoughts and half-formed theories churning inside his head, Vince's stomach was rumbling as he left the wide boulevard that ran down this section of Level 7 and strode up to his office door. As always, he felt a little thrill of satisfaction as he read the words on the small placard mounted beside his door: *Vince Grable, Finder Inc.*

No matter the occasional frustrations and setbacks (or less than helpful authority figures), Vince loved his job. As far as he was concerned, being a Finder was the best possible use of his time, talents, and intellect.

Not to mention the freedom he had being the master of his own proverbial fate—the freedom to choose his own clients and set his own schedule—insofar as one could around the constraints of said clients.

Unlocking the door, Vince let himself into the office. The familiar strains of one of his favorite jazz singers' throaty voice met his ears, along with the smooth sounds of a saxophone. He couldn't restrain a smile—he was slowly converting Bella to a jazz fan. (It had only taken weeks.)

He took a deep breath of clean air as he locked the door behind himself.

"Hey, Boss." Bella abandoned the game she'd been playing on her tablet to lean forward with interest. If Vince hadn't known she was an android, he'd have sworn her dark eyes were alight with keen curiosity. "How did it go?"

"Not quite as expected." Shaking his head slightly, Vince carried the bag containing his lunch over to his desk. Setting it down on the jade green surface, he continued, "Commosky wants my help with the investigation."

"He wants *help*?" Bella blinked her large almond-shaped eyes once, twice, and then looked askance at Vince. "That's not normal, is it?" She folded her arms across her ample chest. She was dressed in black jeans and a scoop-necked red blouse with bell-shaped sleeves today, and her lipstick matched the blouse. "What's the catch?"

"The catch," Vince said grimly, as he headed across the office for the tiny door that led to the hygiene unit, "is that he's aware our client is most likely innocent." He glanced over his shoulder in time to see Bella's look of horror.

"But if that's true—" she shook her head, apparently at a temporary loss for words.

Vince scrubbed his hands clean, feeling like he was washing off the taint of sitting in that Station Authority precinct, and then ducked back out into his office. "I know, Bella."

He stopped at the jade green sideboard long enough to fix himself a cup of plain black tea. "And yet, can you really say you're surprised to hear it?"

Bella considered this a moment before shaking her head again, more slowly this time. "No. Not really." She held up a hand, her silver nails glinting in the light from the glowpanels in the overhead. "And they wonder why nobody trusts Station Authority."

"Exactly." Smiling grimly, Vince carried his tea over to his desk and took his seat. Reaching into the bag of food, he pulled out the container of soup and a bag containing a large slice of fresh-baked bread. "Let me eat and I'll give you the rundown." He smiled again, but the expression didn't reach his eyes. "It's going to be a busy afternoon."

CHAPTER 18

THE OPERATION DENT ANTWERP HAD GOTTEN HIMSELF tangled up in wasn't some newfangled creation. It wasn't even that original. But it *was* successful.

Bella listened in rapt silence while Vince outlined most of what Commosky had relayed to him. Someone—or several someones; Commosky hadn't managed to dig up enough information on the individuals at the top level yet—had built their own private little gambling club inside one of the most popular multiplayer games on Zyga Space Station's servers. By invitation only, the Ruby Gauntlet fostered an air of exclusivity, but that was really just a veneer to make people think they were part of something special and privileged.

The reality, Commosky had explained, was that practically anyone could enter the Ruby Gauntlet and put their credits on the line as long as they were introduced by someone who'd already been vetted by the club.

Gambling itself was illegal on Zyga Station—unless it took place at one of the few casinos authorized to operate aboard the Station.

There were two physical locations and several online venues, and all of them paid a cut to Station Authority and to Zyga Station's governing body for the privilege of being open. The cost of doing business, Vince had heard it described once.

The Oswari and Bok Families each owned—or at the very least owned a vested interest in—one of the physical casinos, and they probably had ties to several of the online operations, though one of *those* was owned by a wealthy playboy who lived on the Rim and had nothing else to do with his life.

The Ruby Gauntlet, however, sought to bypass the authorities and keep all the profit for themselves. They'd gotten away with it, too, for at least a year. What had finally brought them to Station Authority's attention was the fact that they'd grown too popular to stay under the radar.

"Well, that and the bodies." Vince drained the last of his tea and frowned at the bottom of his mug for a second, contemplating whether he ought to go ahead and make himself another cup or wait a while.

"Bodies?" Bella hadn't moved the entire time he'd been speaking. "You mean Dent Antwerp wasn't the first?"

"Oh, no." Vince shook his head. "Not by a long shot. According to Commosky, the bodies didn't start showing up until a few months ago."

Bella snorted softly. "Sorry, Boss, that was a dumb question." She shook her head, frowning. "Of *course* there are more bodies. Why else would a homicide detective be investigating this club?"

"Don't worry about it." Vince decided he *did* want another cup of tea and stood up. "Offhand, I can think of three different reasons why Commosky might be involved, but you're right—he *is* a homicide detective."

"Were the other people who died also informants?"

"No. As far as I know, Dent was the first."

"So who were they?"

Vince shook his head as he rounded his desk and crossed to the sideboard. He chose jasmine tea this time. "A handful of people who couldn't pay and somehow made the Ruby Gauntlet's owners angry enough to take them out."

"Well, that doesn't make any sense."

Glancing over his shoulder, the Finder saw that his assistant was frowning again. His tea finished steeping; he added a dollop of honey. "What doesn't?"

"Them killing people who can't pay." Bella waved a hand. "Don't loan sharks—or whatever these people at this club call themselves—usually like to keep the people who owe them money *alive* so they can get their money back?" She shook her head. "Don't they usually just beat them up and send them home as a warning to everybody else?"

"Usually." Vince favored her with a grim smile. "That's what makes this particular operation so insidious. They've expanded the debts to include their victims' family members—and in one case, friends. So it doesn't matter if the original debtor dies. They'll move on to the family and friends to collect."

Bella's eyes widened with remembrance. "The lien on Mrs. Antwerp's apartment."

"Exactly."

They shared a dire look and then Vince returned to his desk.

"What are you going to do? Try to get an invite into this place?"

The Finder looked over at his assistant. "The thought did cross my mind. I'd rather tackle that as a last resort, however." Vince lifted one shoulder in a pragmatic shrug, smiling wryly. "I prefer to spend the majority of my time in reality, not wandering through some fictional world."

Bella nodded sagely. "I didn't think you were much of a gamer."

"There are a couple of Finders aboard Zyga Station who specialize in hunting people down inside online gaming worlds." Vince shrugged again. "I prefer to track down their physical locations."

He spread his hands. "There are only so many places for a human being to hide. We *do* live on a space station, after all."

"That's true." Bella's gaze drifted past him, her expression going smooth and still.

Vince had the unsettling feeling she was recalling past events that had led to their paths crossing. He also hoped she wasn't about to volunteer to go wandering into this virtual club on her own.

A few heartbeats later, Bella snapped her attention back to the present. "I used to play those games too, when I had the time." Her mouth pursed. "I was never as into them as Cara, though. And since—well—" her hands reflexively flexed into fists, "—let's just say I haven't had the heart." She tipped her head toward her data-pad. "Casual little games are as far as I venture now. Otherwise, I'd offer to help."

"I appreciate the offer." Vince inclined his head toward her. He appreciated her bravery in the face of the memory of how she'd ended up in that body. "Like I said, though, I prefer to track down physical locations. I only ever venture into virtual territory if absolutely necessary."

Which, over the course of his ten year career aboard Zyga Space Station, had only happened twice.

"Besides," he grinned abruptly. "This is why I have informants who enjoy this kind of thing."

Instead of eliciting a smile, however, Bella's eyes widened in almost comical alarm. "You're not sending *Rav* in to investigate, are you?" She shot to her feet, posting her hands on her hips. "I don't care what kind of in-game avatars he's got, he's a kid! He can't—"

"I am not sending Rav into that club." Vince did not raise his voice, but his tone—though mild—had enough steel in it to quell Bella's initial panic. His best informant in the Core was still a teenager—and even if it had been legal, Vince wasn't about to risk Rav's life over this mess.

"Oh. Good." Bella brushed a lock of stray black hair back behind her ear and sank primly back into her seat. "Had me worried for a sec there, Boss."

Vince wanted to roll his eyes, but refrained. Instead, he raised an eyebrow at his assistant. "Rav may be one of my best informants, but he's hardly the only one."

"I know that." Bella had the grace to look slightly chastened. "I just—" she shrugged helplessly, "—the kid kinda grows on you, you know?"

"Oh, I know." Vince permitted himself a small, rueful smile, before clearing his throat and swiveling in his comfortable office chair to face his computer. "Rav may not know anything at all but he can at least help me rule out whether or not one of the Families potentially has ties to the Ruby Gauntlet."

Commosky had danced around *that* subject too—and it worried Vince. From where he stood, it wasn't complicated. Either the Families were involved, or they weren't. Either Commosky knew that, or he didn't.

And if the detective knew and wouldn't say? Well…it did nothing to give Vince peace about his involvement in this operation. Even if his client *was* innocent.

…maybe *especially* since his client was innocent.

CHAPTER 19

Since it would be several hours before he could meet Rav in the Core, Vince decided to do some basic research on the Ruby Gauntlet. He started with a generic ComNet search for the virtual night club and then moved to the next level. What he found wasn't promising.

Not that he'd expected to find much, after his chat with Commosky, but even the little he found was barely more than a few oblique mentions scattered across a handful of gaming forums.

Under ordinary circumstances, that alone would have piqued his interest. Everything had an online footprint. *Everything.*

It was just a question of how deep you had to dig to find the data.

Absently tapping his stylus against the jade green surface of his desk, Vince leaned back in his comfortable chair and stared up at the overhead with unseeing eyes. He let the smooth notes of the music playing softly in the background wash over him while he considered the Ruby Gauntlet. As he'd told Bella, it wasn't often that his job took him into the virtual world. Usually, he simply located the physical bodies of people who were lost to virtual worlds.

But a secret virtual night club? This was out of his league—and he was man enough to admit it.

The tapping of his stylus stilled. This situation called for someone with a lot more experience than he had to pry loose the information he needed.

Someone whose help came with an unfortunately hefty price tag.

Vince snorted softly at his own hesitation to spend more money than he was likely to get back in a fee. How much was a man's life worth? The price of paying an information broker?

Bella recognized the contemplative look on his face. She leaned forward to prop an elbow on her own desk and rest her chin in her hand. "That's a pretty intense look, Boss. What are you thinking?"

"I'm thinking I'm an idiot." Vince flicked his fingers in a dismissive wave before sitting up and swiveling in his chair to fix her with a keen look. "How much is a man's life worth?"

"A lot," Bella said promptly.

"That's what I thought."

Vince reached for his comlink.

Usually, he used texts to communicate with Brill—a need-to-know information broker who lived in a hidden apartment in the Core. But there were occasions when an actual conversation was required—when time was of the essence or the subject matter was too complex.

This was one of those occasions.

The information broker answered the encrypted call after a few rings. "Finder," he said in an almost cheerful voice. "What case are we on now?"

"Murder."

"Murder? That's…unusual for you. Don't you normally prefer the people you Find to be alive?"

"When possible," Vince said dryly. "Today's circumstances are a bit…unusual."

"Must be, if you're calling me. What do you need?"

"Everything you can tell me about a virtual nightclub called the Ruby Gauntlet. I think it's located somewhere in the *Everheart* game world."

Silence greeted this pronouncement. (If he didn't know better, Vince would have almost called it 'stunned'.)

"Let me get this straight," Brill said slowly. "You want to pay me to dig up information on a place in a *game*?"

"That about sums it up."

"Wait." Brill's voice sharpened, as though he'd remembered something. "The Ruby Gauntlet?"

"You've heard of it?" Vince glanced sideways at Bella, who was watching with rapt attention.

"Maybe. I've heard of a lot of places."

His voice was matter-of-fact—a statement of fact, rather than a coy play for a higher fee. That was one of the things Vince liked about Brill. He was—mostly—upfront about his costs.

"Well, I need whatever you can find as quickly as you can find it."

The silence that greeted these words took on a speculative edge. Finally, Brill said, "You've intrigued me, Grable. I'll be in touch."

The line went dead.

"I'm glad I've intrigued you," Vince muttered, dropping his comlink on his desk. Stars only knew what the information broker would have said if he'd been bored.

"Now what?" Bella asked.

Vince shrugged. "We wait."

Bella made a face, only slightly exaggerated.

"My thoughts exactly." The idea of sitting idle while he waited for information had never settled well with him. Sometimes he couldn't help it, but other times he had options.

Vince glanced at his comlink. It was still a little early to leave to meet Rav, but…

It wouldn't hurt to be early.

He rose abruptly from his chair, reaching for his jacket. "I don't expect any trouble, but keep things locked down anyway just in case."

"What if Mrs. Antwerp comes here?" Bella lifted a questioning eyebrow.

Vince considered that for a nanosecond before shaking his head. "She won't, but if she does, let her in. Then call me."

"Got it, Boss." Bella sketched a little salute.

"You're the best, Bella." Vince nodded to her, then exited his office.

Let Brill dig up what he could; there was still plenty for Vince himself to do. Particularly when an innocent man's life hung on the line.

CHAPTER 20

Tʜᴇ ᴛʀɪᴘ ᴛᴏ ᴛʜᴇ Cᴏʀᴇ sᴇᴇᴍᴇᴅ ᴛᴏ take longer than usual, like the oxygen filling Zyga Space Station had somehow thickened and objected to people passing through it. After leaving his office, Vince made his way back to the glass elevator bank and took a cab down to Level 22. From there, he hopped a transporter pod to the Hub.

Normally, Vince would take a moment on a trip to the Core to appreciate the spectacular view of space from the synthglass viewports that ran along both sides of the Hub's bulkheads, but right now he noticed none of it. For one, this was his third trip through the Hub for the day, and for another… His thoughts were occupied with the Ruby Gauntlet.

It occurred to Vince that it would have been nice if he could simply question Rav via a series of texts and save himself a trip to the Core today, but he let the thought pass. Even with end-to-end encryption and messages that deleted themselves after they were read, there were some topics he wasn't comfortable discussing any way other than in person. Particularly if they happened to involve one of the Families or corruption in Zyga Station's government.

In this case, he was fairly certain that the only sensitive topic might be the Families' shady influence, but he wasn't taking any chances. He'd had dealings with members of the Oswari Family and he'd actually met the head of the Bok Family, Bok Chul himself, and he trusted none of them. Both Families had proved themselves fully capable of making people disappear if they got in the way of business as usual.

Bella's cousin Cara fell into that category. The young woman had deserved some sort of punishment for selling Bella to Bok Chul's son in payment for her debts, but Vince wasn't convinced the almost-certain death sentence Bok Chul had meted out was the right answer. It certainly wasn't the *legal* response…and Bok Chul definitely lacked the authority to pronounce such a sentence, much less carry it out.

But that was life in the Core. It operated by a completely different set of parameters than the rest of Zyga Station. Detective Commosky and his fellow Station Authority officers liked to think they were in control, but everyone knew who really ran things down here.

If the owners of the Ruby Gauntlet were flaunting Station Authority *and* the Families…well…Vince had no doubt things were fixing to explode soon.

Dead bodies cropping up across Zyga Station tended to have that effect.

Vince strode down the walkway that led to the entrance to the sphere-like Core, passing the security checkpoints without any issue. He then marched through the Core's uppermost level, which was made up predominately of shops, restaurants, and amusement attractions until he reached the elevator bank. Unlike the elevators throughout the rest of Zyga Station, the Core's elevators were plain, unadorned gray metal streaked with rust.

Vince joined a group of people headed down into the depths of the Core. Some of them were workers, others were returning home from shopping or getting something to eat, and there was no telling what the rest were doing. One or two people glanced sideways at him when he requested Level 19, but otherwise no one paid any attention. It took energy to care what other people were doing, and most people living in the Core didn't have that energy to spare.

The Families had tacitly split control of the Core between them. The Bok Family controlled the western hemisphere, while the Oswari controlled the eastern hemisphere. That meant they each controlled half of each Level, from the top of the Core all the way down until you hit the Authorized-Access-Only levels at the heart of the Core that housed Zyga Station's engines, life-support system, and other important internal workings. Their control then picked up on the other side.

The Core's inner levels were the space station's slums. This was where the detritus of Zyga Station migrated, this was where people disappeared when they were on the run. This was where people tended to actually vanish, as well.

You had to be careful not to get turned around in the Core— most of the bulkheads were the same rusty gray metal and it was easy to get confused in the maze of corridors and mix of large and small compartments that made up the center of Zyga Station. The Core's denizens sometimes weren't all that helpful, either. There were stories (Vince still didn't quite know if they were true or not, though he didn't doubt something like that had happened) about visitors to the Core who got lost and were never seen again after getting faulty information from a Core-dweller.

Rav lived on Level 19, in the half controlled by the Bok Family. Level 19 definitely ranked among the Core's seedier levels, but it was still a few levels up from the worst part of the Core. Vince himself didn't venture down that far unless he was armed and he had a very, very good reason. (A few of the people he'd been hired to find had made their way down that far, but you had to be truly desperate—or reckless beyond measure—to hide out beyond Level 21.)

As the elevator doors opened, Vince braced himself for the smell. Despite the fact that it housed Zyga Station's life-support system, engines, and other important systems, the bulk of the Core lacked many of the amenities found throughout the rest of the Station. Sufficient airscrubbers for the number of people housed here were part of this, and the ones they *did* have were low on Maintenance's list of things to fix when they malfunctioned.

As a result, the air through the Core's lower levels smelled of various foods and unwashed bodies. Walking into that always made visiting down here even more of an…adventure.

Automatically clearing his throat in an attempt to get rid of the tickle that worsened whenever he spent time down here, Vince set off down a gray metal bulkhead marked with the occasional splash of graffiti. Tiny living compartments lined both sides of the corridor and figures huddled in those doorways.

Vince knew better than to make eye contact with anyone. Most of the people he passed were immersed in mobile devices, lost in worlds far richer and more interesting than their own pitiful lives. The bright glow from their screens illuminated hollow eyes and gaunt, dirty faces.

Not everyone down here was jobless. Some people lived down here and worked elsewhere in the Core because they couldn't afford to live anywhere else. Vince also knew that some of the huddled figures he passed had jobs performing various sorts of online work, or else they had in-game jobs that provided a modicum of real-world credit chips. They also earned a few extra credits by collecting trash and selling it to the recyclers, though that could be tricky because trash collecting had its own ecosystem and the Core's levels were split into territories.

Rav collected trash too, on occasion, but he'd also found other ways of making income beyond what Vince paid him to be an informant. He'd had to, now that his grandma was dead.

That's a good thing, Vince thought as he wound his way deeper into Level 19, *because otherwise the kid'll lose that apartment in a few months when his payoff from Magna runs out.*

Several months prior, Rav had proved instrumental in helping Vince and an information broker named Magna track down the location of a secret experimental lab being housed by the Oswari Family on one of the Core's Authorized-Access-Only levels. The kid had allowed himself to be kidnapped—for a price—and Vince had rescued him. Bok Chul's men had found the lab too—and they didn't know that the place had a failsafe security system to take care of intruders.

Vince and Rav had barely escaped with their lives—and the information that not only was this lab indeed where Bella's consciousness had been taken from her living, breathing body and placed in the android shell she now inhabited, but that Bella was also an anomaly.

She wasn't supposed to have lived more than two weeks, and yet somehow she had.

The scientist who had created her would have been very interested in studying her—if Bok Chul's men hadn't killed him. Provided he could find her, of course. The entire reason Vince had been working with Magna in the first place was to create a new identity for Bella and grant her some protection from Bok Chul's son, Orion Lab…and Station Authority.

Androids were illegal aboard Zyga Space Station, after all.

Rounding a corner and offering a short nod to a grim-faced woman wrapped in a dingy brown shawl coming the other way, Vince pulled his comlink from his inside breast pocket long enough to note the time. He still had a good ten minutes to spare before his prescribed meeting with Rav.

More than enough time to reach the Soup Kitchen, one of the kid's favorite meeting spots. He quickened his pace. That was good—it gave him time to scope things out.

CHAPTER 21

Four corridors later, Vince reached a large hatch with a faded mural of a garden painted on it. Pushing the hatch open, he stepped through it into a comparatively large compartment full of long rows of brown metal tables, most of them occupied by people of all ages in worn, grimy clothes. The aroma of cooking food and unwashed bodies mixed with the more metallic tang that permeated the air in this part of the Core. At the far side of the compartment, a group of people holding plates stood in line at a long counter that divided the dining room from the kitchen, waiting to be served.

The hum of conversation filled the air, bouncing off the gray metal bulkheads, but it wasn't what it seemed. At least half of the people filling those tables were talking to themselves. Or seemed to be talking to themselves. Some of them had brain jacks (they'd managed to scrape together enough money for the operation at some point in their lives) and were interacting with a world nobody else could see being projected inside their heads. Others were immersed in hand-held devices, so engrossed that they ate without paying any attention to what they were consuming.

That was probably a good thing—the Soup Kitchen wasn't exactly known for its fine cuisine. It was, however, a place half the Core could go to get a cheap meal that would keep body and soul together another day. A handful of bleeding hearts from more prosperous parts of Zyga Station had started it up a few years back. Those who could afford to buy a meal did, and those who couldn't ate for free.

The Families hadn't quite known what to make of it at first, but after a good deal of suspicious squinting, they'd left the Soup Kitchen and its mostly volunteer staff alone. They even made the occasional donation—all in the name of making themselves look good, of course.

Casually sidling away from the entrance to lean up against the bulkhead, Vince cast a discreet glance around. Rav wasn't here yet, but he would be. The kid tended to be punctual when it involved money. Or food.

The Finder also knew his informant would want his regular cut *plus* a meal. Not that Vince minded. He had a vested interest in keeping the kid alive and in one piece.

He was hoping in a year or two he'd be able to help Rav get away from the Core, help him find good, honest work in one of the Zones or even on a mining ship. True, the Core was all Rav knew, but it didn't have to stay that way. His grandma was dead and he had no other family. Rav could, with a little help, start fresh somewhere else on Zyga Space Station.

Vince smiled slightly to himself. Even if it meant he, Vince, had to find an informant to replace the kid when the time came.

It'd be worth it to know Rav had a shot at a decent life.

After a few minutes, Vince joined the line of people queuing up for food. The line moved quickly; in another moment he had exchanged pleasantries with the servers, made a donation for his food, and carried the tray over to one of the tables near the far wall from the exit. He set the tray on the table and slid onto the bench. Hopefully, his timing was good and the food would still be hot when Rav got here.

Vince eyed the food on the tray in front of him. Steamed greens, a piece of flat bread, and some sort of brown bean mixture he didn't recognize over steamed rice—some kind of curry, maybe? It smelled surprisingly appetizing.

Just as he started to send his gaze around the Soup Kitchen again, someone slid onto the other end of the bench and dropped a worn rucksack to the dingy metal deck.

"That for me?"

Casually, Vince glanced sideways. Rav had joined him at the table. He wore the soft dark green toboggan Vince had found for him after their adventure at Orion Lab jammed over his shaggy black hair, which had grown out considerably since that episode. His jeans, dark blue shirt, and overlarge brown coat were as faded and dingy as the clothes worn by practically everyone else sitting in the Soup Kitchen.

"Yep." Vince set Rav's silverware on top of the flat bread and slid the tray down the table's battered brown surface toward the teenager.

Rav caught it deftly. "Thanks."

Vince suppressed a frown as the kid tucked into his meal with relish. Rav had a slight build and he was perpetually malnourished—he tended to rate spending spare credits on playing his favorite game higher than spending them on things like food— but he looked a little more worn than usual. His wide brown eyes seemed a little larger in his brown face, which seemed thinner than it had been the last time Vince saw him.

Since the Finder knew for a fact that the rent on Rav's tiny apartment was paid up for a while, he had to wonder what else was going on. Where was Rav's money going? Or was this just the result of the kid losing his grandma and being truly on his own for the first time in his short life?

Rav shoveled food into his mouth, chewed vigorously, and swallowed before sending Vince a sideways glance. The fingers of his left hand tapped out restless, imaginary commands on the tabletop. "Whaddya need?"

"The Ruby Gauntlet." Vince kept his voice low and casual. "Ever heard of it?"

By the way Rav's fork paused infinitesimally on its way to his mouth, the Finder guessed Rav had.

The fork continued to Rav's mouth. Once he'd chewed and swallowed, the kid lifted one skinny shoulder in the barest of shrugs. "Yeah. I've heard of it." He risked another sideways glance at Vince. "Never been there." He ripped a bite out of his bread. "Don't play *Everheart*." He shrugged again. "Plus, I think gamblin's stupid."

The flat, matter-of-fact tone of his voice convinced Vince more than anything else that he was telling the truth. The Finder had expected that Rav wasn't likely to be involved with the Ruby Gauntlet, but it relieved him to hear this. That club wasn't something he ever wanted to hear the kid had gotten tangled up in.

"What do you know about it?"

Rav paused again, turning his piece of flat bread around between his fingers as though contemplating just how it had been created. "Enough to know it ain't all it's cracked up to be."

It took a great deal of effort for Vince to restrain the impulse to roll his eyes. Classic Rav, not venturing an iota of real information until he was assured he'd be paid for it. *You'd think he'd have a little more faith in my reliability.*

But, old habits died hard, he supposed. The kid lived in the Core—couldn't really blame him for being cautious.

"Usual fee." Vince leaned back against the bulkhead behind him without looking at Rav. "You know I'm good for it."

Out of the corner of his eye, he caught Rav's slight nod of agreement.

"Don't know much." Rav stabbed his pile of steamed greens without much enthusiasm. "'Sposed to be this great place to hang out, if you can get in." He ate a forkful of greens and wrinkled his nose. "Know somebody who did."

A smile twitched at the corner of Vince's mouth. Of course the kid knew somebody. "What happened?"

Rav shook his head, a quick, slight movement. "Lost most ev-erythin'. Swears he ain't never goin' back."

The refrain of every gambler who'd lost everything plus the shirt on his back. Vince exhaled slowly. Didn't actually stop most of them going back, however. "Anything else?"

Rav gave him a few more details, none of them particularly interesting or helpful, but Vince tucked them away for future ref-erence anyway.

Before he asked his next question, Vince darted a searching glance around the Soup Kitchen. Everything seemed normal; no one was paying the two of them any more attention than any other time he'd been here. "Can you tell me anything about who runs the *Ruby Gauntlet*?"

"Nothin' but rumors." Rav twitched a shoulder as he shoveled the last bite of rice into his mouth. "One of 'em is a woman, goes by the name of 'Starlit'. 'Nother is a guy. Lupin or Lumin, or somethin'."

"Any hint of Family involvement?" Vince asked this as casual-ly as he'd asked everything else.

The kid's gaze skidded sideways at Vince again—long enough for the Finder to see a familiar flash of fear in his brown eyes. It was the same reaction he had every time someone mentioned the Families.

Rav shook his head.

"You're sure?"

This time, Rav nodded. "Never heard nothin' about 'em." Cramming the last of his bread into his mouth, he said around the mouthful, "Told ya. I don't know much, but I know that for sure."

It was a good starting point. At the very least, it eliminated an overt connection to either of the Families. Vince didn't doubt his informant; whispers of Family involvement tended to jump from person to person like fire following a dripped trail of fuel.

The fact that there weren't even any rumors connecting them to the *Ruby Gauntlet* was a tad strange, but Vince was sure he'd encounter an interesting explanation for that soon enough.

He reached into the inside breast pocket of his jacket for his comlink—and the credit chips he'd tucked there in anticipation of paying Rav. Using the table as a shield from prying eyes, he discreetly stretched his arm out along the bench and pushed the credit chips toward his informant. Rav just as casually dropped his hand down to the bench and made the credit chips disappear.

The entire exchange took only seconds.

"Usual fee plus food," Vince said without taking his eyes off his comlink's screen. "Thanks, kid. See you around."

Sliding out from behind the table, Vince crossed the Soup Kitchen and departed. On to the next phase in the investigation…

…as soon as he figured out just what that was.

CHAPTER 22

ON HIS WAY BACK TO THE ELEVATOR, Vince considered half a dozen different names of people he could talk to in the Core in the hopes of acquiring more information about the *Ruby Gauntlet* and its operation. In the end, he discarded all of them. Apart from ruling out Family involvement (which was more for his personal peace of mind than anything else), he couldn't compete with the legion of personnel Detective Commosky had at his disposal to investigate the in-game night club.

He then debated traveling to Zone 4 and visiting the spot where Dent Antwerp had met his fate, but ended up nixing that idea as well. Again, he wasn't likely to discover anything Station Authority officers had missed. Homicide investigations were something they were well-equipped to handle—studying security cam footage, locating potential witnesses, and otherwise combing Zone 4 for Dent's attackers. They had infinitely more manpower to allot to this than Vince could spend in an entire week.

No, his approach had to be different. After all, wasn't that why Commosky had recruited him?

Vince turned a corner down another grimy corridor and skirted a group of ragged children playing tag. He made eye contact with a few of the bolder ones, putting just enough of a hint of sternness in his gaze to let them know he wasn't a mark. Down here, it was likely at least one of them would attempt to pick his pocket.

As the children's laughter faded behind him, it made Vince think of Mrs. Antwerp. She must be reliving memories of her boys as youngsters, her mind taking her back in time as a way of coping with her grief. Dent and Corwin, before addiction and division split their family apart.

Dent Antwerp.

That, Vince realized suddenly, was where he needed to start.

Commosky and his fellow Homicide detectives would be looking into Dent's life leading up to his murder as well, but *this* was where a Finder could go places a Station Authority officer could not. A good portion of Dent's last few months alive had been spent in the Core—

—and everyone knew who was *really* in charge down here. People might not outright laugh in Commosky's face—if they weren't too afraid to talk to him at all—but he wouldn't get anywhere.

And he's unlikely to let his investigation take him much further down than this, Vince thought grimly, as he turned another corner and joined a group of people waiting for the elevator. That was another of the Core's tacit truths—Station Authority officers didn't do well in the lower levels.

The elevator doors opened with a half-hearted ding, disgorging a mixed group of individuals who slid past those waiting in line without making eye contact. One old man with a scruffy beard—probably a former miner, by the looks of him—stuck out his hand to keep the doors from closing and jerked a thumb up. "Goin' up," he said in a raspy voice.

Two-thirds of the waiting crowd streamed forward to cram themselves into the elevator cab. On the verge of joining them, Vince made a split-second decision. Shaking his head at the old miner, he remained where he was instead. The doors creaked shut and the elevator cab departed without him.

The next elevator was headed down. Vince stepped aboard along with a handful of other people, most of whom exited the next few levels. The Finder, however, stayed aboard until the elevator reached Level 23—the first of the levels most denizens of the Core avoided.

Fleetingly, he wished he'd thought to bring his pistol with him. Might have come in handy if things down here got rough. He didn't always carry a weapon, but there were times he deemed it prudent.

This probably should have been one of them.

This is as far as you go, he told himself. If he picked up Dent's trail and it led any deeper, he'd head back to the office for the night.

Probably.

Maybe.

Vince allowed himself a rueful smile, even as the tickle in the back of his throat made him cough. He knew himself too well; it would really depend on how good that lead was.

Besides, it wouldn't be the first time he'd tackled something like this. The key was to keep a cool head.

Just before the elevator doors opened, he sent a brief message to Bella, letting her know where he was. (That was still sometimes a novel concept.) Then he stepped out into a world even more different than the rest of the Core.

CHAPTER 23

THE HEAT WAS THE FIRST THING THAT hit Vince when he stepped out onto Level 23. He rolled his shoulders, basking in the warmth a little. One thing he did appreciate about the Core was the fact that it was warmer here than it was throughout the rest of the Zones. Space was a frigid vacuum, and Zyga Station, while nice, hadn't exactly been constructed as a luxury space station. The Core tended to be a little warmer, probably because of its design and the sheer number of people living inside it.

The second thing that hit Vince was the smell. The aroma of unwashed bodies was a little stronger down here and mixed with the ever-present faintly metallic undertone that permeated the entire space station. Vince cleared his throat, which was tickling again.

Honestly, he was starting to wonder if he wasn't just allergic to Zyga Space Station itself.

Maybe even spaceships in general. Wouldn't *that* be something?

The glowpanels in the overhead gave off a pale, sickly light. At least, the ones that were working, which was only one every five or six meters. As a result, the gray metal corridor stretching off into the distance was dim and shadowy.

Vince mentally shook his head. Compared to the lighting down here, lighting throughout the rest of the Core was positively amazing. If Maintenance *ever* made it down here to fix anything, he'd eat his jacket.

It lent greater weight to the feeling of being in another universe from the rest of Zyga Station. The rules definitely did not apply down here.

Hopefully, his visit would be of short duration.

Faded black lettering on the bulkhead opposite the elevator doors proclaimed this to be Level 23. Two strange symbols had been painted beneath it—a red sun and a snowflake. Fire and ice. The Oswari Family and the Bok Family.

Beneath those was a symbol Vince hadn't seen before—what looked like a stylized purple octopus. He eyed it a little bit closer. Make that an *evil*-looking stylized purple octopus.

Now, *that* was interesting. Who was gutsy enough—or stupid enough, there was a fine line—to openly challenge the Families?

He lingered by the elevator door, rethinking his plan. To be honest, he wasn't really sure he wanted to find that out today. But… he had a client, and a job to do, and this was where the investigation led.

Bracing himself, Vince turned right and set off down the dimly-lit corridor. He took measured, confident strides—the walk of a man who had a destination in mind and wasn't stopping to linger…or interfere with anyone. It was the sort of stride that rendered you mostly invisible.

In a Finder's line of work, hesitation and indecision got you in trouble. Down here, it'd probably get you killed.

It had been a long time since he'd been down this far, but Vince still remembered where he was going. Most of the levels in the Core were laid out in the same way, and he'd spent a lot of time over the years poring over blueprints and maps. His internal map was as good as any official map of Zyga Station.

…maybe not as good as some of the black market maps, or even classified Station Authority maps that showed access corridors, maintenance corridors, and secret things that weren't on any official map, but still. Vince knew Zyga Station better than most.

That was helpful.

His footsteps made little sound on the deck. The corridors down here were grimy with accumulated dust, grease, and a few other things Vince preferred not to think about, but just like elsewhere in the Core, there wasn't much garbage littered everywhere. Not when it was worth money. No, what littered the corridors down here were people.

Or, depending on who you asked about the denizens of this part of the Core, the remnants of people. Scrawny, ragged, and sometimes desperate. People with drug and alcohol addictions, people who owned money to the wrong people, people who were so lost in a virtual world that nothing tethered them to reality anymore.

Vince's goatee began to tingle as a thought struck him. Dent Antwerp had spent weeks down here—and then he'd left.

That was unusual. Once they hit the proverbial rock bottom of the lowest Core levels, people didn't tend to escape. But Dent had.

Why? How?

Was it because of Detective Commosky and the fact that Dent was serving as an informant?

Vince shook his head. He'd just have to add that to the growing list of things that were strange about this case.

A sound caught his attention; he cocked his head to one side and listened. The faint strains of music played in the distance. It was impossible to identify it because it sounded like a dozen different kinds of music all being played at once by different people. But it signified the presence of people.

The doors along this corridor were all shut. Unlike the levels above, people did not seem to want to hang out in doorways this close to the elevator. But, as Vince made his way deeper into the level, patches of light began to occasionally spill out from open doorways. The music grew louder. The air grew a little hazier, and he felt the itch in the back of his throat worsen.

Somebody was smoking down here. He shook his head slightly. Occupational hazard of venturing down this far. Smoking tobacco or anything else was illegal aboard Zyga Station, but that didn't mean that there weren't black market ways around the injunction. And down here, who was going to complain?

The corridor abruptly ended, merging into a sprawling compartment that Vince knew from experience had multiple other corridors spawning off of it. In other levels a compartment like this tended to serve as a marketplace of sorts, but here, it was much different. The grimy deck was covered in makeshift tents and tiny dwellings built from discarded boxes, like some sort of strange fungus had popped up all over the place. There wasn't any rhyme or reason to their layout; they simply existed wherever some poor soul could find—or make—room enough to squeeze in.

It was dim and shadowy in here too, and only partly due to the wisps of vape smoke rising here and there from tents. Only a few of the glowpanels in the overhead actually worked. Music played in a few quarters, but it wasn't as loud as the noise pouring out of the open doors Vince had passed. Here, music being obnoxiously loud was grounds for a fight.

…not that everything was peaceful. The rumble of dozens of conversations filled the compartment, punctuated every now and then by a raucous burst of laughter or the raised voices of people in a heated argument.

Vince eyed the maze of homeless human beings warily. Was it just his imagination, or were there more people squeezed in here than there had been the last time he'd been here? That did not bode well for the current state of affairs on Zyga Station.

Subtly clearing his throat, Vince started to pick his way through the shadowy maze of makeshift dwellings. His destination lay down a dim corridor on the other side of this compartment. Here, too, Vince moved with purposeful steps. Some people noticed him, others ignored him, but no one stopped him.

He let his gaze slide past the people he passed, though he noted everything. Like the man sprawled out on his elbows on a faded green blanket in front of his box house, his glazed eyes staring up at the overhead as though it held the answers to every question in the universe. Or the woman sitting cross-legged just inside her tent, made from a couple of gray blankets, busily tinkering with the disassembled pieces of some small piece of machinery spread out in front of her.

More than half of the people in here were lost to the virtual world. A few of the luckier ones (mostly lucky because they hadn't been robbed yet) possessed headsets, but most people were hunched over handheld devices. Bright screen glows illuminated pale, wan, often grimy, faces.

It was possible that someone here had known Dent Antwerp, but Vince doubted it. This compartment was one of many—and it was close to the elevator and Level 23's link to the rest of the space station. There were other places buried far deeper in this level that would suit someone in Dent's situation much better.

As he twisted his way across the compartment, the Finder noted something mildly disturbing. Here and there, that strange purple octopus symbol marked some of the makeshift dwellings. It might be scrawled onto the side of a box, or painted on the fabric of a tent, or even denoted by a crude pendant on a necklace hanging from an opening, but it was there—and Vince didn't know what it meant.

Yet.

That would be another question for his informant.

Despite the way the hair on the back of his neck was prickling, Vince reached the other side of the massive compartment without incident and started down another corridor. This one didn't look any different, but his internal map told him that it led to an intersection with another corridor that had a large compartment on both ends. The compartment on the left held what passed for a marketplace on this level, though it was hardly a friendly place.

Here, too, the doors that lined this corridor were all shut tight. Vince spared a thought to wonder exactly what—or who—lay behind them, but the bulk of his focus was on keeping his wits about him and finding his informant.

And, hopefully, his informant wouldn't be stoned out of his mind and would actually be of some use. (There had been a few occasions where Vince had braved the trek down here for nothing.) People desperate enough to live down here weren't exactly the most reliable sort.

Vince cleared his throat again as he neared the end of the corridor. He was almost adjusting to the air down here. Almost. (*Don't kid yourself*, whispered a dry voice in the back of his mind.)

Ahead, Vince glimpsed flickering lights through the hazy air and heard snippets of rumbling conversation. Time did not exist down here. Not in any real, distinguishable way. Activity was no gauge of time; people wandered around at all hours of the day and night.

On the verge of stepping out into the large compartment, Vince's keen senses picked up a whisper of movement from behind him. He spun around just as two large, silent figures emerged from a door to his right. They advanced on him, both armed with heavy metal pipes.

CHAPTER 24

VINCE SET HIS JAW, IRRITATED WITH HIMSELF. Of all the days to decide not to take the time to swing by the office and pick up his pistol before he ventured down here… He should have known better.

He held up his hands in an easy, nonthreatening way and backed toward the other side of the compartment. The bulkhead, not another door. The last thing he needed was to back right into another group of thugs.

One of the burly men had pale skin and a shaved head that gleamed slightly in the dim light. He wore a faded black jacket over what had probably once been a white shirt, along with a ragged pair of black pants. A purple octopus had been tattooed on the side of his neck.

The other man had short black hair and coal-black skin darker than Vince's own, but he wore a brown vest over a dark orange short-sleeved shirt that showed off the muscles in his large arms. He hefted his pipe in one hand, eying Vince with an ugly smile on his face. One of those crude purple octopus pendants hung from a necklace of twisted wire around his neck.

Vince met both their gazes in turn, letting them know he wasn't a threat—but that he wasn't afraid, either. He jerked his chin in a nod. "Gentlemen. How can I help you?"

There were only a couple of possibilities. Either he'd inadvertently angered someone, he was being jumped because he was in the wrong place at the wrong time…or he was being summoned.

Summoned by someone who'd seen him coming.

Perhaps by whoever was responsible for all of the purple octopus symbols.

"You don't belong down here," the pale man said in a deep, growling voice. "Folks come down here to get away from the likes of you." His grip tightened on his pipe. "Don't need no Station Authority mongrels meddlin' and pokin' their noses in where they don't belong."

Vince held his ground, hands still slightly raised. "Well, then it's a good thing I'm not Station Authority, isn't it?"

The second man—Orange-shirt, as Vince mentally dubbed him—tapped his length of pipe against his palm in a menacing way, but didn't speak. He only watched Vince and his comrade with cold black eyes.

"Why are you here?" The pale man pointed his pipe in Vince's direction.

It was close enough that he probably could have grabbed it and swung it into the side of the man's head, but Vince ignored the impulse. If he'd wanted a brawl, he didn't have to come all the way down here to find one.

Instead, the Finder lifted one shoulder in an easy shrug. "Don't see as how that's any of your business."

The pale man instantly bristled. Snarling, he took a step forward, raising the pipe over his head. "Oh, ya don't, do ya?"

Vince braced himself for a fight, but Orange-shirt held up a beefy hand. "Hold it, Spurge." His voice was even deeper than his comrade's. "Boss wants to see him, remember?"

Reluctantly, the pale man—Spurge—lowered his makeshift weapon.

Vince wasn't sure what he'd done to rate the look of vehement hate in his eyes. Maybe he hadn't done anything. Maybe it was just the way this guy always looked.

Or maybe the fact that he'd dared to venture down here in the first place was the cause.

"This way, punk." Orange-shirt shifted sideways on his feet, brandishing his length of pipe in the direction of the door through which they'd emerged.

He clearly expected Vince to move, but the Finder continued to stand his ground. His goatee was tingling.

"Who is your boss?" Vince had a passing familiarity with a few names of the major movers and shakers in the Inner Core, but that strange purple octopus gave him pause.

Something had shifted down here lately...the dynamics of power had altered. Whatever had caused that did not bode well for the Core. Or, for that matter, the rest of Zyga Station.

He spared the briefest of thoughts to imagine what a three-way war looked like between the Families and whoever this new-comer turned out to be. It wasn't pretty.

"You'll find out soon enough." Orange-shirt lifted one corner of his mouth in what he probably thought was a menacing smile. The expression was menacing, all right, but it was most definitely *not* a smile. More like a strained grimace.

"All right, then." Vince shrugged again, like it didn't matter in the least bit and he had all the time in the universe. "Let's go." He stepped forward confidently. "I think I'd like to meet this boss of yours."

The two burly henchmen exchanged looks—the slightly confused kind that indicated they were questioning Vince's sanity.

Vince just maintained his pleasantly neutral expression. That was all right. Let them think him a little off. They'd be a little more cautious if they thought he was crazy.

The thought almost made him smile.

"You first, Spurge." Orange-shirt pointed his pipe toward the door again. "Then him."

A flicker of relief curled through Vince, though he was too experienced to let it show. He didn't want Spurge behind him. Interesting that Orange-shirt had the same thought about his partner's trustworthiness.

Spurge's pale face twisted in a snarl, as though he wanted to argue but knew better than to try. Giving Vince one final black look, he stomped toward the door and roughly entered a code into the battered keypad mounted at chest height beside it. The door slid open almost noiselessly—somebody took good care of this one, Vince noted—and Spurge disappeared through it.

Vince almost asked what the pale man's problem was, but refrained. That was a question best left for another time. Instead, he moved forward to follow.

Orange-shirt brought up the rear, his footsteps surprisingly quiet on the metal deck for such a large man.

The door led into what had probably started life as a small living compartment back when the Station was first constructed. The dingy gray bulkheads still held a few cracked family holos, but it was now a small security post. A couple of grimy couches were thrown up against the bulkheads along one side and to the rear, and a battered desk with a computer terminal stood beside the door.

A scrawny young woman with light brown skin wearing a faded magenta jacket over worn brown pants sat at this terminal, hunched over a holographic readout. Her head was partially shaved and she had a black mohawk. She glanced up as they entered, and then just as quickly looked back down.

Vince resisted the urge to wrinkle his nose. The air smelled of some sharp incense he couldn't recall the name of, wafting up from a glass jar on the desk next to the woman. The back of his throat itched fiercely; he willed himself not to cough.

"Keep an eye out in case this one has friends," Orange-shirt commanded from behind Vince on their way through the compartment.

The young woman nodded. "Will do, Tank."

Tank. Vince filed that name away, though he mentally shook his head. Guess they couldn't come up with a more creative nickname for this guy.

He *did* notice that the computer the woman was using looked suspiciously new. Whatever money this mysterious boss of theirs had, at least part of it seemed to be going into security.

Spurge led the way into a short hallway, and then turned right into a small sleeping compartment. This one still had a bed inside, but a rough hatch had been cut into one of the bulkheads.

Vince narrowed his eyes, feeling a sense of sharp triumph.

He'd heard rumors over the years that people down here had founds ways to modify the inner Core's structure—creating their own hatches and escape routes inside each level. While he hadn't doubted the rumors' veracity (that kind of thinking was precisely what you'd expect from paranoid individuals under the influence of something), he'd never been able to get his hands on actual proof.

Neither had anyone else, even though Station Authority strictly prohibited anyone from altering the Station's internal structure and claimed to ruthlessly enforce that policy.

This…this was proof.

One by one, the three men climbed through the hole. Vince was careful not to let the rough metal edges snag on the brown leather of his jacket. They emerged into another grimy, dimly-lit living compartment.

This one was occupied by a handful of jaded-looking teenagers sprawled across the deck and on two rows of gray metal-framed bunk beds with thin mattresses and tattered blankets. Most of the teens looked up from their comlinks, their situational awareness reminding them to be wary of three men passing through their midst, but a few were too obsessed to notice.

Vince winced, expecting Spurge to kick one of the boys on the floor out of his way, but the burly man just growled, "Clear out, all of ya."

Most of the kids scattered out of the way like a school of fish Vince had seen in holodramas and Spurge plowed through the compartment to the other side unhindered.

Vince's goatee tingled. That was interesting—a hint of compassion and consideration the Finder hadn't expected from a man with Spurge's obvious anger issues. The real question was whether it was from Spurge himself or his boss compelling him to act contrary to his belligerent nature.

Just before they exited through the hatch, Vince glanced over his shoulder in time to see the teenagers settle back into their spots as though they'd never been disturbed. He almost smiled. Just like a school of fish.

The only question was what they were doing hanging around a crew like this.

CHAPTER 25

As his bulky guards led Vince through the bowels of Level 23, part of him couldn't help but wonder if their mysterious boss planned to let him live when this was over. After all, Tank and Spurge took no pains to hide their tracks. They just marched through the warren of corridors and compartments with a grim sort of determination.

They ducked through yet another makeshift hatch and Vince found himself wondering how the people down here had managed it. The kind of equipment this modification had to have required wasn't something you could easily get your hands on and then just casually cart through the Station. It required organization, planning…and connections with someone in the mining industry.

He was seriously considering asking Tank about it when their journey came to a sudden and abrupt end at a worn hatch in the middle of a corridor that looked identical to the last three corridors they'd passed through.

Vince glanced around with equal parts mild curiosity and keen interest. There was nothing to indicate it was anything special. Not even one of those strange purple octopus insignias. (He'd half-expected one.)

Spurge pounded four times on the door—two long raps and then two shorter ones—before entering a code into the lockpad mounted into the bulkhead beside the hatch. The door slid aside with another one of those unusually quiet whispers for a door down here, and the big, pale man stepped inside.

"Follow him," came Tank's growling voice from behind Vince.

The Finder did not hesitate. Moving with his usual easy stride, he followed Spurge through the hatch. He'd faced down the head of the Bok Family himself; he could handle whoever was waiting for him inside.

The first thing that hit him was the smell of garlic and soy sauce. Someone was either cooking in here or else they'd brought food in from somewhere else. More than a little intrigued, Vince glanced around.

They'd entered another small living compartment with a few battered pieces of furniture scattered about the living area. Several narrow doors led to what Vince guessed were the hygiene unit and at least one sleeping compartment. The tiny kitchenette in one corner of the room was empty, which meant it couldn't be the source of the smell.

His gaze was immediately drawn to a gray blanket with a large purple octopus painted on it that hung on the far bulkhead. Unless he was very much mistaken, this compartment, too, had been altered to suit its inhabitants. That makeshift curtain probably covered another crude hatch. The faded gray bulkhead beside it was covered with what looked like pieces of paper with…

Vince squinted. Were those *children's* drawings?

He didn't have time to study them further.

Spurge raised his deep voice in a bellow. "Boss, we've got him."

Seconds later, the gray curtain rippled as someone pushed it aside.

A young man of medium height emerged from the compartment beyond and came to stand the center of the deck. His skin was a creamy brown and he had a wide face with sharp, appraising dark eyes. Black dreadlocks hung down to the middle of his back, held away from his face by a purple bandana tied around his head.

The young man put his hands on his hips as he looked Vince up and down. He wore black trousers and a faded purple and gold striped vest over a cut-off black shirt that left his muscular arms bare. Dark geometric tattoos curled along his skin.

Vince couldn't help but notice that a crude purple octopus pendant hung around this man's neck too.

"So, you are Finder Grable." The young man had a light, mellow voice at odds with his comrades' baritones. He pursed his lips, his dark eyebrows drawing into a frown. "What are you doing down here?"

"I'm looking for someone," Vince said calmly. If they knew who he was, that shouldn't come as a surprise.

"Who?"

Vince just smiled slightly. "Before I answer that, I'd like to know who I'm talking to." He tilted his head to one side. "I don't believe we've met before."

The younger man laughed, his hard smile revealing a glimpse of his teeth. He was missing at least two.

Tank and Spurge laughed too, the deep sound bouncing off the bulkheads. But when the younger man held up a hand, they both quieted instantly.

That was also interesting.

"I am Zaslo. These are my friends, and this is our home." The young man indicated Tank and Spurge and their surroundings with a sweep of his hand.

Zaslo.

Vince ran the name through his mental database, but came up empty. He didn't think he'd ever heard of this guy before—and he knew without a shadow of a doubt he'd never encountered the purple octopus insignia before.

Behind Zaslo, the gray curtain shifted again, drawing Vince's gaze. A slender teenage girl with coppery skin and a narrow face emerged into the compartment. She wore a faded green sweater over brown pants, which were tucked into worn brown boots. A thick black braid curled over one shoulder. Her dark eyes held an unfriendly, almost haunted look.

Zaslo glanced over his shoulder and his frown deepened when he saw her. "I thought we agreed you'd wait."

The girl lifted one shoulder in a shrug. "They took too long." Her voice was surprisingly husky.

Zaslo shook his head once, making the ends of his dreads dance, and turned his attention back to Vince. Folding his arms across his chest, he drilled Vince with a hard, piercing stare the Finder would have expected from a man several decades his senior. "Why are you down here? Who are you looking for?"

It was Vince's turn to shake his head. "That isn't how it works. I maintain my clients' confidentiality unless there is a very good reason to disclose information pertaining to my cases." He gave an apologetic shrug. "You understand."

This did not go over well.

Off to the side, Tank and Spurge both stirred menacingly. Behind Zaslo, the girl's expression grew colder. If looks could kill, Vince would have turned into a smoldering pile of ash.

Zaslo himself remained cool and collected. His expression gave nothing away; somewhere along the line, the young man had developed an excellent poker face.

"I'm afraid it is you that does not understand." Zaslo directed a casual hand to his companions. "You are on our turf." His quick smile was all sharp edges. "If you disappeared down here…well…" It was his turn to shrug. "Who will care? Or know?"

Vince's goatee began to bristle again. Something was off about this whole situation. He flicked a glance around the compartment again, and then focused on Zaslo.

"You could make me vanish," he said slowly, "but I don't think you will."

"Oh?" Zaslo arched a dark eyebrow, folding his arms across his chest again.

"No." Vince shook his head again, this time with confidence. "You have quite a presence down here, from what little I can see, but I haven't heard anything about you." He offered the younger man a slight, sardonic smile. "And I would have heard at least a whisper about purple octopuses."

"That tells me two things." He held up a finger. "One, you're not in direct competition to either of the Families. And two…" He held up another finger. "You're keeping a low profile. A *very* low profile."

Zaslo said nothing, just watched Vince with his eyebrow still raised.

"Which means whatever you're doing, it's not drawing Family attention."

"Yet," the girl said darkly.

Zaslo flicked another glance over his shoulder in the girl's direction. "You have to have faith, Zuzu."

"Oh, I've got plenty of faith." The girl folded her arms tightly across her chest. "I just happen to have a lot of common sense, too." She scowled at Vince. "And common sense says that a Finder poking his nose around down here is trouble."

"I'm looking for information about a young man named Dent Antwerp," Vince said abruptly.

It was a random shot in the dark—given what Dent had been caught up in, he couldn't have been part of whatever this Purple Octopus group had going on—and yet… The way Vince's goatee tingled told him it was worth a try.

Complete silence met this pronouncement.

Vince surveyed the small compartment, taking in everyone's reaction. Zaslo's face remained neutral, but the girl narrowed her eyes, setting her jaw in a stubborn line. Tank and Spurge both shifted uneasily on their feet.

The Finder covered the rush of shock he felt. They *knew* Dent's name.

He hadn't actually expected that.

CHAPTER 26

"**W**HY?" ZASLO SHRUGGED CARELESSLY, APPARENTLY UNAWARE that Vince had gotten the answer he wanted. "What's this guy done?"

"He's dead." Vince didn't move, but his awareness of the compartment expanded to soak in every single detail. "Station Authority arrested his brother this morning."

This time, Tank and Spurge failed to react, but the girl's eyes widened in shock.

Zaslo huffed a sardonic laugh, his gaze now drilling into Vince again. "And you obviously have a client who thinks the brother didn't do it." He cast a glance around the compartment before returning his attention to Vince. "Or why else would you be here?"

Vince inclined his head. Let them think that, if they liked. "Why, indeed?"

Another deafening silence filled the compartment, unbroken save for the ever-present hum of the engine far below their feet at the Station's center. Then, somewhere beyond the gray curtain, a baby cried.

Unbidden, Vince's gaze flicked toward the curtain. His mind raced, trying to work out exactly what was going on here. Purple octopuses…and young people. In fact, now that he thought about it, most of the people he'd seen on his way here with those purple octopuses were young. Tank and Spurge were actually on the older side of the spectrum.

But what did that mean? Vince frowned mentally. He just didn't have enough information yet.

Prompted by a sudden thought, he said, "Dent wasn't a bad kid. He just lived his life in a game and got in too deep with the wrong people. I'm trying to find out what really happened to him." He shook his head. "His mother doesn't need to spend the rest of her life thinking that one of her sons murdered the other."

The silence that met these words was a little deeper and more profound than the last one. Finally, Zaslo stirred, as though holding a mental debate with himself. "And you think he came down here?" He indicated the entirety of Level 23 with a sweep of his hand.

"Yes." Vince didn't have to say more.

"Do you have a holo of him?"

In lieu of answering, Vince carefully reached into his breast pocket to retrieve his comlink. Tank and Spurge both tensed at this movement, but Zaslo didn't flinch. He just watched as Vince brought up a holo of Dent and handed him the comlink.

Zuzu left her post by the curtain and drifted forward a few steps to see as well. She peered at the comlink display around Zaslo's shoulder. Her control over her expression wasn't as good as Zaslo's; she looked a little shaken.

"He looks vaguely familiar." Zaslo lifted one shoulder in a prosaic shrug. "But so many people come and go down here every day, and most of them want to be left alone." He handed the comlink back to Vince, shaking his head. The movement made the tips of his dreadlocks dance. "Can't help you, Finder."

Vince couldn't say he was surprised.

"I understand." He inclined his head in a nod, but his eyes were on Zuzu. Her gaze followed the comlink and he saw deep confliction in her dark eyes. He decided to press a little harder.

"I'm not down here to cause trouble for anyone. I'm just looking to find out what really happened to Dent and keep his brother from going down for a crime he didn't commit."

There was no point in mentioning anything else. Not now.

"We can't help you," Zaslo repeated, his voice a little firmer.

Vince's goatee was still bristling. He just needed a little more *time*. He was on the verge of a breakthrough; he could feel it.

He met Zaslo's eyes again. "Then perhaps you can answer a question for me."

The change in the atmosphere inside the compartment was instantaneous. Tension flooded everything.

"Depends on what the question is," Zaslo said quietly.

Vince nodded to the pendant that hung around the younger man's neck. "What does the purple octopus mean?"

Another silence met this, but it was a different silence—the kind of silence that had just been disarmed. Tank, Spurge, and even Zuzu relaxed fractionally.

For his part, Zaslo just threw back his head and laughed. Still smiling, he regarded Vince with new eyes. "You are not what I expected, Finder."

"I can only imagine what that was," Vince said dryly.

Zaslo folded his arms across his chest and leveled a piercing look at the Finder. "Do you know why you're here?"

That had to be one of the dumbest questions Vince had heard in a long time. He almost said as much, but swallowed his impatience and turned one hand palm up. "No. But if I had to guess—"

Zaslo's dark eyes sharpened and both Tank and Spurge seemed to freeze into hulking rocks.

"—I'd say it has something to do with you making sure I'm not going to interfere with anything you're doing."

Zaslo didn't move. "Why not something concerning the Families?"

That was blindingly obvious, but Vince kept this thought to himself as well. "Call it a hunch." He shrugged, but didn't take his eyes off the younger man. "I'm a Finder, remember?"

Zaslo considered him for a moment. The compartment was completely quiet, save for the sound of their combined breathing and the ever-present hum of the Station's engine beneath their feet. Finally, he inclined his head in acknowledgement.

"You have good instincts, Finder."

Vince shrugged again, a casual, *what can you do?* gesture.

Unfolding his arms, Zaslo spread his hands wide. "We are the Haven, Finder."

"Zaslo—" the girl began, her voice sharp and a little worried.

"It's all right, Zuzu." Zaslo offered her a reassuring smile that vanished as quickly as it had come before he addressed Vince again. His voice grew hard. "People down here aren't safe from the Families. They take what they want—take *who* they want—and no one stops them."

Spurge and Tank both nodded in agreement.

"You asked about this, Finder?" Zaslo held up his octopus pendant, a momentary undercurrent of anger contorting his expression. "This was my little brother's favorite animal. He disappeared ten years ago, just like dozens of other children disappear every day in the Core."

"So we decided to do something." Zaslo's dark eyes burned with sudden fire. He swept a hand in a circle to indicate the entire level. "We take care of the ones everybody else neglects. We take care of the ones everybody else exploits."

Vince glanced around without turning his head. Tank and Spurge had straightened at these words, as though hearing them had given both men a shot of encouragement and adrenaline.

Behind Zaslo, by the curtain, Zuzu straightened as well. She settled into a stance Vince could only describe as defiant.

Zaslo seemed to grow taller in his passion. "The Families sell our children and our women and even some of our men into slavery. They kidnap them and ship them off Zyga Station to God only knows where throughout the galaxy and nobody stops them. Station Authority looks the other way." His lip curled in a sneer. "The officers who should be protecting the citizens of Zyga Station turn a blind eye to the people who need their help the most."

"You're not wrong," Vince said quietly. Zaslo was an eloquent speaker; he could feel the younger man's passionate energy spark an answering fire inside his own chest. Running headlong into injustice always had that effect on him. "However, I must point out that Bok Chul does not condone human trafficking."

It was Zuzu's turn to snort. Everyone turned to look at her as she said, "Buying and selling bodies, maybe, but souls?" Grimacing, she shook her head. "You're delusional, Finder, if you think that the Bok Family's hands are clean just because the head honcho frowns on human trafficking."

Vince's mind immediately traveled to Bella and what had happened to her with Bok Seung. "I am aware of that."

His goatee began bristling again as the first part of Zuzu's statement registered. It gave him an idea. "Dent Antwerp lost his soul to someone. I'm just trying to figure out who."

"And I already told you we can't help you," Zaslo retorted, an edge sliding into his voice. He narrowed his eyes at Vince.

"Maybe *you* can't," Vince said evenly, "but I think *she* can." He jerked his chin toward Zuzu.

CHAPTER 27

"**W**HAT?" ZUZU'S EYES WIDENED IN SHOCK—AND more than a touch of fear—before they narrowed in anger at Vince. "No, I don't." Posting her hands on her hips, she sent a fierce glare in his direction before turning to Zaslo. "He's talkin' crazy. You gonna let him stay here an' do that?"

"You know him." Vince remained planted in the center of the compartment—a calm, implacable force. He continued to look at her. "How do you know him?"

Zuzu bristled like a feral cat. "I *told* you, I don't—"

"Just tell him already," came a voice from behind the curtain. "Can't possibly make things worse now."

Everyone turned as the curtain rustled again and a dark-haired, brown-skinned older woman emerged, carrying a scrawny baby wrapped in a faded pink blanket. Vince judged the woman to be a decade or so older than he was, and the baby…well, it was hard to say. The tiny little thing had a head of curly black hair, dirt-stained caramel skin, and was chewing on her fingers as though hoping to get milk from them.

"Areba—" Zuzu's gaze fell to the baby. "You can't—"

The baby whimpered in the older woman's arms and resumed chewing on her fingers even more vigorously.

Areba leveled Zuzu with a hard stare. "Tell. Him."

Zaslo shifted on his feet, his dark eyebrows drawing together in concern. "Areba—"

"No." The older woman held up an imperious hand. "If what he says is true—" she indicated Vince with a tip of her head, "—then he needs to know."

Still bristling, Zuzu looked at Zaslo. After a second, he gave her the barest of nods. The girl's mouth took on unhappy slant, but she turned to Vince.

"I didn't know Dent personally. Just saw him a few times here and there." Zuzu's arms were crossed so tightly Vince wondered if she was losing circulation. "He was friends with a girl I know. Got her knocked up."

After all the things he'd seen in ten years as a Finder, this shouldn't have surprised Vince, but somehow it did. His eyebrows rose slightly as he regarded Zuzu, weighing whether or not to believe her. "Are you telling me Dent surfaced from his game long enough to show interest in a woman?"

He found himself on the receiving end of unfriendly looks from both Zuzu and Areba.

"You're a bigger fool than you look if you think that don't happen down here, Finder." Zuzu scoffed derisively.

Vince didn't deny that. He just hadn't expected it, given Dent's history. He nodded to the baby. "You're saying she's Dent's? Where's her mother?"

"Gone," Areba said flatly, swaying from side to side to calm the baby. "Went out looking for Dent a while back and never came back." She shook her head. "Doubt she will."

All eyes were on him now. Vince glanced around, a surreal feeling stealing over him. What were the odds of him coming down here and stumbling across Dent's *child*?

He spread his hands. "Is that all? You don't know anything else?"

"Isn't that enough?" Zuzu asked tartly.

Vince smiled without any real humor. "Not in the slightest."

Zaslo regarded the girl with raised eyebrows. "Zuzu?"

"I don't know anything else." She held her hands up. "I swear. I only saw him a few times and heard Mariella talk about him."

Vince's goatee bristled. "Did she talk about him much?"

Zuzu rolled her eyes. "All the flippin' time. But it was nothin'—just his grand plans for a future that ain't never gonna happen."

The baby let out a cry; Areba hushed her.

"Like what?" This was important; Vince could feel it, a nebulous wisp of *something* hovering just beyond his reach.

"I don't know." Zuzu shrugged, a little savagely. "Somethin' about some big game he was helpin' test and a place called Ruby somethin'. He thought he was gonna hit it big." She scowled at Vince as though he was personally responsible for stringing her friend along. "But it was all space dust—just the kind of made-up junk men tell women to get in their pants."

Normally, Vince would have agreed…except for the bit about the Ruby Gauntlet. That had a ring of truth to it. He filed the boast about the game testing away for future investigation—he had yet to stumble across any evidence of that. "Anything else?"

"Yeah." Zuzu pointed to the baby. "What you gonna do about her?"

Vince tilted his head in a silent question. *What do you expect me to do?*

"Don't give me that look." Zuzu narrowed her eyes at him again. She swept her hand toward the baby again. "She's Dent's kid. Dead or not, he's got family. They oughta take her instead of lettin' her be a burden on us."

"Zuzu…" Zaslo said her name as a sigh.

"You know it's true, Zaslo." Zuzu folded her arms across her chest again, her dark eyes defiant. "We got enough babies down here to worry about who ain't got any family."

Behind the hard edges of her words, however, Vince sensed actual concern for the child's welfare. He posed another question. "How do you know Dent's family is any good?"

"He talked about 'em." Zuzu shrugged again, this time a trifle self-consciously. "At least according to Mariella. Loved his momma, for sure."

But not enough to stop gambling. Vince held back a sigh. Wasn't that the way it always went?

He motioned to the baby. "I can't just walk out of here with her."

"Why not?" Zuzu shrugged, her lean, coppery face hard with a jaded expression that belonged to someone much, much older. "The Families do it all the time. Nobody says a word."

Zaslo started to speak, but Areba beat him to it. Throwing the younger woman a chiding look, she said, "The Finder isn't the Families."

"We don't know that," Zuzu retorted, posting her hands on her hips again. "Not really."

"There's a procedure," Vince said slowly.

Zuzu scoffed. "What, like getting a paternity test? Trust me," she said scathingly, "she's Dent's."

Vince leveled her with a look. "You can't possibly expect me to take that baby to his mother and claim it's her grandchild without a paternity test."

"Or paperwork?" the young woman sneered.

Zaslo sighed. "Zuzu..."

Vince had the distinct impression that this topic was something that had come up before, though not with this baby. He looked from one face to another before returning to Zuzu.

Paperwork wasn't the issue, exactly—after all, Vince knew it was possible to create an identity for someone. He'd done it for Bella, hadn't he?

No, the real problem was much bigger. And more dangerous.

Slowly, the Finder shook his head. "You're forgetting the most important thing."

"Oh, yeah?" Hands still on her hips, Zuzu met his gaze head on. "And what would that be?"

"Dent Antwerp was murdered."

The silence that greeted these words was deep, with an element that indicated they really had forgotten that part. Death, disappearance, and tragedy were such regular staples of their lives down here that one more lost life had hardly registered.

Vince nodded to the child in Areba's arms. "Can't take the risk of putting that child in danger." His conscience wouldn't let him.

Even if he *could* think of half a dozen ways to potentially use the child's existence to help him solve this case.

He took a deep breath. What he was about to say could be a problem later on, but... He gave a mental shrug. Family was family.

"When this is over..." he glanced from Areba to Zaslo, his meaning perfectly clear. "When this is over, I'll come back and collect the child. Take her to her grandmother and her uncle." His gaze turned steely. "If she's Dent's kid."

"She is," Zuzu said, with the impatient air of someone who had repeated the same thing too many times to count. She abruptly spun and stalked over to Areba and the baby, pulling something small from her pocket on the way. It glinted in the dim light from the overhead.

Areba gave her a warning look and instinctively turned away to shield the baby, but Zuzu just huffed impatiently. "I ain't gonna hurt her." Reaching out, she took hold of one of the baby's dark curls and snipped it off. "There. All done."

Turning around, she stomped over to Vince and held the lock of hair out on her palm. Her dark eyes were full of a challenge again. "Can we trust you to tell the truth, Finder?"

In answer, Vince reached into his left breast pocket for a small, clear evidence bag. He opened it, and Zuzu dumped the tiny lock of hair inside. He then sealed the bag and replaced it in his jacket.

Glancing around at the silent Tank and Spurge, Zaslo, Areba, and Zuzu again, he lifted his eyebrows. "You satisfied I'm not a Family man?"

No one answered. After a few heartbeats, Zaslo lifted a shoulder in a shrug. "Reasonably." It was his turn to level Vince with a challenging stare. "You won't tell anybody about us."

It wasn't a question.

Vince shrugged. "No reason to."

"Good." Zaslo nodded to Tank and Spurge. "They'll take you back and you can leave."

Ah. There it was. Vince had been waiting for this. He shook his head. "Can't leave yet."

At this, the atmosphere in the compartment grew cold. Zaslo's expression turned forbidding, but Vince didn't let it bother him.

"Haven't found the person I came all the way down here to talk to."

Instead of getting angry, however, Zaslo let out a short bark of laughter, as though he found this amusing. "You have stones, Finder, I'll give you that." He waved a hand to Tank and Spurge. "Take him back to the Cave and let him go."

Vince turned to follow them out, but felt someone's glare burning into his back. He glanced over his shoulder—and his gaze met Zuzu's. Her dark, angry eyes seemed to say, *You'd better come back.*

He nodded to her. *I will.*

CHAPTER 28

Rᴜᴇ ᴛᴏ Zᴀsʟᴏ's ᴡᴏʀᴅ, Tᴀɴᴋ ᴀɴᴅ Sᴘᴜʀɢᴇ marched Vince back the way they'd come. When they reached the compartment where the girl with the mohawk still sat hunched over the display screen, they both gave him menacing looks. Wordlessly, Spurge opened the hatch and Tank shoved him unceremoniously into the corridor beyond.

The force of the shove nearly sent Vince into the opposite bulkhead, but he caught himself in time. Straightening his brown leather jacket, he spared a glance over his shoulder in time to see the metal door slide shut. With a mental shake of his head, he set off toward the end of the corridor and the cavernous compartment beyond. The Cave, Zaslo had called it.

Vince had lost an hour of his time, but it wasn't a complete waste. If the Purple Octopuses—the Haven—were to be believed, Dent had not only spent time down here, but he'd mentioned the Ruby Gauntlet. That was the confirmation Vince had needed.

Now, he could only hope that his source could tell him more—and that his source was relatively sober.

And alive.

One never knew, in the desperate chaos that was life down here.

Like the massive compartment near the elevator bank, the Cave too was filled with an array of dingy tents, boxes, and other piles of scraped-together belongings. Vince was used to the overall smell at this point, but every so often he got a whiff of something new. A heavy perfume, or the sharp smell of alcohol, or the aroma of food.

This deep into Level 23-A, more people were milling around now. Vince was dressed a little better than some of them, but for the most part he blended in with the crowd. He kept his head down and his shoulders hunched, making himself smaller and more un-obtrusive. He also avoided meeting anyone's eyes, though his deep brown gaze took in every detail.

His source was an old man who preferred to pitch his ragged tent on the Bok Family side of Level 23-A. Niko Beka was fairly re-liable…except for when he managed to get his hands on spice pow-der and went on a bender that usually lasted two or three weeks. Vince *really* hoped this wasn't one of those occasions. The old man wasn't terribly helpful when he was high, though sometimes Vince still managed to pick up something of use.

Sometimes the Finder felt guilty giving the old man credits for his information. Part of him felt like he was enabling old Niko to keep getting high on substances that would land him in prison if Station Authority ever got a hold of him. The other part of Vince recognized that he wasn't responsible for the old man's actions.

The sensible thing was for Niko to buy himself food, clothes, and the like. If he chose to do something different, well…Vince had learned a long time ago that you couldn't force people to be sensible. And so he always paid Niko just like he would any oth-er informant and hoped that this time maybe the old man would make different choices.

Someone (Vince couldn't remember who) had once said that was the triumph of hope over experience.

Vince couldn't say he expected anything different this time.

As he picked his way deeper into the bowels of Level 23-A, Vince kept an eye out for anyone tailing him. His business with Niko was nobody else's business—not the Bok Family's, or the Oswari Family's, or the Haven's, for that matter. To that end, he doubled back and wove around more than usual.

He also kept an eye out for anyone who might want to mug him simply because they wanted whatever they thought he might have on him.

It wasn't safe to wander around this deep in the Core. (That was why Station Authority mostly left this handful of levels alone. They'd lost a few officers down here and never quite figured out who was responsible.) Bad things happened down here in the shadows, amid the grime and the poverty and the desperation of people who'd hit the bottom and couldn't figure out where else to go.

Really, it's a wonder Zaslo and his people want to stay down here, Vince thought as he slipped through the shadows of a narrow corridor that emptied into another larger compartment where another mass of people congregated in little groups beneath the dim lighting from the two lone functioning glowpanels in the overhead. *You'd think they'd want to find someplace a little safer.*

Especially if they were trying, as they claimed, to protect children and other vulnerables.

Dent's child remained on Vince's mind throughout his journey. The infant's big dark eyes, that shock of curly black hair. Such innocence in a part of Zyga Station he hadn't thought had any claim to even a brief association with the word.

Had Dent known about his little girl? Zuzu thought he had, but she wasn't sure. The child's mother had been missing for several weeks. There was no telling what had happened to her, though Vince suspected Zaslo and his Purple Octopuses believed she'd been kidnapped and shipped off-Station.

That though alone set something in the pit of his stomach to churning in horror, but there wasn't anything he could do about it now. There were some wrongs in the galaxy one man couldn't right on his own.

Making a mental note to talk to Sergeant Anita Rychek, his friend in Station Authority in Zone 5, later, Vince set the issue of what to do about Dent's possible child aside for the time being.

He had more pressing matters to consider just now—such as making sure he made it out of Level 23-A in one piece with the information he was seeking.

CHAPTER 29

Fifteen minutes later, Vince almost found himself wishing he'd stayed out of the Core entirely. Niko was still among the living, but he was high. Higher than Vince had ever seen him, in fact. The old man had gotten his hands on something good.

Vince found the old man's tattered, grimy tent, tucked away in a corner of the large compartment known as the River. (Vince wasn't sure why it bore this name; the only thing he could figure was that the large pipe in one corner had something to do with it.) Corners were prime sleeping locations, depending on your perspective, so Vince was always a little surprised when he found out Niko was still there. He kept waiting for some young, arrogant upstart to kick the old man out of his spot and claim it for his or her own.

Of course, given that Niko had made it to this advanced old age while surviving in the Core, it was entirely possible that he had methods of ensuring his own safety that Vince wasn't privy to.

Coming up to the tent, Vince surveyed the thin, begrimed figure sprawled happily on a dingy blanket at his feet. Either that or the people down here regarded the old man as harmless—and not worth robbing.

At this stage of his life, Niko Beka was so wrinkled that it was impossible to tell how old he actually was, but his vision was still sharp, as was his hearing. He was a small, slight man who was even shorter now that he was old and his shoulders stooped. He had a shock of surprisingly thick white hair, and his wrinkled tan face often bore an inscrutable expression. That didn't change when he was out of his gourd, other than occasionally he smiled more.

Holding back a sigh at the tell-tale scent of spice, Vince squatted near the old man and debated whether or not to even engage in a conversation.

Niko took the decision out of his hands. He happened to turn his head slightly so that instead of staring off into the overhead with eyes that clearly did not see said overhead, he glimpsed Vince instead.

It took a second for Vince's face to register. When it did, a broad smile broke out over the old man's wrinkled face.

"Ah, you've come to visit, have you?"

It was hard not to answer that wide, almost childish smile. Vince nodded. "Thought I'd drop by."

"Have a seat, have a seat." The old man slapped the blanket beside him and turned his gaze back up on the overhead. "Watch the lights with me. Pretty lights today." He squinted suddenly, cocking his head to one side like an old bird. "Can you see them lights, Finder? Or is it just me?"

He laughed, and Vince smiled, but made no answer. It wasn't necessary. In this state, it didn't matter what he told Niko; the old man wouldn't remember.

In some respects, it was a good thing Niko wasn't much help when he was like this. People could take advantage of him.

Vince smiled again, and rested his hands against his knees, leaning comfortably into his squat. Good, too, that he was honest enough not to cheat the old man out of anything.

"What can I do for you today, Finder?" Niko waved an airy hand toward the overhead without looking at Vince.

Vince maintained his pleasant expression. *Not call me 'Finder', for one*, he thought, but he kept it to himself. Instead, he leaned in a little closer. "Looking for somebody named 'Dent'. Ever heard of him?"

"Oh…" Niko drew the syllable out with happy delight. "Oh, of course. You're always lookin' for somebody, ain't ya?" He gave Vince a much-exaggerated wink.

"Yes." It went without saying that work was the only reason Vince ever dared to venture down here. "Dent Antwerp. Heard of him?"

"No, can't say as I have." Niko's glassy stare transferred briefly from the overhead to Vince's face. "Wish I could help." He laughed suddenly, and slapped his knee. "Come back in a few days." The laughter continued; he thought his little joke was hysterical.

Mentally, Vince shook his head. In a couple of days, obviously, Niko would run out of whatever he was taking and be in the market for more.

Well, he'd known it was a long shot.

He started to get up, to tell the old man goodbye and hightail it out of Level 23-A, but a thought flashed across his mind, freezing him in place. He sent a casual glance at the large compartment around them. No one was currently paying them any attention.

That was good.

"Niko," he lowered his voice, "what can you tell me about a place called the Ruby Gauntlet?"

The effect this had on the old man was astonishing. The glazed, happy expression on his face melted away, to be replaced with abject fear. Niko transferred his gaze to Vince again, and the fear seemed to have jolted a modicum of sense into him. He started shaking his head, leaning toward Vince like he was afraid someone would overhear them.

"Stay away from it," he said in a fierce whisper. "Stay away, Finder. No good'll come out of you going there."

"Have you been there?" Vince asked, even though he doubted it; Niko wasn't exactly a technological whiz. But he *did* spend a lot of time around young people who were.

Niko just blinked at him. "I look that stupid?" He resumed shaking his head. "Place just causes trouble." His glazed eyes darted around the compartment, looking hunted. "Lots of trouble. Don't want no part of it." He scooted away from Vince, folding his arms and legs in to make himself smaller.

A small spike of alarm shot through Vince. In all the years he'd been using Niko as a source, the old man had never had a reaction quite like this before. Not even when it involved the Families. (The Families scared him, true, but not to this degree.)

Frustration swelled in Vince's chest, but he bit back the impatient words that rose to the tip of his tongue. He had a dozen new questions, but it wouldn't any good trying to push the old man for more information. Not right now. All he'd do was get Niko all worked up—well, more worked up than he already was—and draw unwanted attention to both of them.

Instead, he nodded solemnly to the old man. "Don't worry. I won't." He put as much calming assurance in his voice as he could.

It worked. Niko stopped shaking his head, and blinked slowly at Vince. He drew one shuddery breath, and then the newly-found awareness receded from his eyes again. He laughed once and sprawled out on his blanket again, content to stare up at the pretty lights only he could see.

Vince pushed a credit chip into the old man's hand and departed.

CHAPTER 30

EVERYTHING, THE FINDER THOUGHT AS HE WOUND his way back through the dark corridors of Level 23-A to the elevator bank, *hinges on the Ruby Gauntlet.*

That virtual nightclub was the key to all of this—and it was one of the very few places on Zyga Station Vince couldn't find a way into.

A fresh wave of frustration mounted and coiled inside him. He was good, but he wasn't a miracle worker. Detective Commosky was asking too much. To let an innocent man take the fall for a crime he didn't commit when Station Authority knew he was being framed?

Vince wasn't too upset, however, to fail to notice the figure that separated from the shadows of an intersection near the spot where he'd encountered Tank and Spurge and began tailing him. The hair on the back of his neck prickled uncomfortably, as did his goatee. He rubbed his chin thoughtfully, a corner of his mind sifting through everything he'd learned today, even as the rest of him remained on high alert.

That was one problem with a place like the Core—there were only so many places to run. Not that Vince was running, but he had no intentions of letting whoever was following him get the drop on him.

To that end, he doubled back and cut through narrow access corridors, sometimes nearly tripping over the body of some poor soul passed out tucked up against the bulkhead. Most people tended to stay out of these narrow corridors because anything could happen in them, but there were times they came in quite useful.

It was hard to keep his pace even, to look like he was headed somewhere with a purpose but not a mission. Haste and quick strides drew attention as easily as obvious attempts to go unnoticed. But, Vince had a lot of practice. He managed, even though a large part of him urged him to walk faster, to reach the corridor that led to the elevator bank before whoever was following him could beat him to it.

As he neared the elevator bank, he wondered who would be following him—and why. He didn't frequent this part of the Core often, but it wasn't unheard of for him to visit. Apart from Commosky or someone paying close attention to Commosky, who even knew he was investigating Dent's murder?

His client certainly didn't, although it was possible someone had spoken to Corwin's mother.

That brought up an entirely new slew of questions. *Why* would someone other than Commosky be keeping an eye on Mrs. Antwerp's apartment?

He rounded a corner and the dingy, battered gray bulkheads that framed the elevator bank came into view. A couple of people in worn, mostly gray clothes stood waiting for it. None of them made eye contact with anyone, though most of them sent the occasional jittery glance around as though they expected some danger to melt out of the bulkheads and pounce on them.

Vince neatly infiltrated this group, hunching his shoulders and ducking his head as he joined them. Gone was Vince Grable, the Finder. In his place was a man hoping to make it to another level without running into any trouble.

He didn't see any. Trouble, that is.

Sending a surreptitious glance around, Vince couldn't spot anything out of place. Either he'd lost his tail, or they'd hidden themselves away somewhere around here and would attempt to pick up his trail at a later time.

Either way, he'd nearly made it out of the depths of the Core unscathed.

He almost started when he felt a soft vibration inside his jacket. Someone was calling him. He let the comlink buzz; something told him this wasn't the moment to be pulling it out.

Seconds later, one of the elevators' doors slid open with a rusty squeak. Vince shuffled forward along with the rest of the people waiting. They piled into the cab and stood there without looking at each other, though Vince wagered almost everyone was hyper-aware of everyone else.

The young man in the corner, with stringy, greasy black hair, a pale face, and dull eyes, was probably the most out of it, but everyone else—regardless of their game, drug, or drink of choice—was paying attention without *looking* like they were paying attention.

That was a fine line—and not everybody could walk it.

Everyone was headed up. Vince chose Level 12-A—given the parameters of this particular investigation, it was probably wise to refrain from heading straight all the way back up to the upper levels of the Core. Best to first make yet another detour and completely ensure he'd lost his tail.

Vince cleared his throat with a soft rumble, drawing a couple of suspicious, darting glances. The ever-present tickle in the back of his throat grew worse now that he was confined in this metal cab with a handful of people who hadn't bathed in God only knew how long.

Plus, he really needed to check his comlink and find out who'd called him. If it was Bella, he needed to talk to her anyway.

As soon the elevator's doors opened on Level 12-A, Vince slipped out and set off at a brisk walk. Once he found a quiet spot to call Bella, he could loop around to the elevator bank again and get out of the Core. His goatee was still bristling.

As soon as he was out of sight of the elevator bank, the Finder picked up his pace. A normal trickle of people streamed back and forth through the corridors. Level 12-A was predominantly a housing level, mostly for the families of mine workers. The people here were poor, but not as destitute as most in Levels 16-A through 21-A. The air still held the faint scent of food, even though it was between mealtimes.

As he worked his way a couple of corridors over from the elevator bank, Vince extracted his comlink from inside the jacket he'd worn beneath the coat. His assistant *was* the last person to call. He tapped the screen to return the call and waited.

Bella answered immediately. "Boss! Are you all right?"

The concern in her melodic voice was touching. Like most citizens aboard Zyga Station, Bella believed the lower levels of the Core were incredibly dangerous.

She's not exactly wrong, Vince thought wryly. Though to be fair, it mostly depended on what one was doing in the lower levels that determined the danger level.

Even he had to admit, however, that he'd scored more than a few points on the danger scale today.

"I'm fine," he said in a low voice. "Anybody call while I've been gone?"

"No, not a soul. I thought for sure we'd hear from Mrs. Antwerp, but so far she hasn't called."

"I don't expect she will. Not this early." Vince recalled the lost, grief-stricken look in the older woman's dark eyes. She was still reeling; her brain wouldn't start inventing questions until later.

Commosky hadn't called either, but Vince wouldn't lose any sleep over it. He didn't need the detective pestering him right now.

Vince rested a shoulder against a bulkhead between two apartment doors for a moment. "Have you found anything else out about that night club?" He wasn't about to say "Ruby Gauntlet" aloud down here.

"Yes and no."

Vince narrowed his eyes, even as he casually scanned the faces coming and going past him along the corridor. "Meaning?"

Bella hesitated…and Vince *knew*. "Bella…"

"I'm being careful," she protested. "Honest."

"Bella—"

"I had to start from scratch when—everything—happened, but I have a few friends online now. All I'm doing is asking some questions. Most of them don't know anything, but one of them does. We're talking now."

Vince took a deep breath, tamping down the brief flicker of protective frustration that had sprung to life inside him. Bella was a full-grown woman…well, android…and he certainly wasn't in charge of her life, but the idea of her using her new online persona to poke around searching for the Ruby Gauntlet made him nervous.

As he stood there, Vince forced himself to examine *why* it made him nervous. Was it the fact that he knew she'd gotten into trouble once already online—with dire consequences? Or was it the fact that wandering about game worlds was out of his league?

No, he realized, with dawning grim certainty. Mostly it was the fact that this cluster of pixels in the online gaming world had real, physical teeth—and wasn't afraid to use them.

Vince felt something harden inside his chest. Good thing he'd called in reinforcements.

"...ss? Boss? Vince?"

Vince came back to himself with a start. His fingers tightened around his comlink, and then he consciously relaxed his grip. "Okay. See what you can find out—but don't do anything risky."

"Got it." Bella paused, as though searching for the right words to delicately phrase whatever she said next. "What are you going to do?"

"Talk to that old friend of mine."

He didn't have to say more; Bella read between the lines.

"Okay, Boss. I'll be waiting for further instructions."

"Thanks."

Vince ended the call, a fresh feeling of resolve swirling through him. Time to talk to Brill.

He sent a quick, encrypted text. ::*Anything yet?*::

The response came almost immediately. ::*Oh, yeah.*::

Grim satisfaction curled through Vince's resolve. ::*On my way.*::

His comlink immediately buzzed again. ::*No need, Finder. I'll send everything to you. Call when you're in your office.*::

Vince considered that for a full second before mentally shrugging. He'd have preferred to have this conversation in-person, but if Brill didn't, he'd have to concede defeat. The information broker lived and worked in a hidden apartment connected to a little cantina on Level 6-A. If he didn't want visitors, Vince wouldn't be able to get past the cantina's barkeeper.

Besides, Brill was not someone he wanted to upset if he could help it.

::*Fine. Talk to you soon.*::

CHAPTER 31

VINCE MADE HIS WAY BACK UP TO the top levels of the Core without incident, but he still couldn't shake the feeling that he was being followed. It was a particular feeling, a pervasive itch that refused to leave him alone. He didn't spot anyone, but that didn't mean anything.

Either his tail was very good, or he, Vince, was just being paranoid. (That old saying about paranoia came to mind: Just because you're paranoid doesn't mean they *aren't* out to get you.)

The evening meal rush was in full swing by the time the Finder strode through the broad boulevard lined with shops and eateries that led through the center of Level 1-A. If he hadn't been in a hurry to get back to his office to talk to Brill, he might have stopped in one of these places just for the novelty. Plus, he was hungry. His stomach gave an appreciative rumble as he inhaled a jumble of inviting smells—cooking meat, fried food, garlic, baking bread.

Vince assured his stomach he'd get something to fill it once he made it back to Zone 5 and marched on.

There were some occasions Vince wished somebody would figure out how to invent a teleporter. This was one of them. After all, human beings had figured out how to travel faster than the speed of light, so why not teleportation?

He was on the verge of…something. He could feel it in his bones. This could be the break he needed, the break *Corwin* needed.

A feeling of grim anticipation thrummed in Vince's veins as he journeyed back through the Hub to Zone 5 and then up the glass elevator bank to Level 7-A. He was almost to his office when his comlink buzzed.

His attention mostly fixed on his office door, which had just come into sight, Vince pulled his comlink out and glanced at the display. A freezing sensation, like he'd just been doused with a bucket of cold water, swept over him.

Commosky.

That couldn't be good.

For a split second, Vince considered not answering. The detective could hardly have expected him to crack this case wide open after less than a day on the job. He, Vince, had an excellent reputation, but even for him this was way beyond the realm of possibility.

That said, he'd rather not rub Station Authority the wrong way right now.

Suppressing a sigh, Vince looked both ways before answering the call as he crossed the boulevard to his office door. "Detective?"

"Somebody just forced their way into Mrs. Antwerp's house and threatened her."

Vince blinked, his hand freezing above the keypad beside his door. "In broad day-cycle?"

"Yep."

"Is she all right?" Vince imagined several scenarios—all of them terrible. He thought of that poor woman's slight frame and her sad, dark eyes and felt anger twist in the pit of his stomach.

"Shaken up, but otherwise unharmed. They wanted to scare her, not hurt her."

Commosky's voice was grim—but Vince detected a faint note of satisfaction. He narrowed his eyes, even as he let himself into his office. "You're pleased."

"They've finally tipped their hand." The note of satisfaction lacing Commosky's voice grew. "They didn't know we had the apartment under observation. I've got men following them now. We'll know who they are and who hired them soon enough."

"Station Authority is eminently suited for that task," Vince said, nodding to Bella, who had looked up from her desk at his entry. She'd realized, however, that he was on a call and waved instead of greeting him verbally. Her lipstick was still as red as her blouse.

Locking the door behind him, Vince headed over to his desk. His stomach rumbled again, but he ignored it. Now was not the time for food. "What do you want from me?"

In his mind's eye, he could see Commosky shrug. "Maybe nothing, now. If this lead pans out, we'll have what we need." A pause. "Unless you've come up with something already."

There it was. The expected nudge for information. One corner of Vince's mouth lifted in a sardonic smile. "Pursuing a couple of leads."

He didn't mention Brill. The information broker preferred to let Station Authority think they were the only ones who ever called on his services—even if nobody actually believed it. Better to let them assume than to provide concrete proof.

The Haven, on the other hand… Vince's slight smile turned into a frown. "I *have* found evidence that Dent may have recently fathered a child."

At her desk, Bella's dark eyebrows shot up into her hairline. She widened her eyes at Vince in a silent question; he nodded in return.

"Unless that has something to do with his death, he could have fathered a dozen children and it wouldn't matter."

In other words, Vince thought, *you don't care.* He hadn't really expected the information to get much of a reaction from Commosky, but being confronted with callous indifference always saddened him.

He cleared his throat. "Supposedly, he mentioned the Ruby Gauntlet and claimed to be helping beta test a new game."

"A *game*?" Commosky snorted derisively. "Sounds like a line of space dust he'd spin to a girl."

Vince's spine stiffened, and he narrowed his eyes again. *He* suspected as much as well, but he still intended to look into it. That Commosky was dismissing the claim right out of hand was… troubling.

But then, the detective obviously thought his men had cracked the case wide open.

Commosky seemed to realize the silence that greeted his words was more than a little frosty. "Ah, well. Go ahead and investigate, Finder. A lead's a lead, regardless of whether or not it pans out."

"Thanks," Vince said dryly. "How magnanimous of you." He narrowed his eyes again at his jade green sideboard, struck by a chilling thought. "You *let* those men threaten Mrs. Antwerp and her friend, didn't you?"

It was Commosky's turn to fall silent. After an uncomfortable pause, he cleared his throat and said, "Well… We couldn't tip our hand. They had instructions to step in if things got out of hand."

He had the grace to sound slightly abashed. Emphasis on the *slightly*.

Vince found himself wondering exactly what the detective considered 'out of hand'. His eyes narrowed further, a feeling of helpless indignation flooding his nerves.

No, he thought suddenly. *Not helpless.*

He was already helping. He could find the real culprit and restore Corwin to his mother—before anything else happened to the Antwerps because of Commosky's myopic focus on only the macro level of events.

His comlink beeped softly, indicating he had another incoming voice call.

"Excuse me, Detective, but I've got work to do." Vince didn't wait for the other man to respond, but switched over to the other call. "Grable, here."

"Finder?" asked a tearful, angry voice. "This is Cora Antwerp."

CHAPTER 32

Vince straightened in his chair. "Mrs. Antwerp." He started to ask if she was all right, before remembering that she didn't know about his involvement with Commosky.

It didn't matter anyway. Mrs. Antwerp immediately loosed a torrent of words.

"They came into my house, Finder! Into my *house*! Two of them! Big, hulking men reeking of cheap cologne with dead eyes and they told me that if I don't pay the money they will come back and do…things….terrible things to—to me and my apartment and my friends." She paused long enough to draw a shuddery breath. "Is it not enough that they have killed my son? Must they now hound the living?"

Vince opened his mouth to reply, but Mrs. Antwerp swept on. Gone was the tragic, silent woman of earlier. In her place was a woman whose shock and grief had morphed into fiery anger.

And she *was* angry. There was no doubt about it.

Vince mentally shook his head. Hadn't taken long for *that* emotion to set in.

He waited for a break in the onslaught of words to ask a question he already knew the answer to. "Have you told Station Authority?"

"Yes. I called them." Mrs. Antwerp's voice shook with suppressed anger. "They said they would look into it." She let out a derisive laugh that choked on a sob halfway. "Just like they 'looked into' my—my—"

Vince heard a muffled sound, like Corwin's mother had pressed a hand to her mouth to stifle a sob. He glanced sideways in time to see Bella drop her gaze to her tablet and pretend to be engrossed in the display.

"Mrs. Antwerp." He had to say her name twice before she answered. "Is your friend still with you?"

A sniffle, and then, "Yes." A hint of gratitude and pride filled her voice as she added, "She is the best friend and stayed. Even though those terrible men frightened her too."

"Good. I'm proud of both of you." Vince rose from his desk and crossed the office to the credenza to brew himself a cup of tea. He needed tea right now. "Have her stay as long as she can."

"Do you think they'll come back?" Mrs. Antwerp asked, almost hesitantly. "Station Authority said they would not, but I—I don't believe them."

"I don't blame you." Vince picked a bag of tea at random, which turned out to be green tea. "I don't think they'll come back again tonight."

"But tomorrow?"

It was his turn to hesitate. Should he give her the stark truth or a gentler version to tide her over until the next day? He shook his head. The woman had already received one of the biggest shocks a human being could have.

The stark truth, by comparison, was nothing more than a not-so-minor inconvenience.

"They might return tomorrow," he said at last. "Depends on how long they said you had to come up with the money and how much…motivation…they think you might require."

"I see." Another pause, and then Mrs. Antwerp asked, even more hesitantly, "Have you made any…progress?"

Vince thought of the baby girl down in the worst part of the Core, the baby girl who might be this woman's grandchild. "Too many things in flux to give you any certainties, but, yes, I believe so. I hope we'll have this cleared up soon."

He cleared his throat softly before she could say anything else. "If you'll excuse me, Mrs. Antwerp, I have a very important call to make. "

"I—" the woman drew a deep breath, seeming to pull herself together. "I understand. Thank you, Finder."

"You're welcome. I will check in with you later to make sure you're all right."

Dropping his comlink onto his desk, Vince leaned back in his chair and exhaled slowly. Whoever was behind the Ruby Gauntlet wasn't wasting any time ensuring Mrs. Antwerp knew who was in charge. He imagined the scene that had just played out in that tiny apartment and felt a twinge of nausea.

He had to stop these men.

Hopefully he could do that with whatever information Brill had dug up.

Before he called the information broker, Vince reached down into one of his desk drawers and withdrew a protein bar. He consumed it in a couple of large bites and washed it down with a few just-this-side-of-scalding sips of tea. His stomach protested, but he ignored it. That would have to do for now.

Out of the corner of his eye, he caught Bella shaking her head. He grinned at her, a quick flash of white teeth. "Part of the job."

Reaching for his comlink, Vince noticed for the first time a little plastic tub with a lid sitting to one side of his desk. Unmarked, the tub was a shade of green just a tad darker than the jade green of his desk. He frowned. He was reasonably sure that tub hadn't been there when he left that morning.

"What's this?" Vince picked it up between his thumb and forefinger and held it up for Bella to see, swiveling in his chair.

"Oh, you found it." Bella straightened in her chair, her face brightening. The expression was almost normal instead of exaggerated. "That," she said, nodding to the little tub, "is for you."

"Figured as much," Vince said dryly. "Doesn't answer my question." He shook the tub lightly. Whatever was inside didn't seem to move. "What is it?"

"It's a salve I got from an old friend of mine." Bella's face fell before Vince could feel a stab of concern. "Well, she doesn't *know* it was me. All I said was that I'd heard about her shop and I needed something for my boss."

It took effort to maintain a pleasant expression. Any other time, Vince wouldn't have minded hearing this story, but the weight of his impending conversation with Brill left him itching to get on with it. His fingers tightened slightly on the tub. "Bella…"

"It's for your throat," his assistant explained in a rush, self-consciously tucking a lock of shining black hair behind her ear. "I've heard you cough, sometimes, after you get back, and you've mentioned something in the Station's air bothers you. Figured that's why you've got the airscrubber in here." She tipped her head toward the tub. "That will help."

A flood of warmth filled Vince's chest at her thoughtfulness. Before he cracked the lid, however, he raised an eyebrow at her. "Nothing illegal in this stuff, right?"

Probably not a good idea to go wandering around Zyga Station wearing something that would get him into trouble.

Bella cocked her head to one side, her expression thoughtful. "Would you really care if the salve worked?"

This time, both of Vince's eyebrows shot up in surprise. He stared at Bella, but before he could do more than blink at her, she dissolved into laughter.

"The look on your face is priceless!" She held out both hands, still smiling. "It's fine, I promise. I have no idea what's in it, but old Lola has been selling healing salves out of her apartment since before I was born. She's never had a problem with Station Authority."

He'd have to take her word for it, for now. Vince opened the jar to reveal a pale cream. A pungent scent wafted up to meet his nose; he immediately grimaced and turned his face away. "That is… powerful."

"It's very effective," Bella said brightly. "You're supposed to apply a dab behind your ears and under your nose every time you leave the office."

He wouldn't be able to smell anything else. Worse, people might smell *him* coming. There wasn't any way to tactfully say that to Bella, however.

Vince turned his head to regard the jar again. Now that the first shock of the smell was over, he took another tentative sniff. The cream was a jumble of earthy scents, but one predominantly rose above the others—and there was something familiar about it.

Eucalyptus.

Vince had barely recalled the name before the memory of the last time he'd smelled eucalyptus slammed into his mind. There had been a eucalyptus tree in Dr. Faust's office in Orion Labs. He recalled the scent of smoke and laser fire and scorched flesh, as clearly as though he'd just escaped from the lab again with an unconscious Rav in tow.

"What?" Bella asked anxiously. "What's wrong?"

Vince blinked again and the memories dissipated like smoke. "Nothing." He offered her a smile over the top of the jar. "Thank you, Bella. This was…incredibly thoughtful of you."

She beamed at him and turned back to her tablet.

That warm glow still burning faintly inside his chest, Vince capped the jar and set it aside. Regardless of whether or not it'd be practical for daily use (and he wouldn't know *that* until he tested it later), it was a kind, thoughtful gesture. Nobody had done anything like this for him in a long time.

In fact, Anita—Sergeant Rychek—was the last person to—

Vince cut that thought off at the knees. He had work to do and a man's life to save, and a stroll down memory lane wouldn't help him get it done.

He reached for his comlink. At this rate, Brill would think he wasn't interested in the information he'd dug up.

A slight smile tugged at the corners of Vince's mouth. Of course, that could be a good thing. Maybe Brill would charge him less.

CHAPTER 33

$\mathbf{B}$RILL ANSWERED HIS COMLINK ALMOST IMMEDIATELY, A tell-tale sign that he was still intrigued enough to prioritize Vince over his other clients. "Took you long enough," he chided.

Vince shrugged, even though the other man couldn't see him over a voice-only call. "That's life. What do you have for me?"

"Enough to get you into a mess of trouble."

That sounded promising. Vince unconsciously straightened in his office chair. "Well?"

"I'll have you know, Finder, I really had to work for this one."

Vince raised an eyebrow, his gaze fixed on his jade green sideboard. "Even more than you did digging up info on Terrell Roda a while back?"

Brill paused, considering. "Well, maybe about the same. Which surprised me, because Roda had a lot more pull."

Vince could almost picture the information broker's long, pale fingers dancing over a keyboard. He waited, knowing from long experience that the other man did not like to be rushed. Unless he was being paid otherwise (and beyond extravagantly, at that), Brill found the information he was hired to acquire and presented it in his own way.

It was annoying at times, but part of the price one had to pay for his services.

At her desk, Bella gave up all pretense of working. She leaned forward to rest an elbow on her desk and cup her chin in her hand while she stared across the office at Vince.

"Where to start?" Brill mused through the comlink. "This story has a bit of a circular bent."

To hold back an impatient reply, Vince reached for his tea, which had cooled considerably. He took a silent sip and let the warm liquid wash down his throat. Only then did he permit himself to speak. "I'm surprised you called instead of just sending everything over."

"This job requires context." Brill paused. "Also, like I said, I'm intrigued. The best word I can think of to describe what you've stumbled into is 'audacious.'"

Vince refrained from shaking his head. If Brill was going to walk him through it after all, he'd have preferred the information broker do it in person.

"I've sent you what I turned up," Brill continued.

The instant he opened the first set of files, Vince knew what Brill had done. He sat back in his chair, sucking air in through his teeth. Brill hadn't just scoured the highways and byways of Zyga Station's ComNet for traces of the Ruby Gauntlet. No, no, that would have been too easy.

The information broker had actually *gone* there.

How he'd done it, Vince could only speculate, but the evidence was right there in front of him.

Brill had taken screenshots. Vince leaved closer to his computer display, both a little awed and a little irritated. Waltzing right into the place was liable to tip them off—even if Brill *was* a genius.

Vince swiped through the screenshots, which were all of the inside of a dimly-lit nightclub packed full of people. The inside of the Ruby Gauntlet itself. At first glance, everyone looked normal, but then he spotted horns, wings, and a host of other decidedly inhuman features. Avatars, all of them.

"I'm impressed," he said grudgingly. "How did you find the place?"

Brill waved that aside. "Finding it wasn't the issue. Neither was getting inside. I've played *Everheart* myself and I have contingencies set up for something like this."

That news didn't surprise Vince. He'd eat his jacket if Brill didn't have a handful of character profiles built up for every major—and probably most of the minor—games available on Zyga Station.

"The operation itself isn't even that complicated," Brill said. "Check the rest of the screenshots. Practically every game they've got can be played anywhere else in the galaxy."

Vince continued to look through the screenshots. Unlike the other casinos on Zyga Station (real or virtual), the Ruby Gauntlet maintained its nightclub feel by eschewing the slot machines and other automated trappings. It had a geologically-based decor—all jeweled tones and glittering gemstones of green, blue, red, yellow, and white—and a large dance floor.

"It *is* predominantly a nightclub. And it doesn't take much to get in."

"What's the issue, then?" Vince narrowed his eyes, sensing the impending problem.

"The issue is that the owners—or somebody they hired—hacked the game." Brill's tone said he was impressed. Before Vince could ask to what purpose, the information broker said, "All in-game currency is supposed to run through official channels on the game's servers."

"So it can be tracked and recorded in the real world. I know." Vince was familiar with this. Station Authority hadn't wanted anyone—including the Families—being able to launder money through a game.

"Exactly. Except money transfers inside the Ruby Gauntlet are handled completely differently. The payment portal doesn't connect to the outside game at all. It's a fancy bit of coding. Takes the money someplace else."

"Where?" Vince rubbed his chin thoughtfully; his goatee was bristling. *Follow the money.* People lied, cheated, and deceived, but money never lied. It had to come from somewhere, and it had to go somewhere.

The question was who was handling it?

"That, I'm not sure yet. They've done a damn good job of hiding their tracks."

"Brill, that doesn't help me."

"Hang on, hang on." The information broker's voice took on a slightly wounded edge. "Who said I was finished? Look at the next set of files I sent you."

Vince pulled them up and found himself looking a list of names. "What is this?"

"Look at it. Notice anything familiar?"

Biting back a frustrated retort, Vince scanned through the list of names again, more carefully. He still didn't recognize any of them…except… That one. Third from the bottom.

His eyes narrowed. *Str33twarrior8.*

That was Dent Antwerp's username.

CHAPTER 34

Vince leaned back in his chair, sucking in a breath through his teeth. *Str33twarrior8.* As usernames went, it wasn't particularly imaginative. Commosky had given that information to him, but up until now there hadn't been much he could do with it.

"Brill, where did you get this list?"

"Like I told you, Finder, I maintain a presence." He could almost see Brill shrug on the other end of the line. "Got a couple of the right people talking and found out there's a Wall of Shame. Sent you a screenshot of that too." The information broker's voice took on a grim note again. "Doesn't say how much they lost—and I doubt any of the club's regulars known the truth—but it lists everybody who's gone into the Diamond Gem Room and come back out with nothing."

It only took Vince a moment to find the screenshot the information broker had mentioned. He stared at it, taking in the twinkling lists of avatars and usernames. "Why would they track this?"

"It's a *game*, Grable," Brill said impatiently. "People track all kinds of loony things in games. High scores, how many times someone's failed a level, how many times somebody's bombed something, you name it. Something like this is probably considered a badge of honor. 'I bombed out in the Diamond Gem Room in the Ruby Gauntlet.'"

"The fact that they even made it there is a big deal." Vince nodded in understanding, thoughtfully narrowing his eyes at the list of usernames.

In the background, his airscrubber kicked on, but he didn't even consciously register the sound. The implications of this were dawning in his mind with all the fiery glory of a sunrise seen from the Rim.

"Any way we can trace these to the people behind these names?" he asked abruptly, and then paused. "Legally, I mean?"

He'd faced down Family goons and survived. A couple of un-named—albeit rich and powerful—casino owners didn't intimidate him. He just didn't want them to get away and ooze back into the dark corners of Zyga Space Station.

Brill paused as well. "You'd need a court order to make the game company give up that kind of information."

"And otherwise?"

"Risky. Don't get me wrong, it can be done, but they're pretty stringent about maintaining security."

Vince nodded again, even though the other man couldn't see him. He'd expected as much.

The Finder glanced over at Bella. She'd straightened at her desk, her posture radiating concern mixed with excitement. Over the months they'd been working together, Vince had come to the realization that his assistant enjoyed the adrenaline rush that came with narrowing in on closing a case almost as much as he did.

Even though, as a woman stuck in an android body, Bella couldn't actually *feel* adrenaline anymore.

Quickly, Vince scanned through the rest of the data the information broker had sent him. There wasn't much. A few screenshots of a beautiful female elf avatar Brill suspected might be the mysterious Starlit, one of the club's owners, and a shot of a tall, stately orc Brill suspected might be Lumen.

"Brill," Vince said, shaking his head, "I must admit, I'm impressed."

"You should be," Brill said promptly. "Anything else you want me to keep an eye on?"

Vince considered, trading glances with Bella. "Keep working on the money angle, will you?" he said at last. "And log everything, no matter how inconsequential you think it is."

"That'll cost—"

"—extra, I know." Vince smiled wryly. "This is important, Brill. Peoples' lives are on the line, not just their money. If we can find out where the money is going, maybe I can figure out how Station Authority can legally catch them."

Brill was silent for a moment. "Sometimes, Finder," he said at last, "I think you're entirely too softhearted for this business."

Vince thought of Corwin Antwerp's earnest face, his mother's sad eyes, and that scrawny baby girl orphaned in the heart of the Core. Somebody had to help them get justice.

"Maybe." He shrugged. "Good thing I know talented people, eh?"

The information broker just scoffed.

On the verge of signing off, Vince paused. "Brill."

"Yes?" Brill sounded just a touch suspicious.

"Any way you can figure out where Starlit and Lumen's messages are originating from?"

"No. Already tried that."

Vince digested this. "Okay," he said at last. "Thanks. Send me a bill."

"Is that it?" Brill sounded both dubious and curious.

"I'll let you know," Vince promised, and ended the transmission.

Dropping his comlink onto his jade green desktop, he leaned back in his chair and absently rubbed his chin while he stared unseeing at his drinkmaker on the credenza on the opposite side of the room. The information he'd just learned swirled around his head, bits and pieces of it slotting themselves into place with what he already knew. A picture emerged, its edges slowly sharpening and coming into focus, like a telescope focusing in on a cluster of stars across the galaxy.

"I know that look," Bella said abruptly. She pushed back her chair and stalked around her desk to perch on the corner of her boss's desk. She pointed a long, slender finger at him. "You've figured it out."

"No." Vince shook his head. "Haven't gotten that far yet."

"But—?" she asked knowingly.

"But…" Vince smiled slightly. "I have a better idea of where to go next."

"And where is that?"

"Track down other losers from the Diamond Gem Room."

Bella's eyes widened. "Of course." It was her turn to shake her head. "Should have thought of that earlier."

"I know." Vince picked up his comlink again. "I've got to call Detective Commosky."

CHAPTER 35

On the face of it, Vince's epiphany was simple. Hiring Brill to hunt down the real people behind the usernames on that list inside the Ruby Gauntlet would most likely result in the information being considered tainted by the judicial system. Station Authority wouldn't be able to use it for the murder trial—*any* of the murder trials that would likely result from cracking this case.

Therefore, Vince would have to take what information he could get legally and hunt the people down himself—the old-fashioned way. It would take a lot longer…but it would be admissible in court.

But that didn't mean he couldn't see if Commosky could speed things along a little.

The detective answered on the second ring. "You got something for me?"

"Are you aware there's a Wall of Shame inside the Ruby Gauntlet with a list of usernames of people who've lost money in the Diamond Gem Room?"

Commosky grunted. "And here I thought you had something good for me." He grunted again. "We've had that for a while. Dent brought it to us."

Vince's goatee bristled again; he rubbed his chin. "From your dolorous tone, I take it you weren't able to do much with it?"

"No. Need a damn court order to get identities."

Which meant they definitely didn't have enough for probable cause. Vince narrowed his eyes. "Aside from the fact that getting a court order might have tipped somebody off that you were poking around?"

"I resent that implication," Commosky said coldly. "I might have used Dent, but I'd get a court order in a heartbeat if I could."

In the background, Vince's airscrubber kicked on, softening the smooth jazz notes filtering through the office.

"Fair enough." The Finder lifted one shoulder in a shrug. "For the record, Detective, I believe you."

Commosky grunted again, as though he couldn't care less whether Vince believed him or not. "Hope you've got something better than that, Finder, or your boy is going down."

"I may have had an idea," Vince said slowly. He wasn't sure if he wanted to reveal it to Commosky or not. It was *possible* this had already occurred to the detective…but then again…perhaps not.

This was, after all, why Commosky had wanted him on the case. He didn't think inside the same box Station Authority did.

When Vince didn't elaborate, the detective said, "Well, I'm warning you—better make it quick."

"You got anything for me?" Vince asked by way of answering.

"Nothing you could use," Commosky said curtly, and with that, he ended the transmission.

Vince looked over at Bella, shaking his head. "He could let me be the judge of that."

Bella just smiled. "That'd be too easy, Boss."

"Tell me about it." Vince blew out an irritated breath, rolling his shoulders to relieve some of the tension that had formed in them. It wasn't like he and Commosky were on the side of justice or anything.

Shaking his head again, he looked down at his comlink display. Time to explore his idea. He was running out of options.

On the verge of diving in, Vince hesitated—just long enough to consider a sobering fact. Surely, *surely*, this option had occurred to Commosky too. Vince didn't deal much with murder cases, but from what he *did* know, all the possible motives in the galaxy boiled down to a few main themes.

Money was one of those.

Wouldn't Commosky follow the money too?

Disgust curled through the Finder. *Not when he's got me*, he thought. *Not when he's got Corwin—the perfect patsy.*

And Vince knew from experience that Station Authority as a whole didn't care about certain things and people groups as much as they should.

Commosky might want to dig deeper, but if someone in his command chain thought that the case was closed, or, worse, someone in his command chain was getting money from the people behind the Ruby Gauntlet, his hands might be tied.

Vince paused a second longer to wonder if this could possibly be a trap. Surely the people behind the Ruby Gauntlet wouldn't leave a trail that could be followed so easily.

He shook his head. Dent.

It all came back to Dent—and his murder.

Vince reached for his mug of tea, discovered it was empty, and set it back down on his desk. Dent's murder was a crime of passion—a result of some catastrophic revelation. It hadn't been planned.

But the default plan to intimidate his family into paying the lien had gone on regardless.

Something stirred deep in the Finder's chest: grim resolve. If the owners of the Ruby Gauntlet could be said to have made a mistake, Vince had a feeling this was it.

He just had to figure out how to use it to track them down—and he knew exactly where to start.

"Bella," he tipped his head toward her. "Get ready to do some digging."

Then he pulled up Mrs. Antwerp's comm details.

Corwin's mother answered immediately. "Yes, Finder?"

Vince didn't waste any time. "Did those men who accosted you this morning give you any paperwork regarding the lien Dent supposedly put on your apartment?"

A brief pause greeted these words. Then Mrs. Corwin said in a stronger voice. "Yes. Yes, they did."

A wave of grim satisfaction flooded Vince. "Good. Give me everything you've got."

He felt his goatee bristle. This was the break he'd been searching for.

Either the Ruby Gauntlet's owners were selling the properties they acquired…or they were building a rather respectable array of rental properties. Both options meant money flowing to them from somewhere or someone else—a real-world connection to money lost in a virtual world.

He allowed himself a grim smile. *Follow the money.*

CHAPTER 36

ONCE VINCE KNEW WHAT TO LOOK FOR, it didn't take an information broker like Brill to turn up information on Nasard Mutual. All it required was a little patience, Zyga Station's public records—and access to a few things that weren't exactly public record.

Having a Finder's license did come with a few perks.

"They have an office," Bella said presently, from her desk. "Over in Zone 4. It's tiny and only has two employees," she added thoughtfully, "but it does exist."

"It'd have to exist to pull something like this off," Vince said grimly. "Just enough appearance of the truth to keep anybody from digging too deeply."

His fingers flew over his own keyboard. "If that's the case, then there's a list of properties they've handled."

"Got it," Bella said a few seconds later.

Vince shot an impressed smile in her direction. "You beat me to it."

She beamed back at him. "Hey, gotta justify that salary you pay me somehow. Sending it to you now."

A second later, a link to the information she'd found popped up on Vince's own tablet display. He brought it up and scanned through it, frowned, and then scanned through it again.

In the last year alone, Nasard Mutual had bought and sold a few small businesses and a large number of apartments all over Zyga Station. More than just the number of losers posted on the Wall of Shame inside the Ruby Gauntlet. Vince's frown deepened. Either there were more losers than recorded, or Nasard Mutual handled a few more…legitimate…deals as well.

The Finder leaned back in his chair and rolled his shoulders before jumping to his feet and beginning to pace the length of his office. He'd been sitting too long; he needed to get up and get his blood pumping.

Preferably to his brain. He couldn't shake the feeling that he was missing something.

Struck by a sudden thought, Vince glanced over his shoulder. "Bella, cross reference that list with the list of people who've died aboard Zyga Station in the past…. Let's say nine months."

"Got it, Boss."

While his assistant handled that, Vince made himself another cup of tea. Strong tea, this time. He smoothed a hand over his chin while he waited for it to brew; he had a feeling he'd be out in Zyga Station's corridors before long.

"There are four," Bella said after a moment. "Three deaths under mysterious circumstances, tentatively ruled homicides, and one death that looks like the cause was genuine old age."

Four deaths—and all of them were connected to property that was subsequently sold through Nasard Mutual.

That wasn't a coincidence.

Vince took his tea back to his desk and settled down in his chair. "Cause of death for the homicides?"

Bella consulted her datapad. "All three of them were shot to death." She grimaced. "Execution style. And Station Authority doesn't have any real leads on who was responsible."

"Execution style," Vince repeated. A spark ignited inside his head. "You're sure of that?"

"Positive." Bella shot him a look, but didn't remind him that this was a fairly dumb question—Station Authority reports were usually cut and dry—emphasis on the 'dry'.

Vince didn't notice. His gaze had turned inward, reviewing everything he'd learned so far in light of this startling new piece of information.

Three homicides—and Station Authority had no leads. His expression darkened. Either that or, like Commosky, they had leads they couldn't—or wouldn't—pursue.

Three homicides—most likely connected to the Ruby Gauntlet. Three victims who had more or less been *executed*. Presumably for failure to pay, and to send a *very* clear message to their relatives.

Ruthless and coldhearted, but just business.

They hadn't been beaten to death.

Vince swiveled in his chair to face Bella, nearly spilling his hot tea. "Dent's death *was* personal. I don't know why yet, but I don't think this has anything do with the Ruby Gauntlet's general operation."

Bella frowned, her red lips pursing. "But Commosky—"

"—has got the Ruby Gauntlet on his brain. Dent was his informant when he died, and that's all the detective can see." Vince set his tea down on his desk and ran a hand over his close-shorn hair, a mix of excitement and frustration swirling inside him. "We've been looking at this all wrong."

"What do you mean?" Bella's frown deepened. "Wouldn't these people—Lumen and Starlit—have a vested interest in keeping Dent from reporting to Station Authority?"

"They would if they'd known about it." Vince shook his head. "I don't think they had a clue he was investigating them."

It was Bella's turn to lean back in her chair. She held out a silver-tipped hand. "Okay, Boss. You're going to have to explain the thought process on this one."

"If Lumen and Starlit wanted Dent dead, all they'd have to do is shoot him—just like everybody else who's crossed them has died so far." Vince stood and pushed his chair back, before moving around his desk to pace the length of his office while he talked. Pieces were clicking together inside his head, almost too fast for him to verbalize. "They've gotten away with it up to this point— why break pattern?"

"Because they were angry with him." Bella held a hand palm up. "He was reporting to Station Authority and he could get them into a lot of trouble."

Vince shook his head. "He didn't know them well enough to rate that kind of reaction." He held up a finger. "And what's the other thing that's different about this case?"

Bella tilted her head to one side, her almond-shaped eyes narrowing as she thought. After a few seconds, she said, "Station Authority arrested Corwin?"

"Exactly." A grim sense of finality coalesced in Vince's chest. "Somebody murdered Dent and framed his brother for it." He held out his hands. "Why would the owners of the Ruby Gauntlet bother doing that?"

"They wouldn't." Bella shook her head. "Too much work. And—" she straightened, her eyes widening. "They'd have had to know who Dent was in order to find him."

"Yes." Vince bestowed her with a proud nod. "We don't have any evidence they knew who he was outside of the *Everheart* game."

They both fell silent for a moment, the gentle rumbling of the airscrubber and soft strains of jazz the only sounds in the office.

Bella finally broke it. Pushing a lock of glossy black hair over her shoulder, she leaned forward and rested her elbows on her jade green desk. "So now what do we do?" She shook her head. "We've just eliminated our biggest suspect."

"It goes back to Dent and Corwin."

"Does that mean we have to start all over?"

"No." Vince drew in a breath, then exhaled slowly. "But it *does* mean I have to call Commosky again."

Bella shook her head again. "He's not going to like this at all."

"No, he's not." Vince grimaced. "But, there's no getting around the fact that the truth is the truth. And, whether he likes it or not, it's looking like the truth is, the Ruby Gauntlet's owners had nothing to do with Dent's murder."

"The game," Bella said abruptly, sitting bolt-upright in her chair. She looked at Vince and her dark eyes were wide in her pale, heart-shaped face. "He told the girl he got pregnant that he was helping to test a game."

Vince nodded. "That's what I'm thinking too." He paused, held out a hand palm-up. "That's if he was telling the truth about the game."

"How do we figure that out?"

In lieu of answering, Vince reached for his comlink.

CHAPTER 37

COMMOSKY ANSWERED ON THE SECOND RING. "YOU better be calling to tell me you've figured it out, Finder, because I don't have—"

Vince cut him off before he could finish his brusque opening. "Did you recover Dent Antwerp's comlink with his body? Or any mobile device at all?"

A brief pause greeted this. Then, slowly, almost suspiciously, Commosky said, "No. Figured the killer or killers took it."

The Finder nodded; he'd expected as much. "Anything else you can tell me about Dent and Corwin's lives leading up to the night of the murder?"

Another pause, this one longer. "What are you playing at?" the detective asked at last. "The last time you called, you were asking about the Ruby Gauntlet. Now you want what my men have dug up?" His voice sharpened. "What changed in the last half-hour?"

"Give me what you've got and I'll tell you." This was the only way to negotiate with the detective—Commosky was liable to shut off lines of communication like an air hatch closing against the vacuum of space as soon as he found out his pet theory was toast.

The detective seemed to sense this. "You *have* found something." His baritone voice deepened a little in disgust. "I'm not going to like it, am I?" It wasn't a question.

Vince bit back a hint of a smile. Never let it be said Commosky wasn't intelligent. Brusque and dogmatic, perhaps, but not dumb.

"Detective," he said, "I could go dig up what I need myself, but we both know that your men are eminently trained for this sort of thing. There's no sense in me wasting my time."

There was another pause. Vince could feel time ticking away while Commosky dithered, seconds slipping past them, never to be recovered. He glanced at Bella, to find her watching him. Her expression was sober, her chin propped in her hand.

To his credit, Commosky seemed to also sense they were wasting time. He blew out a frustrated breath. "Fine. We'll play it your way for now, Finder."

"Thank you," Vince said, but the detective barreled right over him.

"We don't know much about Dent's whereabouts or doings when he's in the Core. It's only when he comes back to the Zones that he pops up on our radar again. He was pretty reliable about checking in and reporting." Commosky's voice turned grim. "Wanted his money."

Vince nodded. "What about Corwin?"

"Don't get ahead of me, Grable. In the last couple of months, Dent showed up at his mother's apartment and at the noodle shop where Corwin works. A few arguments ensued, but nothing dramatic. That is, until a couple of weeks ago, the last time he was at the noodle shop."

"He got into a fight with his brother." Vince's goatee bristled; he smoothed a hand over his chin. "Mr. Pho told me about it."

"Did he tell you that Dent was already fighting with somebody else before Corwin intervened?"

Vince went very still. "No," he said at last. "Mr. Pho failed to mention that bit. Any idea what the fight was about?"

"No," Commosky said flatly. "And when I asked Corwin about it, all he said was that his brother had come in for a loan and somebody else had come in after him."

That was…odd. Vince ran through his memory of his talk with Corwin that night in this very office. He didn't remember the young man mentioning anything about somebody else coming into the noodle shop to accost Dent.

"Have you—"

"Checked the noodle shop's security footage?" Commosky sounded both smug and weary, all at once. "Done and done. Couldn't get a good view of his face."

Which meant he either was incredibly lucky, or he knew where all the noodle shop's security cams were. Vince narrowed his eyes. "Have you—"

"Investigated? What kind of newbie do you take me for, Grable? Of *course* we've investigated. I've got men looking for this guy, but so far they haven't found him. Noodle shop owner said he'd never seen him before. Couldn't describe him, either."

Vince let the detective's prickly irritation bead off of him like condensation dripping off the synthglass panels inside the greenhouses in Zone 2. It told him how badly the detective wanted to take down the Ruby Gauntlet. He shook his head slightly. It was a pity it couldn't be done by finding Dent's murderer…but that didn't mean things were hopeless.

"Do you have holo stills of him?"

Commosky paused. "Yeah." Vince pictured him shrugging. "I'll send you one."

"That would be much appreciated. What about my client?"

"Corwin's fairly clean. Far as we can tell, all the kid does is work and study. Other than a couple involving his brother, he hasn't had any altercations with anyone."

That was good. Vince was sure his client was being framed, but there was always that chance…

"That's all I've got," Commosky said gruffly. "Your turn, Finder."

Vince glanced across the office at Bella, who gave him an encouraging nod. He shook his head. "I've got good news and bad news, Commosky. Good news is, I think I've eliminated a suspect."

"Bad news is…" He took a quick, bracing breath. "I don't think Dent's death had anything to with the Ruby Gauntlet."

Vince was right—Commosky was not happy. When the Finder finished his story, the detective peppered him with a series of increasingly bad-tempered questions, before abruptly ending the transmission. He did, however, keep his word.

Five minutes later, Vince's comlink buzzed with an incoming message. Commosky would be investigating Nasard Mutual further. A holo still from Pho's Noodle Shop was attached.

"Look at this, Bella." Vince motioned for Bella to join him.

His assistant hopped up, a little more enthusiastically than was perhaps warranted, and crossed the office to lean over Vince's shoulder. Vince pulled the holo still up on his datapad, and together, they inspected the holo still in silence.

"Well," Bella said presently. "That's completely useless." She gestured to the datapad display. "All that confirms is that it's probably a man. Too broad-shouldered to be a woman." She tapped her long fingernails on the surface of the jade green desk. "And they asked the noodle shop owner if he knew the man?"

"They did. No luck there." Vince stroked his goatee, which had begun to bristle, as he recalled Commosky's exact words. "Mr. Pho couldn't identify him."

He leaned back in his chair. "Now, that's interesting."

Bella glanced sideways at him. She was close enough that if she'd still been human, he would have felt the heat emanating from her body. As it was, if he closed his eyes, the only physical indicator she was standing beside him was a faint hint of a plastic smell.

He wrinkled his nose. Not to mention the tickle of her hair, which brushed his neck and shoulder as she straightened as well. It felt like a near-invisible spider crawling over him.

"Why is that interesting?"

"Because Mr. Pho is one of the sharpest restaurant owners on Zyga Space Station." Vince shook his head. "That man remembers his customers and he remembers what they like."

"Ah." Bella folded her arms across her chest and leaned a hip against his desk. "So you think he lied to Station Authority."

"Something like that."

Bella shook her head. "I understand why he lied. People are scared of Station Authority. Or," she added darkly, "they're more scared that talking to Station Authority means going against one of the Families. But—" she pointed to the holo still. "Who's Mr. Pho scared of?"

"That," Vince said, rising from his chair and reaching for his jacket, "is what we're going to find out."

Bella brightened immediately. "We?"

"Yes." Resolve crystallized in Vince's chest. The office could take care of itself just fine in their absence. It was time for Finder Grable and his assistant to make a formal appearance somewhere.

Pho's Noodle Shop was just the place.

It was just a crying shame Bella wouldn't be able to eat anything.

CHAPTER 38

During their transport pod to the elevator bank, Vince realized with a start that the last time he'd been out someplace with Bella was the day she'd moved into her new apartment. He'd helped her carry a few pieces of furniture inside—all of which she'd had to purchase, since her old life and belongings were lost to her. If she still needed to do human things like eat, it probably wouldn't have been so long, but the fact that she didn't need to eat made getting lunch or dinner together rather awkward. And he couldn't blame Bella for wanting to keep a low profile.

Magna might have succeeded in helping her get a new identity, but Bella couldn't do much to change the android shell her mind occupied. And while Bok Chul might have let her go, Vince suspected Bella wasn't so sure Chul's son would leave her alone if he happened to stumble across her again.

The Finder took a deep breath, inhaling the faint scent of eucalyptus. He'd smeared some of the cream Bella had given him under his nose and behind his ears before he walked out of the office. This was as good a time as any to test it out. He'd give just about anything to not experience an itchy throat every time he left the clean air of his office.

Bella had been staring out of the transport pod's viewport, but she turned to consider him. Her pale skin glowed against her red scoop-necked blouse with its bell-shaped sleeves. With her black jeans and boots, she looked ready for an evening out; you'd never know she'd been in an office all day. "What do you think?" She raised a dark eyebrow. "Can you tell a difference so far yet?"

"Not sure." Vince took another couple of experimental breaths. The transport pod smelled of lingering perfume and old cologne, mixed with a trace of body odor, but it wasn't bad enough yet to bother him. Either that or her friend's concoction was actually working. "I'll let you know."

Bella nodded and turned back to look out the viewport. She was sitting with one leg crossed over the other, and her booted foot bounced in excitement. "Thanks for letting me come with you, Boss."

"You're welcome." Vince smiled wryly. "I'm hoping the presence of a beautiful woman will help loosen Mr. Pho's tongue."

Bella just snorted. "I doubt that, but I'm happy to help."

With evening traffic, it took a little while longer to get to Level 22, through the Hub, and into Zone 4 than it had earlier. Bella kept pace with Vince as they stepped out of Zone 4's elevator bank on Level 4 and caught another transport pod. Vince stopped the pod two blocks from Pho's Noodle Shop and paid their fare before they disembarked.

It was only once the pod had glided away in search of another fare that Vince set off up the sidewalk on one side of the boulevard toward the restaurant. Bella shot him an appraising sideways glance, but didn't say anything. By now, she was used to his precautions— or at least *hearing* about them. She didn't have a lot of in-person experience.

At this time of the evening, business was booming in the restaurants scattered up and down the boulevard. Pho's Noodle Shop was three-quarters full; it would be completely full in another hour. Vince knew his timing was problematic—Pho certainly had plenty to occupy his time—but the Finder was betting that the very fact that the restaurant was so busy would put Pho at his ease.

With so many people eating dinner, there were more distractions. It wasn't as likely that anyone would pay attention to a quick conversation between the noodle shop owner and two customers who'd just walked in.

"They look really busy," Bella said in a low voice as they pushed through the door into the dimly-lit restaurant. "Are you sure he'll have time to talk to you?"

"Oh, I'm sure." Vince took a deep, appreciative breath, savoring the smell of sautéing meat, garlic, soy sauce, and the other rich flavors permeating the air. "If nothing else, his curiosity will get the better of him."

He strode over to the hostess desk, where a slip of a girl in a black waiter's uniform stood waiting. Bella drifted after him.

The girl greeted him with a cheerful smile. Her black hair was done up in a waterfall braid. "How can I help you?"

"I'd like to place a to-go order." Vince waited until she gave him an expectant look and then rattled off his favorite meal.

"It will be a few minutes," the girl said. "That okay?"

"That'll be fine." Vince paused, then said conversationally, "Would you tell Mr. Pho that Vince Grable would like to speak with him, if he has a moment?"

By the way the girl's eyes widened, Vince knew she knew who he was. She ducked her head in a bow. "I'll be right back."

She disappeared into through a cleverly concealed door behind her. Vince caught Bella's eye and nodded to a few chairs that had been placed near the entrance door. They both settled down to wait.

Bella looked around with interest. "It smells wonderful," she said softly. "It's a shame I can't eat here."

Vince wholeheartedly agreed with that sentiment.

"How did you ever find this place?"

"Stumbled across it while working a case a few years back." Vince smiled wryly. "Always wished it was closer. I'd be here a couple of times a week, if I could."

"If it tastes half as good as it smells—"

"Oh, it does."

"—then I can see why." Bella crossed one leg over the other and clasped her hands around her knee. "In fact, I—"

At that moment, the door behind the hostess station opened and Mr. Pho emerged. He hurried around the station and crossed the entrance floor toward Vince and Bella, one hand outstretched in greeting.

"Ah, Finder Grable. It is good to see you back so soon." He nodded to Vince and then turned to Bella with a smile. "And who is this lovely lady?"

"This is my assistant, Ms. Escovedo." Vince motioned to Pho. "Bella, this is Mr. Pho, and this shop is the best eatery in Zone 4."

"Ah, well, that is perhaps a slight exaggeration." Mr. Pho brushed the praise aside, though his face flushed slightly with pleasure. He bowed to Bella, before accosting Vince with friendly censure. "Why have you only ordered a meal for one?" He gestured to Bella. "Surely Ms. Escovedo is hungry too."

Bella smiled. "I thank you, but unfortunately I already made dinner plans." She shook her head. "A decision I truly regret, now that I've arrived."

Mr. Pho nodded knowingly. "You will have to come back." He then glanced toward his dining room before addressing Vince. "You wished to speak with me?" His face creased in concern. "Do you have news of Corwin?"

"Yes, on both counts." Vince inclined his head in a respectful nod. "Would it be possible for us to speak in your office?"

If this request gave Mr. Pho cause for concern, he hid it well. The restaurant owner only swept a hand toward the door behind the hostess station in a wordless invitation.

Bella started for the office first, and Vince followed. Mr. Pho brought up the rear. They stepped into a small, cramped office with a dark wooden desk taking up most of the space on one side and a series of gray metal filing cabinets along the other side. It smelled of cooking oil and soy sauce.

Mr. Pho closed the door behind them and looked at Vince expectantly. "Have you cleared him? Will Station Authority let Corwin go?"

"Not yet." Vince shook his head grimly. "At the moment, he's their only viable suspect."

"I still do not believe he had anything to do with his brother's death," Mr. Pho said stubbornly. "Corwin is a good boy."

"I agree with you." Vince pulled out the holo still, which he'd printed before they left. Unfolding it, he held it out for Pho to see. "I think this man is involved."

To his credit, Mr. Pho hid his reaction well. If Vince hadn't been scrutinizing him closely, and if he hadn't had as much experience with people as he did, he probably would have missed it. Mr. Pho's smooth face only slackened a fraction, his dark eyes widening ever so slightly, before his expression smoothed into polite non-recognition.

"I'm sorry, Finder." He shook his head. "I'm afraid I can't help you. I told that detective with Station Authority the same thing."

"That would be where I got this." Vince indicated the holo still. There was no point in hiding it; the key here was to help Mr. Pho understand how badly he'd miscalculated by keeping this information to himself. "But unlike Detective Commosky, Mr. Pho, I know how good you are with customers."

Mr. Pho's face remained expressionless, but Vince saw his pulse jump in his throat.

He took that opportunity to press his advantage. "I love this restaurant, Mr. Pho. You know I do." He held the older man's gaze. "The last thing I want is for any trouble to come down on your head because you didn't identify a potential suspect in a murder investigation."

Beside him, Bella leaned against the edge of the desk, her gaze tracking back and forth between him and Mr. Pho.

Vince let his words sink in for a few seconds before he tipped his head toward the holo still. "Who is he?"

"I don't know." Mr. Pho was breathing a little faster, his calm facade showing the first signs of cracking. "I truly don't know, Finder."

"But you've seen him before." Vince continued to hold out the holo still. "This wasn't the first time you'd set eyes on him." When Mr. Pho started to shake his head in protest, he held up a finger. "Ah, ah, ah. If you didn't know him—or have a good idea—you'd have had no problem reporting him to Station Authority."

He deepened his voice. "Especially if it would benefit Corwin."

CHAPTER 39

For a heartbeat, Mr. Pho stood motionless, his face stricken. Then he rubbed a shaking hand over his face and the rest of his facade abruptly crumbled. "I don't know who he is, Finder. That part is true. You must believe me."

Vince darted a glance at Bella; they both heard a 'but' coming.

"But—" Mr. Pho drew in a shaky breath. "I know who he works for."

Vince waited, but the noodle shop owner did not immediately continue. Bella shot him a questioning look; the Finder only gave his head a minute shake. Silence was powerful in situations like these. Confession might be difficult to start, but once the proverbial well was primed, words tended to pour out like liquid.

That silence swelled around them while Mr. Pho wrestled with himself. In the quiet, Vince became acutely aware of the Station's hum beneath their feet and the faint chatter of customers and clatter of dishes beyond the closed office door. Tension began thrumming in his veins. If the noodle shop owner was this fearful, they were definitely getting somewhere.

At last, Mr. Pho straightened and moved around the desk to his chair, brushing past Bella like a man in a daze. He collapsed into his chair and rested his arms on the desk, as though drawing strength from its solid surface. He breathed in once, twice, and then squared his shoulders and met Vince's gaze full on.

"Zone 4 gets all kinds of regular space traffic. Many of them come here to eat." He waved a hand to indicate his restaurant. "You know this, Finder."

"I do." Vince inclined his head.

"You may also know there are…rumors…" Mr. Pho chose his words carefully, "…that human trafficking occurs on Zyga Space Station. Mostly people from the Core, as I understand." He shrugged, as though to apologize for peddling gossip.

"We've heard those rumors too," Bella said softly.

Mr. Pho looked at her, but his dark eyes didn't seem to see her as much as see *through* her. "Most people don't know what to think about such things. If they think about them at all."

Vince inclined his head. That was another unfortunate human truth—the tendency to not consider the painful or uncomfortable things in life until you were directly confronted by them.

"But being so close to the hangar bays…" Mr. Pho shook his head. "One hears things, over the years."

Bella did not shift position, but Vince could tell she didn't understand the need for the circuitous explanation. He, too, wished Mr. Pho would hurry up and get to the point, but the older man had his own way of explaining things. He would get to it when he got to it.

"That man—" Mr. Pho pointed to the holo still with a surprisingly steady finger, "—works for an import/export business here in Zone 4." He shrugged eloquently. "If the rumors are to be believed—and they are rumors whispered in dark corners by hushed voices—the business is owned by a member of the Oswari Family."

The Oswari Family. Vince resisted the urge to shake his head. Of *course* there was a Family involved, after all.

He pursed his lips. "How do you know this guy works for them?"

"Because I have seen him before with his boss." Mr. Pho's confidence faltered. "They have eaten here. He is…not a man I would cross, Finder."

A comlink on the desk rang. Bella jumped, startled, but Vince controlled his own surprise. Mr. Pho glanced at the comlink, his expression clearly stating that he'd prefer to end this conversation by taking the call.

To keep him on track, Vince asked calmly, "What did he want with Dent that day?"

To his surprise, Mr. Pho shook his head. "It was the other way around. Corwin's brother followed this man inside." He pointed to the still. "He was here to order dinner and Corwin's brother accosted him."

The comlink rang once more and then stopped.

"Really?" Bella straightened, her face brightening with excitement. "What did he want?"

"He started yelling all kinds of things at the man, calling him a slave trader and demanding to know what they'd done with her."

"Her?" Vince and Bella asked at the same moment. Vince felt something catch in his throat; his goatee began bristling again. Beside him, Belle leaned forward a little. The Finder knew she'd had the same thought.

Mariella. The mother of Dent's child who had vanished some weeks before.

Mr. Pho shrugged again, holding out his hands in mute helplessness. "He never said her name. But he was angry—very angry. Corwin rushed over to help defuse the situation and his brother began shouting at him too."

Something crystallized inside of Vince; Corwin had failed to mention the extent of this altercation. "What happened to the man?"

"He left without buying dinner." Mr. Pho shrugged a third time, though this time with complete understanding. "I would leave too."

"What did Corwin do?"

Mr. Pho made a sound in the back of his throat. "They had an argument that resulted in them coming to blows." He shook his head, disapproval written into every line on his face. "It was bad for business. Scared several of my customers. After it was over, I told Corwin that I understood his feelings, but his brother was not allowed to ever set foot on my property again."

"Understandable." Vince inclined his head. "Anything else?" He paused. "Like where I can find this man?"

Mr. Pho actually blanched, and then he stretched out a placating hand to Vince, shaking his head. "You don't want to find him. I know Corwin had nothing to do with his brother's death, but..." he trailed off, still shaking his head. "These are dangerous men, Finder."

"Not going after them would be the greater wrong," Vince said softly. He waited until the noodle shop owner met his gaze again. "You think they killed him too."

It wasn't a question.

That dreadful silence filled the office again, and then Mr. Pho nodded once, a small shaky motion.

"If they did, and if they're involved in these other horrible things, they deserve to meet justice." Vince lifted his eyebrows. "Don't they?"

Beside him, Bella made a small sound, as though the magnitude of what Vince was proposing had just hit her.

Mr. Pho rocked back in his chair, looking miserable. "You cannot bring them to justice, Finder. They are untouchable." He shook his head. "You will lose your life just like Corwin's brother and I will lose a good customer." He spread his hands in resigned surrender. "There are some laws of Zyga Station that are as immutable as the stars."

"That's the thing, Mr. Pho," Vince said with a grim smile. "I've learned lately that people aren't as untouchable as they think they are. Where can I find this group?"

"If I tell you," Mr. Pho said quietly, "I am sending you to your death."

Vince's eyes hardened. "Let me be the judge of that."

A knock sounded on the door.

CHAPTER 40

MR. PHO COMPOSED HIMSELF. "COME IN."

The door opened far enough for the hostess to stick her head around it, letting wonderfully scented air waft toward them. Her eyes scanned across Vince and Bella before landing on her boss. "Finder Grable's food is ready."

"Ah, excellent." Mr. Pho rose to his feet. "We were just finishing."

The hostess withdrew, closing the door behind her, but Vince did not budge. "Where can I find them?"

Mr. Pho pressed his lips into a thin, dubious line, but behind his eyes, Vince saw the sudden flicker of hope spring to life. "Saroyan Imports. They have an office on Level 2."

Of course they did. One corner of Vince's mouth curled in disdain. Scum like them should have been ashamed to show their face outside of the deepest levels of the Core, much less flaunt their business on the topmost levels of Zone 4.

Mr. Pho correctly read his expression. "Yes." He exhaled, looking suddenly ten years older. "It is most unfortunate."

"They're not untouchable." Vince shook his head. "No one is above the law, no matter how much they think they are."

The noodle shop owner just regarded Vince gravely, before rising to his feet. "I hope you are right, Finder." He gestured to the door. "Are you sure you will not stay here and eat?"

"I'd love to, but we have other business." Vince opened the door and held it for Bella and Mr. Pho.

At the hostess station, a bag of boxed food sat waiting for Vince. Faint wisps of steam curled out of it. He paid for the food with a creditchip and the hostess handed it to him with a smile.

"Enjoy," she said brightly.

Vince's mouth watered at the delicious smell wafting from the bag. He inclined his head toward the girl and Mr. Pho, who still stood behind her. "Thank you, I will."

He and Bella departed the restaurant. In the large corridor outside, the glowpanels in the overhead had dimmed, indicating the beginning of the night cycle. Pedestrian and transport pod traffic had increased; a steady stream of people flowed up and down the sidewalks on either side of the boulevard, while dozens of silver transport pods drifted up and down the center.

"What's the plan now?" Bella glanced from Vince to the bag of food in his hand. "Seems to me like you'd have been better off staying there and eating that."

Vince cast his dinner a regretful look. "I'd have loved to, but it wasn't a good choice. Not after that conversation."

"Understandable." Bella hoisted her oversize purse a little higher on her shoulder and glanced up and down the boulevard. "Now what?"

"I have a friend who works in the dock hangar bays." Vince glanced left and right before crossing the boulevard to the sidewalk on the other side. Bella hastened to keep up with him. "We're going to have a little chat."

Out of the corner of his eye, he caught the funny look Bella gave him. "You think your friend is involved?"

"No. But I do think he might have heard a few things here and there."

Bella's gaze dropped to his bag of food. "I may not need to eat anymore, Boss, but even I know that's not quite enough food for two people."

Vince shot her a grim smile. "He wouldn't eat it anyway. We'll stop and get something else."

"Food—the universal conversation starter." Bella shook her head in amusement, and then her expression darkened. "You think Mr. Pho was telling the truth about that guy?"

"More or less."

"Oh, *that's* helpful." Bella rolled her eyes. "How do you tell the difference?"

Vince paused his constant scanning of the boulevard around them to glance down at her. They were a full block from the noodle shop now; in another block they would turn left down another corridor and make their way back to the elevator bank. His friend lived down on Level 8.

"Experience." The Finder lifted his shoulders in a shrug, the movement stretching the brown leather of his jacket across his shoulders. "Half of this job is figuring out what people are really saying—especially when they don't say much of anything."

"So what's the other half? Putting the pieces together?" Bella tossed her head to get a lock of black hair out of her face. She looked beautiful—the picture of a perfectly healthy young woman. Again, Vince found himself marveling at how *real* she looked.

He pushed that thought out of his head. Bella *was* real. Her mind *made* her so. It didn't matter what Station Authority—or anybody else, for that matter—said about androids. Bella was *real*.

"Yes." He gave his assistant an encouraging nod. "Putting everything together. You research things and you take what you learn and put it all together. That's how you arrive at the solution." He frowned. "And we don't have enough pieces of this puzzle yet."

Struck by a sudden impulse, Vince hurried down the sidewalk a handful of meters and then stepped out of the flow of traffic into a narrow access corridor. He leaned up against the smooth metal bulkhead, its silvery surface tarnished by accumulated grime and fingerprints from who knew how many people who had wandered through here since the station was built. Bundles of cables stretched overhead, forming a ceiling as dark as if it had actually been metal.

Propping one booted foot against the bulkhead, Vince pulled his comlink from his breast pocket with his free hand. Time for a quick ComNet search before they did anything else.

"So, this brings back memories." Bella settled up against the bulkhead beside him. She glanced around, her mouth pulling into a distasteful grimace. "Don't think I've been in an access corridor since the whole…" She inscribed a vague circle in the air with one hand. "…Cara thing."

Vince was barely listening. The chatter of dozens of conversations flowing up and down the boulevard beyond the narrow access corridor faded away as he tapped in Saroyan Imports and did a general search. Several items pulled up immediately, one of them the business's main listing. He scanned it briefly, but apart from a glowing history of the husband/wife team who owned it and a list of the many places they bought from and sold to, there wasn't much there.

Bella peered over his shoulder, reading along with him. "Looks expensive." She kept her voice low, so as not to carry far down the access corridor.

"Their clientele is definitely upper-Zone," Vince agreed. "Probably Rim too."

He opened another search engine, one that most citizens on Zyga Station didn't have access to. This one contained reports from Zyga Station Authority officers, official Docking Bay reports, and other information his Finder license gave him access to.

At first glance, nothing appeared to be out of order. At second glance, it was still the same. Saroyan Imports didn't appear to have caused any waves—bad or otherwise.

"They look clean," Bella said after a moment, echoing Vince's thoughts.

He glanced at her, frowning. "Doesn't mean they actually are." He shook his head. "Just means that if they are dirty, nobody's been brave enough to file an official report."

Vince paused, a darker though flitting through his mind. Or if anyone *had* been brave enough, someone *else* had suppressed it. Somebody in either the Docking Bay or Station Authority.

Money had a tendency to do that, here on Zyga Station.

"What about asking—" Bella glanced from side to side before leaning in closer to him and dramatically dropping her voice, "—Brill?"

"No point." Vince shook his head again and slid his comlink back into the breast pocket of his leather jacket. "He might be able to acquire more information, but I doubt it would be enough to bust open a trafficking operation." His frown deepened. "That's not something we could tackle in a day."

"And not with Corwin facing murder charges." Bella posted her free hand on her hip, matching his frown.

"We'd need more time."

Bella tilted her head to one side, her dark eyes narrowing. "Would Detective Commosky be interested in a human trafficking operation?"

"He would if he gets credit somehow."

"Then we'll have to make sure he gets credit."

Vince surveyed his assistant, the way she had straightened and the suddenly fierce look on her features. She probably didn't *intend* to look that fierce, but then again…

"Wait." Bella paused to look askance at him. "We *are* going to see what we can do about this, aren't we?"

For the first time in what felt like a long time, the Finder felt a genuine smile tug at his lips. Her enthusiasm was encouraging. "Baby steps, Bella. We'll get there."

He stepped out of the access corridor onto the sidewalk and resumed walking. Bella joined him.

Shifting his grip on his bag of food, Vince smiled wryly. "It'll take Commosky a while to reassess and move on with his investigation, but—" he trailed off, struck by a sudden, electrifying memory that had risen out of his subconscious.

Niko's terrified face floated in front of his mind's eye.

Vince recalled that his elderly informant had been so frightened by the mention of the Ruby Gauntlet that it had temporarily jolted him out of his drug-addled state. The Finder frowned; in the past few hours, he'd forgotten that in the rush of determining Dent's murder had *probably* had nothing to with the nightclub.

"Boss?" Bella rested a hand on his forearm. Her dark, almond-shaped eyes were wide in her pale face. "Are you okay?"

They'd stopped on the corner. Vince stepped out of the way of the flow of traffic again, his shoulder pressing up against the wall of the repair shop that occupied the coveted corner compartment. He looked down at Bella, his bag of food and his growling stomach temporarily forgotten. "*Why* are people so scared of the Ruby Gauntlet?"

CHAPTER 41

Bella stared at him, her eyes narrowing in confusion. "What?"

"They're terrified. Of a virtual nightclub. *Why?*"

"Umm…well, they *have* taken a lot of people's property." Bella looked askance at Vince, like she thought he'd suddenly lost his mind and wasn't quite sure what to do about it. "And we know they *probably* murdered at least three people."

But did that warrant the level of fear that had penetrated all the way down into the Core's deepest levels? Vince shook his head. "Something's not right."

"Tell me about it." Bella's free hand clenched into a fist. "Human trafficking shouldn't exist on this space station."

"Aside from that." Vince shifted his weight from foot to foot, unable to put a finger on what was bothering him exactly. His goatee bristled, his every instinct shouting, *wrong, wrong, wrong!*, yet he didn't know *why*.

What could a human trafficking ring and a virtual nightclub with an off-the-books casino *possibly* have in common?

Apart, of course, from Dent Antwerp?

Just a few hours before, Vince had been so sure that the Ruby Gauntlet had nothing to do with this case that he'd told Detective Commosky so. But now…now the very foundations of his brain had suddenly been shaken.

Were the two connected? Vince wasn't sure. He had been so sure they were not, but now…he found himself doubting his earlier theories.

He pressed his lips into a thin line. If they were *not* connected, did that mean that there was a second mystery here—the mystery of the strange, fearful hold the Ruby Gauntlet had on people?

"Boss?" Bella stood at his elbow, her face full of concern. "Are you okay?"

Vince wanted to tell her he was fine—he was just experiencing a minor existential crisis. Before he could even open his mouth, a gleaming silver transport pod pulled up at the curb beside them. The door opened, and a large man in a gray jacket and dark brown pants climbed out.

Even with his head spinning, Vince recognized him.

The man Dent Antwerp had accosted in Mr. Pho's noodle shop.

"Get in." The man spoke to Bella, but kept his eyes on Vince.

When neither Finder nor assistant moved, the man lifted the front of his jacket. Just enough to show them the pistol holstered there.

"Get in," he repeated.

Bella's gaze flicked to Vince. In her eyes, he saw reflected the same question racing through his head. How had this man known to come get them?

There were only two possible answers. Either his employers had been watching Pho's Noodle Shop, or Mr. Pho had called them himself.

"Good evening to you, too." Vince finally found his voice. "What's this about?"

"Boss wants a word with you," the man said in a deep baritone. "If I was you, I'd cooperate."

"I'll have to eat on the way." Vince hefted his bag of food. "This stuff is best when it's hot."

The henchman—it was the best possible description for him Vince could think of—narrowed his eyes and his craggy face became even more forbidding. "Now, Finder."

Vince shouldn't have been surprised the man knew who he was. They *always* knew who he was. He looked at Bella. "Run along back to the office and lock up. You're off the clock."

His gaze bored into her. If they thought Bella was simply a pretty little receptionist, perhaps they'd let her go.

Bella looked back at him, nonplussed. She quirked an eyebrow; she knew what he was doing and she clearly didn't think it would work.

It did not.

"Both of you," the henchman growled. "Now." He batted a meaty hand in the direction of Vince's food, but the Finder yanked the bag out of his reach just in time.

"Now, now. No need for violence." He fixed the man, who was at least eight centimeters taller than he was, with a chiding look. "You know who I am, so you know I'm in the location business. I'm always happy to speak with prospective clients."

It was the henchman's turn to look nonplussed. He blinked at Vince, his upper lip curling into an expression that spoke volumes. His boss wasn't some 'prospective client.'

Vince knew that too, but this was how you played the game. All bravado and nonchalance until you had enough information to determine what was *really* going on.

"Saves us a trip, anyway," Vince said as he slid into the transport pod, careful to avoid upsetting his bag of food. "Believe it or not, we were just on our way to see your boss."

The henchman merely grunted as though he seriously doubted that, watching warily as Bella shoved the straps of her oversize purse higher on her shoulder and climbed into the pod after her boss.

Bella took the seat next to Vince, pressing herself into the corner. Her control of her facial expressions had improved greatly over the past few months, but she couldn't quite hide her anxiety. She slid her purse straps off her shoulder and clutched the bag to her chest instead.

"Gimme that." A meaty hand reached into the transport pod and swiped the purse out of her grasp.

Bella squeaked in protest. "Hey!" She started to lean forward. "That's—"

Vince put a hand on her arm. Her eyes darted to him and he gave his head a minute shake. It wouldn't do any good to argue.

The henchman riffled through Bella's purse, pausing over several items—namely her tablet and her comlink. These disappeared into his coat pocket, and then the henchman climbed into the transport pod, seating himself opposite them. He shoved Bella's purse at her and she folded her arms protectively over it.

"Hey, I better get those back." Her red lips pulled into a scowl. "You—" She broke off as the henchman casually pulled the pistol from his waistband and aimed it at her.

The man's cold gaze, however, was on Vince. "Your turn, Finder. Comlink. Any other devices or weapons. *Slowly*, or she gets it."

No subtlety here at all. Resisting the urge to roll his eyes, Vince balanced his bag of food on his lap with one hand while he plucked his comlink from his breast pocket with the other. The heat from the containers soaked into his lap. He extended the comlink to the other man.

"Weapons?"

"I'm unarmed today."

This was both a good thing and a bad thing. Vince doubted they'd be sitting in this transport if he'd been carrying a pistol.

But…this cretin's boss was probably the head of Saroyan Imports, and Vince needed to talk to him anyway. So, really, things were working out.

And, he wouldn't even have to pay for the trip there.

The henchman eyed him suspiciously, but apparently decided to take his word for it. At least for the moment. Without taking his eyes off of Vince and Bella, he leaned over and tapped a button on the pod's AI display.

A second later, the pod glided away from the curb, carrying Vince and Bella off into unknown territory.

CHAPTER 42

VINCE MADE A SHOW OF SETTLING BACK against his seat's dark green cushion, as though he hadn't a care in the galaxy. Dimly, he registered that this transport pod smelled suspiciously clean. He'd wager good money it was owned by Saroyan Imports.

On the upside, the concoction Bella had gotten for him seemed to be working. The back of his throat hadn't itched once since he left his office. He made a mental note to thank his assistant again for her thoughtfulness when this was all over and proceeded to consider his options.

There weren't many.

To distract himself, Vince looked over at the henchman. "Surprised they sent you by yourself."

Usually, whenever a boss of something sent men after him, they sent at least two. Sometimes more, but definitely no less than two.

The man smiled. It did nothing to improve his features; the smile was just as ugly as he was. He cracked the knuckles of one hand and then proceeded to crack the knuckles of his other hand, making Bella wince. His knuckles were bruised, particularly on his right hand.

"Don't need anybody else," he said, looking Vince up and down, his expression scornful.

"I can see why." Vince tactfully refrained from mentioning that the big guy was in trouble if somebody ran a coordinated play on him. The way the henchman's eyes bored into him, as though at any moment he expected Vince to jump up and do something crazy, told Vince he operated on a hair trigger.

The transport pod swept on through Level 6's corridors until it reached the main elevator bank. Just as Vince had suspected, the pod was privately owned. Instead of stopping and allowing them to disembark and take the elevator on foot, the pod bypassed the main line and glided into the transport pod line.

In less than a minute, their pod had settled in a synth-glass elevator cab specifically designed for transport pods and they were soaring up to Level 2.

Vince spared a glance at Bella. Her eyes had widened; she craned her neck slightly to see out the viewport without trying to make it *look* like she was trying to see out. This was probably the first time she'd ever ridden a transport pod on the elevator.

It was only Vince's second time; normal people didn't have that kind of money. His mind flashed back to the last—and only other—time he'd done this. He and Rav had just escaped the massacre at Orion Lab in the heart of the Core and were being escorted up to Level 1 to be questioned by the head of Zone 5's Station Authority Headquarters Precinct.

In another moment, their transport pod arrived on Level 2 and departed the special elevator cab. Vince couldn't see much of Level 2 out of the pod's viewport, but from what he could tell, the pod's course left the main thoroughfare running through the level and snaked off through a series of brightly-decorated corridors leading toward the Rimward end of Zone 4. Ritzy apartment complexes and high-end shops, offices, and eateries flashed past.

Mentally, Vince brought up his internal map of Zyga Space Station. He had a rough idea of where they'd ended up, though he wouldn't know for certain until they exited the transport pod. He suppressed the urge to whistle. If their destination was in fact Saroyan Imports, this group *definitely* had money and power.

An image of Terrel Roda came to mind, followed by Bok Chul's face. Vince squared his jaw. He'd faced worse. (The head of the Bok Family *definitely* counted as worse.)

The Finder's gaze slid sideways to encompass Bella. Granted, he hadn't counted on his assistant being part of the process, but… they'd manage. Somehow.

The transport pod's hatch slid open and the henchman gestured with his pistol. "Out. Both of you. Slowly." He nodded menacingly to Bella.

Vince did not dignify that with a response. He gestured for Bella to exit ahead of him, and then followed her out. They found themselves on a sidewalk beside a stretch of multi-story office buildings with reflective synthglass windows for walls that were so shiny they practically gleamed in the dim glow from the glowpanels in the overhead far above. This entire section of Level 2 oozed money and an air of assumed respectability. Potted plants and potted trees ran along the edge of the sidewalks on both sides of the corridor, providing a welcome break from all of the metal that otherwise comprised the space station.

Vince's eyes narrowed as he glanced up and down the building in front of them. If the rumors were true and the Oswari Family was running a human trafficking ring out of this place, it was just another example of how horrible, rotten things could hide behind pretty, expensive exteriors.

Behind them, the transport pod settled down beside a cheerful little sycamore tree sitting between the corridor's gray metal deck and the strip of sidewalk—made of slabs of real rock, Vince noted.

He didn't wait for the henchman to speak, but instead offered Bella his elbow. "Shall we?"

Bella placed her hand in the crook of his arm, flipped her glossy black hair over her shoulder, and hiked her purse up on her shoulder. Then, together, they marched straight for the double doors leading into the building. The doors were made out of the same reflective synthglass as the windows; in their reflection, Vince had the satisfaction of seeing the henchman's jaw drop before he grimaced and strode forward to catch up with them.

He'd caught the man off-guard. Vince allowed himself a tiny smile. Good. Let him reevaluate things. That man might have brought the Finder and his assistant here, but that didn't mean he was in charge of this situation.

As he and Bella approached, the double doors slid apart. The two of them stepped into a large, gleaming foyer, all glass, chrome metal, and pristine white, except for the floor, which was tiled in swirls of white and teal. The air was warmer in here, with a faint minty scent. An elevator bank stood on the left, while on the right, white chairs and a sofa formed an artfully arranged waiting area. In the center stood a long, silver reception desk with a fancy placard that held only one name: Saroyan Imports.

Behind this desk sat a beautiful dark-skinned woman with lipstick the same shade of scarlet as her sheath dress. She glanced up with vague curiosity as they entered.

Vince took in the opulence of their surroundings and felt something hot ignite in his stomach. There was a good chance every bit of this had been paid for by illegal—not to mention unspeakable—means. The very thought of it made him ill.

Beside him, Bella lifted her chin. She returned the reception's curious stare with cool indifference, making the other woman glance from her to the henchman behind them.

"They're with me," the henchman grunted.

As the receptionist showed no sign of fear, Vince guessed their escort had temporarily holstered his pistol. The receptionist's gaze lingered on both him and Bella, but she only offered a short nod to the henchman before glancing back down at her comlink again. Clearly, she knew this man.

She didn't like him—that much was obvious by the tension that had entered her slender frame, and the way she was watching them from beneath her eyelashes as though to make sure she knew where they were going. But, she knew him.

Which meant he was a regular, trusted fixture here.

"Elevator," the henchman said in a growl. He quickened his pace, reaching out a meaty hand to grab Bella's upper arm.

"Don't touch me," she snapped, jerking away from him and closer to Vince. The man was a head taller than she was, but she glared haughtily up at him. "I am quite capable of walking myself into an elevator."

His expression turned ugly, but Vince hit the button for the elevator doors and they opened immediately. Bella stepped inside and Vince followed, keeping his body between her and the henchman. He didn't like this. He didn't like this at *all*. He could suddenly—and with complete clarity—think of a dozen different ways this could go completely wrong.

In most of them, he ended up dead and Bella ended up with a fate worse than death.

Don't go there, Finder, he told himself. *Focus. No need to jump to the worst-case scenario.*

Not yet, anyway.

CHAPTER 43

THE TRIO TRAVELED UP THREE FLOORS TO the top of the office building. When the elevator doors opened, Vince and his assistant found themselves in a sumptuous waiting area. Out of the corner of his eye, Vince saw Bella's red lips part and her eyes round in amazement.

He understood her reaction. This place reminded him of life on the Rim—the most expensive part of Zyga Space Station. If he hadn't already gotten a taste of the extravagance of some of the living quarters in the Rim, he'd have been awed as well. As it was, his gaze scanned the waiting area with a practiced eye.

Burnished hardwood floor, spread with a colorful—and expensive—deep-pile rug; probably from the Temeda system. Two deep brown leather chairs and matching couch up against the wall to the left of the elevator, with burgundy, gold-trimmed decorative pillows. A few pieces of statuary in silvery metal, marble, and what looked like real ebony.

A smattering of framed artwork hung on the cream walls. Vince didn't recognize any of it (not surprising, given the scope of the galaxy), but that was beside the point. It all screamed money.

Floor-to-ceiling windows draped in gauzy gold curtains tied back with matching cords provided an excellent view of the boulevard corridor below and the buildings across the corridor. Soft strains of unimposing, unremarkable music played in the background, and the air up here held that same faint minty scent.

Vince felt something settle inside his chest. If he didn't know any better, he'd think this place was exactly what it pretended to be: an upscale import/export business on a space station at the edge of a mining system.

He glanced to the left. A reception desk made of some dark wood polished to a high shine stood on the other side of the elevator, beside a heavy door made of actual wood that looked darker against the cream walls. Another beautiful woman occupied the chair behind this desk, though this one was dressed in a shade of emerald green that set off her coppery skin to perfection. A mass of curly black hair tumbled around her shoulders.

The receptionist raised a dark, manicured eyebrow at the henchman and tipped her head toward the door. "About time you got here. They're waiting."

Darting a glance at the henchman, Vince wasn't sure if the burly man's craggy face had actually paled or if he'd just imagined it.

"Got here as fast as we could." The henchman's growling voice seemed a little muted.

The receptionist waved a hand—her nails were tipped in gold—as though she couldn't be bothered to hear excuses. Rising from her chair in a swirl of rustling fabric and perfume, she crossed to the door, rapped sharply on it, and then twisted a gold knob and pushed it open.

"The Finder and—" she cast a half-curious, half-disdainful look at Bella.

"The Finder's assistant," Bella said coolly, lifting her chin and hiking her purse a little further up on her shoulder.

The receptionist waved her free hand again, as if to say, *There you have it.*

"Come in," said a low, melodic female voice.

Bella sailed through the doorway ahead of Vince—the picture of assured grace. The Finder followed, admiring her poise in the face of the unknown. That wasn't something that had come with her android body. He suspected Bella would have glided in the same way even if she'd been wearing the cleaning uniform of her former profession.

Vince cast a quick, appraising look around. More of the same decorations that filled the waiting area hung on the walls, or were scattered tastefully around, but this office was large enough that he suspected his entire apartment would fit inside. A large, mahogany desk was the focal point of the office, located in the center of the floor-to-ceiling windows that stretched the length of the compartment here too. Behind this desk sat not one, but two, matching wingback leather chairs. Even from here, the tan leather looked buttery soft.

A man and a woman occupied these two chairs. Vince judged them both to be in their early fifties, but they could probably pass as younger. The woman was a slender and wiry, with straight black hair pulled back in an elegant chignon, and dark eyes set in a narrow, olive-toned face. She wore a simple, elegant dress of some shimmery cream material that Vince knew had to cost at least as much as the annual salary of some of Zyga Space Station's poorer workers. She wore a ring with a massive princess-cut diamond on her left hand.

The man (her husband? Vince wondered) was taller, and looked to be in equally good shape, though he had an obvious paunch. A black goatee came to a sharp point on his chin, standing out against his skin, which was a shade or two darker than his wife's. His curly black hair was cut long and streaked with silver. He wore an expensive bespoke pin-striped gray suit with shoes that probably cost more than Vince made in an average month.

Vince kept the scorn he felt from his face. The import/export business on Zyga Station must be doing *very* well.

"Ah. Finder Grable," the man said. His voice was pitched surprisingly higher than Vince would have expected. "Thank you for joining us."

"Didn't exactly have a choice," Vince said, keeping his tone pleasant. Beside him, Bella surveyed the scene with cool curiosity.

The man waved a hand to the burly henchman, who immediately moved two hardback mahogany chairs over in front of the desk before retreating over to the door. "Please, have a seat."

"I'd prefer to stand," Vince said.

"That was not a request." This from the woman, who straightened in her seat, as though even a hint of implied defiance roused her ire. Her voice was still melodic, but stern.

Ignoring her words, Vince glanced back and forth between them. "I'm at a disadvantage here. You know who we are, but I'm afraid we can't say the same."

The pair exchanged glances. "Why," said the man, "we're the owners of Saroyan Imports, of course." He indicated himself with a careless gesture. "I am Taro Saroyan, and this is my wife, Kari."

The woman inclined her head in a graceful, if aloof, nod.

Saroyan eyed Bella, an appreciative glint in his dark eyes. The man's expression set Vince on edge; he could only imagine how it made Bella feel. The Finder resisted the urge to shift protectively in front of his assistant.

"And you, Finder's assistant, who are you?"

"Does it matter?" Bella canted her head slightly to one side.

"No, it does not," Mrs. Saroyan said crisply, before reaching over and placing a hand on her husband's arm. "Taro, dear, we really haven't the time for this."

"I told you already, love, we'll have to make time." Mr. Saroyan patted her hand with his other hand. "Sometimes life forced us to rearrange our schedules. This is one of those occasions."

Listening to the two of them gave Vince a surreal feeling. He cleared his throat. "To say nothing of my time as well." He looked at each of them in turn. "Was it necessary to bring us here at gunpoint? I'm sure Station Authority would have something to say about *that*."

"Oh, Station Authority has plenty to say about everything." Mrs. Saroyan flicked her fingers impatiently. "It's ridiculous, frankly."

Vince thought the people who were likely being shipped off-station into bondage would disagree with that, but he kept silent and waited. He had, after all, been on his way here to talk to them. Let them hang themselves.

Detective Commosky, he knew, would be *most* grateful.

CHAPTER 44

Mr. Saroyan drilled Vince with a hard look. "I understand you are currently investigating the death of some poor unfortunate a few levels down."

"A 'poor unfortunate' who had an altercation with your enforcer here not long before his death." Vince jerked his head toward the henchman.

"That proves nothing," Mrs. Saroyan said dismissively.

"Kari." Her husband held up a quelling hand.

His booted feet sinking into the luxurious pile of the carpet, Vince's surreal feeling increased. He glanced from Mr. Saroyan to his wife again. "As you said, Mr. Saroyan, time is money. Why are we here?"

He wasn't even going to bother asking if they were interested in hiring a Finder. All that would do was waste even more time.

"You and your…" Mr. Saroyan peered appreciatively at Bella, whose spine stiffened a little further, "…lovely assistant here are wasting your time on this particular case." He shrugged casually. "I've read the news reports. Dent Antwerp was a useless excuse for a human being. Besides, Station Authority already has his killer. I believe they arrested his brother?"

When Vince only stared at him, unspeaking, the businessman continued, "There is no need for you to go poking around this any further. Griffin here had an altercation with Antwerp because Antwerp accosted him in a restaurant." His dark eyes were cold and hard as he pressed his hands into a steeple. "That is as far as it went."

Vince didn't buy that for a hot second, but of course, how in the galaxy was he supposed to prove otherwise? "I'm a Finder," he said at last.

"And a good one, at that." Mrs. Saroyan spoke again. "You have quite the reputation." Something flashed through her dark eyes, too quick to categorize. "Particularly now that Terrell Roda is on trial for murder."

Vince felt his goatee prickle. He lifted one shoulder in a shrug, let it fall. "I don't usually investigate murders."

"And yet you did." Mr. Saroyan spread his hands. "And are again."

Bella was glancing from person to person, taking in every detail. If for some reason Vince couldn't recall a detail himself, he knew he'd be able to ask her later and she'd describe everything perfectly. One of the few upsides to being an android.

"My involvement with this case predates murder." Vince kept his expression serene, but his sense of confusion was only growing. What was the angle here? What possible reason could they have for bringing him—and Bella—all the way up other than to warn him off the case?

But why do that? Why openly confirm any suspicions Vince might have about their man Griffin's involvement—or their own— by going out of their way to tell him they weren't involved? And at gunpoint at that?

It didn't make any sense…and the fact that it didn't make any sense set off all Vince's internal alarm bells.

Were they trying to awe him into cooperating by showing off this opulent office? Sure, it was great, but it wasn't a Rim office.

Mr. Saroyan pulled a slim comlink from the breast pocket of his jacket and set it on the burnished wooden surface of his desk. "You're unlikely to get your fee, with your client in jail facing murder charges."

"Not if they find the real killer," Vince said.

Mrs. Saroyan laughed, a light, musical sound. "We all—" she gestured to the four of them, "—know they won't." Her cold eyes grew amused as she looked at Vince. "They have no incentive to find another killer when they've already one in hand."

That was, to some extent, depressingly true. Even without the pressure Commosky was putting on Vince.

Eying the two business owners, Vince decided to take a gamble. It was a sudden, abrupt decision, borne out of the strangeness of this entire conversation and the fact that at this point he didn't have anything to lose. Even if the Saroyans turned out to be running a human trafficking ring, there wasn't any way he could currently prove it.

"Dent Antwerp accosted your man because he believed your business is responsible for kidnapping people from the Core and shipping them off Zyga Space Station."

Neither of the Saroyans reacted to this. Not that Vince had expected them to react. He was positive they knew full well what Dent had been shouting.

"Oh, that." Mrs. Saroyan made another dismissive gesture. "It's ridiculous. The ravings of a man addled in the brain with—" she fluttered her fingers again, "—whatever he was on. We deal in antiques and luxury items, as you can see." She nodded to the office at large. "Not human beings."

"He had to have gotten the idea from somewhere," Bella said softly.

Mrs. Saroyan favored her with a thin smile that was dagger-sharp around the edges. "You'll find as you get older, my dear, that all it takes to start vicious rumors are a few careless words." Her smile thinned further. "Or a few deliberately chosen words, designed to stir up trouble."

Vince just looked at her. It didn't answer the question of how Dent could have known who Griffin was—or who his employers were—for him to even track the man down to yell at him. His goatee bristled again. What had Dent known—or discovered—that Vince and Station Authority didn't yet know?

"What's your point, Mrs. Saroyan?" he asked in a low rumble.

Mr. Saroyan answered instead. "Our point is that vicious rumors hurt our reputation, which in turn affects our bottom line." He tapped his comlink. "What were you going to charge your client? We'll double it."

Vince had seen that coming. He lifted an eyebrow. "In return for?"

"Close this case." Mr. Saroyan smiled genially, but the expression didn't change the hard look in his dark eyes. "Let it go. If Station Authority has enough proof to arrest Antwerp's brother, can you really prove otherwise?"

Something cold and hard settled in Vince's chest.

He could certainly try.

"We'll even throw in a bonus for your assistant here." Mrs. Saroyan smiled at Bella, but it was an appraising smile, the sort of expression that said she had put a value on the younger woman.

Knowing what they were likely involved in, it raised the hackles on the back of Vince's neck. He wondered which one of them was related to the Oswari Family. "And if I choose to keep going?"

Mr. Saroyan shrugged, stretching the expensive fabric of his pinstriped suit. "You'll miss out on a hefty fee." One side of his mouth curled in something that was probably supposed to be a smile, but came off looking more like a sneer. "Your reputation as a man with principles precedes you, Finder, but principles can be… problematic."

CHAPTER 45

Vince offered the older man a thin smile. Before Gemma Roda's kidnapping, his name hadn't been as well known as it was now. (He had no illusions about how long *that* would last; life on Zyga Space Station was just like life elsewhere in the galaxy. It had rhythms, and sometimes you rose to the top of the heap before getting churned over into the bottom again.)

Of course, there was also the not-so-inconsequential fact that the Saroyans were involved with this somehow.

"You'd be foolish not to accept our offer," Mrs. Saroyan said placidly, though her dark eyes remained ice-cold. "I understand your business has been excellent lately, but the money you've earned from those fees won't last forever."

Vince acknowledged this with a nod. He didn't bother pointing out that as a man with principles, he could hardly accept their offer, now, could he?

Instead, he glanced at Bella. "It is curious how events have unfolded this evening, isn't it, Bella?" He looked back at the Saroyans, his thin smile still in place. "There we were, on our way to visit Saroyan Imports, and before we even reach the elevator bank, their…associate…shows up to escort us the rest of the way."

"It's very curious, Boss." Bella wasn't smiling. She just tightened her grip on the straps of her purse and continued to face their ersatz hosts, her dark almond eyes darting from one to the other. "Almost like they knew we were coming."

"Yes. I was thinking that same thing." Vince's expression turned chiding. "You've been monitoring Pho's Noodle Shop."

Mrs. Saroyan gave a light, blasé laugh. "I think you're imagining things, Finder."

"Oh, I doubt it," Vince said pleasantly, though he felt the muscles in his face hardening. "I don't believe in coincidences."

It was Mr. Saroyan's turn to laugh. "You can hardly deny that they exist, Finder." He looked askance at Vince. "That seems a rather far-fetched assumption, especially for someone in your occupation."

"It's because of my occupation that I don't believe coincidences exist." Vince shook his head. "There's always a connection, always a cause. You just have to dig deep enough to find it."

"Well, you're traveling up the wrong space lane if your investigation has led you here." There was a note of finality in Mr. Saroyan's voice.

"Then why offer to pay our fee?" Bella shifted on her feet, her fingers tightening further on her purse straps. If they tightened any further, Vince suspected she'd snap the straps all together.

Mrs. Saroyan looked at her husband. "It's a shame what society has come to, when you can't even do a kind gesture for someone without your motives being questioned."

Bella narrowed her eyes, her lips flattening into a thin line. "Maybe you mean well, but it looks suspicious."

Vince had to agree. "And then there's the matter of you bringing us here at gunpoint."

"Oh, please." Mrs. Saroyan waved a dismissive hand. "That was nothing."

Vince and Bella traded sideways glances out of the corners of their eyes. "Station Authority would likely disagree," Vince said.

The atmosphere in the spacious office turned colder.

"No need to be rude," Mr. Saroyan said icily.

That surreal feeling swept over Vince again. The room felt like it was spinning around him; he blinked once to make sure he wasn't actually dizzy. This was, without a doubt, one of the *strangest* conversations he'd ever had.

He struggled to focus, to parse through the double-speak and fluff to the truth. "You still haven't mentioned *why* you want me to drop the case." He held a hand out palm-up. "There's a woman on Level 6 who thinks that one of her sons killed the other. Surely you wouldn't want that to stand."

"It is *so* unfortunate that these things happen." Mrs. Saroyan's voice practically oozed fake sincerity. "But they *do* happen, and there isn't much anyone can do about them."

Vince eyed the pair of them. Dent Antwerp had been convinced that this pair and their business had something to do with Mariella's disappearance. And the disappearance of many others.

Why? Where had he gotten the idea? It had to have come from somewhere.

And *why* were the Saroyans bothering to offer him a bribe to close this case? They had to know he didn't have much to go on.

The answer dawned on Vince with the sudden, blazing light of Cartha's sun slipping past the gas giant to shine its full glory on Zyga Space Station.

The Saroyans were *afraid*.

They were afraid of *him*.

Vince drew in a sharp breath through his nose. For all their power, for all their casual arrogance when it came to other people's lives, a simple Finder like himself had managed to rattle them.

Well, said a small voice inside his head. *Not so simple when you think about it. Terrell Roda is answering for past sins, isn't he?*

The Rodas. The *Juggernaut* and its crew. His attempt to save little Gemma had led to solving a decade-old mystery.

The repercussions of *that* were still rippling through Zyga Space Station.

They don't want me digging any deeper because they're afraid of what I'm going to find.

More than the identity of Dent Antwerp's murderer, it was looking likely.

But even that made no sense. These two had consciences calloused enough to render them impervious to any feelings of guilt over trafficking fellow human beings. Why would something as small as a murder shake their cages?

Mr. Saroyan drew Vince's attention back to himself.

"You're sure you won't take the money?" The older man arched a thin, dark eyebrow at Vince, one hand idly tapping the surface of his desk.

"You haven't given me sufficient reason to drop my case."

Mrs. Saroyan laughed her tinkling, melodic laugh again. "Oh, yes, because a large sum of money isn't enough of a reason."

"He *is* a man of principles, remember, my love?" Her husband tipped his head toward her.

"Oh, yes." Mrs. Saroyan sniffed disdainfully. "How…quaint."

Bemused, Vince shook his head. "You do realize that essentially kidnapping us at gunpoint and bringing us to your office makes you look guilty." He glanced sideways at Bella. "I find myself a little concerned now, actually. This is the second—"

"Third," Bella said flatly.

"—third time in the past few months that someone I've been investigating has taken it upon themselves to bring me in." Vince continued to shake his head. "Talk about coincidence. Makes my investigation a lot easier."

Mrs. Saroyan sniffed again, as though she couldn't believe his impertinence.

Mr. Saroyan drilled Vince with a hard look. "If you refuse to work with us, then you're of no further use." He flicked his fingers in Vince and Bella's general direction. "Griffin, get them out of here."

"Sure thing, Boss." The henchman started forward in their direction, cracking his knuckles again.

"No need." Vince held up a hand that wasn't holding his now-cold dinner. "We'll show ourselves out."

"Visitors," Mrs. Saroyan said in a sickly sweet voice, "are not permitted to wander our premises unescorted."

Bella offered the older woman a smile that was just as sickly sweet. "Of course not. You wouldn't want them getting into any trouble."

"No, indeed," Vince said. He nodded to the Saroyans. "Evening." Then he turned on his heel and stalked toward the door. He didn't wait for Griffin to get there first.

A fierce, almost reckless fire licked his insides. The Saroyans were as guilty as sin. He couldn't prove it yet, but they were. And he *would* prove it.

Somehow.

CHAPTER 46

GRIFFIN EXITED THE OFFICE ON THEIR HEELS, shutting the heavy wooden door behind him as he went. "Back to the elevator," he growled, but Vince had already motioned for Bella to precede him across the waiting area.

Vince was hard-pressed to keep from reeling again. That they'd actually walked out of the office alive and in one piece was…surprising. He'd half-expected one of the Saroyans to produce a pistol and *shoot* them.

He could definitely see Mrs. Saroyan dispatching them with a kind of cool efficiency—and her husband praising her for it.

They reached the elevator. Vince caught Bella's eye and gave her the faintest of approving nods. She'd done well.

One corner of her cherry red lips tilted up in a hint of a pleased smile. Then she reached out and tapped the elevator's call button with a silver-tipped fingernail before hiking her large purse a little higher on her shoulder.

The elevator dinged and the doors slid apart just as Vince faced Griffin and extended a hand, palm up. "I'd like our comlinks back now."

Griffin's craggy face could have been carved from granite. "Not until we're out of the building."

Vince narrowed his eyes, but he knew instinctively there would be no arguing this point. Griffin apparently had his orders—and he was not the sort of hired minion to buck the orders handed down to him. The Finder held his gaze a second longer and then deliberately broke the look to nod to Bella.

His assistant gracefully stepped into the elevator and Vince followed, keeping the henchman in view in case he attempted to pull anything funny. The man didn't—he took up position in the front left corner and stood still and unmoving.

No one spoke as the elevator doors closed and they descended with a faint lurch.

Seconds later, the doors opened on the downstairs lobby. Griffin pointed a meaty finger at the doors. "Out. Both of you."

Bella shot him a withering look. "What do you think we're going to do, stand here all night?" She sniffed and flipped a lock of her black hair over her shoulder before sweeping out of the elevator. Her shoes made little click-clacking sounds on the white floor.

The all-white floor.

Vince had taken two steps forward before it hit him. The artful swirls in the tiled floor were gone. The receptionist's desk was empty.

This *looked* like the lobby…but it wasn't.

They'd been tricked.

"Bella—" he began, whirling around just in time to see Griffin produce a small silver pistol from an inside shoulder holster. It had been so small Vince hadn't realized it was there—and he usually picked up on that sort of thing.

Two soft 'pffths' filled the air as the henchman shot Vince and Bella in rapid succession.

There wasn't time to move. There wasn't even time to think.

All Vince could do was stare at Griffin, a stinging pain in the base of his throat.

"Boss?" Bella sounded terrified.

Vince glanced down at himself, but didn't see anything. His hand came up to rub at the source of the stinging pain and encountered a slender needle with a tufted end. He yanked it out and held it up in the air. The tiny red feather in the end of the dart almost glowed in the cool light from the glowpanels in the overhead.

A tranquilizer dart. Or possibly a poisoned dart.

No way to be sure.

His gaze fell on Bella, who sported a second dart, which had pierced her pale skin just above her exposed collar bone. Her face was blank and shocked.

His gaze then traveled to the source of the darts.

"You—" Vince began, but his tongue was already growing thick, his mouth sprouting a horrible cottony feeling. His head filled with muzzy fog; the floor began to spin beneath his feet. Darkness flickered around the edges of his vision, as though Griffin and the fake lobby were beginning to retreat into the distance.

"Boss!" he heard Bella say again, but there wasn't any stopping his freefall into oblivion.

The last thing Vince saw before darkness claimed him was the smug, satisfied look on Griffin's craggy face.

CHAPTER 47

Awareness returned to Vince slowly. His mind took its time to return to its mortal bonds, preferring instead to float freely, independent of his body. His subconscious used this time to bring a few things to the forefront for his consideration.

Cases were mysteries Vince loved—and lived—to solve. Mysteries in which people's actions and sequences of events were puzzle pieces that, when put together in the right order, revealed all their secrets. Missing a few crucial pieces of the puzzle made solving it a great deal harder, but not impossible.

Never impossible.

Every mystery had a solution.

The key was finding it.

Vince was good at that. He'd been called the best Finder on Zyga Station. But even he had to admit that not every mystery could be solved. There were some mysteries that would probably remain mysteries until the end of time itself.

This case, however, this mystery of who had killed Dent Antwerp and *why*…was not one of those unsolvable mysteries.

A vivid memory of Griffin's hands came to mind. His knuckles had been bruised. Particularly the ones on his right hand. Griffin had either been in a fight recently…or else he'd beaten someone up recently—most likely on his employers' command.

Was it proof positive Griffin had beaten Dent Antwerp so badly that he'd killed him? No. But it *was* a curious coincidence.

If you believed in coincidences, that is, which Vince did not.

And then there was the matter of who was responsible for framing Corwin Antwerp.

Whoever it was would have needed to gather physical traces from Corwin without the young man's knowledge.

In his mind's eye, Vince rewatched the vid of the altercation between Dent and Griffin at Pho's Noodle Shop, complete with Corwin sailing in at the end to help pry the two men apart. Even if Dent had been strung out on something—which he probably was—Griffin was strong enough that he shouldn't have needed Corwin's help. He was over twice Dent's size.

Either Griffin had been exceedingly quick on his mental feet—

—or the fight had been staged to entrap both Antwerp brothers.

If that was the case, it had worked spectacularly.

Dimly, Vince became aware of a throbbing in his head, situated what felt like right behind his eyes. He raised his hands to rub his eyes, but his hands bumped into something solid. And flat.

…something that felt suspiciously like the lid of a *box*.

Despite his throbbing headache, Vince opened his eyes. It made no difference; he was still enveloped by complete and total darkness. He blinked once, twice, but nothing changed.

He was lying on his back on a hard surface, in warm, surprisingly stuffy darkness. The air smelled of his own laundry detergent and a musty scent he couldn't quite recognize. The back of his throat itched faintly.

Vince grimaced. That was just what he needed. Bella's concoction must be starting to wear off.

Tentatively, he lifted his hands to explore his surroundings. His questing fingers encountered three flat surfaces—one on either side of him, just brushing his shoulders, and another stretching out over his body as far as he could reach until the top of his head smacked into it.

He *was* in a box. Vince laid his head back down, his heartbeat beginning to quicken inside his chest at the thought of being trapped. He forced himself to take calm, slow breaths.

No way of knowing how much oxygen he had left. Best to conserve as much as possible.

Beyond the thundering of his pulse in his ears, Vince strained to catch a snatch of any other sound. Voices, footsteps, the rumble of machinery—something, anything.

He thought he heard something that could have been voices. The thump of something that *could* have been cargo being loaded or unloaded. He wasn't sure.

Vince felt his throat threaten to close up and forced himself to inhale slowly. Up until now, he hadn't thought he was claustrophobic. The idea of being essentially trapped aboard Zyga Space Station, unable to leave it except in a spaceship, had never really bothered him. The space station was big enough that he'd never felt like the corridors were closing in on him.

Being trapped inside a box barely large enough for his solid frame was another story.

Vince grimaced. Probably an airtight box at that.

Was this how the Saroyans planned to dispose of them? Let them suffocate in a box being shipped to God only knew where?

Them.

His eyes opened wider in the darkness. *Bella.*

What had they done with her? Surely, they hadn't discovered she was an android.

Vince's headache worsened. The way Mrs. Saroyan had looked at Bella, appraising her… If they didn't think she was too dangerous to let live, they were probably shipping her off to sell her to someone.

Something twisted in the pit of his stomach. He couldn't let that happen.

He had no illusions as to their plan for him. They wouldn't sell him; they couldn't. And while putting a laser bolt through his brain was probably too messy for them, letting him suffocate in an airtight box was surprisingly efficient.

No one knew where they were.

No one would be able to help them.

Vince thumped the top of the box with a fist. "Bella? BELLA? Can you hear me?" He took a short breath. "CAN ANYBODY HEAR ME?"

His voice seemed impossibly loud in the dark confinement of the box. It made his ears ring. He held his breath, listening for an answer—for anything.

Nothing.

He shouted again. "HELP! BELLA? WHERE ARE YOU?"

Still nothing. And now his ears were ringing again.

Vince patted himself down in the darkness. He still had his wallet, with his identcard, which surprised him. No comlink, of course. Clearly, there hadn't been any point in Griffin giving them back.

Vince blew out an aggravated breath, which he immediately regretted. He shook his head slightly instead. At least the Saroyans wouldn't be able to do anything untoward with their comlinks.

With the fee he'd gotten from Jewel Roda, Vince had been able to implement some major security measures. If the Saroyans attempted to break into his comlinks, the devices would essentially brick themselves.

Losing the devices wasn't ideal, but it *was* a backup plan for precisely this sort of situation.

Now if only he had a backup plan for *this* part of the situation.

Was it his imagination, or was the air in here getting stuffier? Vince's heartbeat quickened again, but he gritted his teeth and forced himself to regulate his breathing. Panicking would only use his precious oxygen all the faster.

Think, he told himself. *Think. There has to be a way out of this.*

He refused to give up. He *refused* to let the Saroyans win—to let them shove him in a box and make their problems disappear.

He refused to let them hurt Bella.

Think.

He needed more time. More air. His was rapidly running out, and he didn't have a clue where he was.

Vince jolted in sudden realization. They hadn't bothered to take his wallet. Probably hadn't wanted to have anyone caught disposing of it. A logical thought. After all, if he disappeared, so did his wallet.

And what's the harm in a wallet, right?

He allowed himself a tight, triumphant smile. Nothing—unless you were a Finder who'd recently come into some money and figured out ways to guard against some relatively hairy situations.

One of those was a smooth, gray rectangle about the same size as an identcard, but triple the thickness. It fit into his wallet perfectly, and unless someone already knew the secret, they'd never guess that it unfolded into a tiny laser cutter.

Other than test it out on a few pieces of trash, Vince had never used it before. He'd purchased it on a hunch not long after the Gemma Roda case. He often carried a knife, but a hidden laser cutter had a practical—and mysterious—appeal.

Besides, you never knew when something like that might come in handy.

Apparently, Vince thought as he reached into his breast pocket, his fingers instinctively locating his wallet, *today's the day.*

CHAPTER 48

Laying his wallet on his chest, Vince flipped it open and ran his fingers over the contents. On the right, he felt the smooth, cool plastic panel where his identcard resided. On the left, a series of tiny little pockets for creditchips and slightly larger pockets for card-sized objects.

Vince wheezed a little as he exhaled. He was starting to get lightheaded. He gritted his teeth again. No way to tell how long he'd been out.

It occurred to him that if he hadn't woken up—if he'd just continued to sleep—he would have run out of air and suffocated without knowing it.

The thought made something twist in the pit of his stomach.

His only real consolation in this entire mess was that Bella didn't need to breathe. If his assistant was trapped in a box like he was, she'd be fine until he got her out.

Vince just hoped she really *was* trapped in a box and not trapped on a ship leaving Zyga Station for parts unknown.

His questing fingers skimmed over the top of the cards, searching for the hidden laser cutter. With his head starting to spin a little, he couldn't recall exactly where he'd put it. The seam where it fit together was practically naked to the invisible eye, but it could be felt. He distinctly remembered feeling it when he'd turned the cutter-card over in his hands.

His index finger touched a faint line running across a card. A jolt of triumph shot through him like an electrical pulse. Vince held his breath as he pulled the card out, leaving his wallet lying on his chest.

It took him precious seconds to reassemble the tiny laser cutter. Having to do it all by touch, with no idea what it looked like, was harder than he would have thought. Vince made a mental note to practice this later.

He had to breathe again.

Vince exhaled and then filled his lungs with what was left of the air in his box. Scooting sideways as far as he could against the left side of the box (which wasn't far), he brought the laser cutter up to shoulder height with his right hand.

On the verge of flicking it on, he paused.

His head throbbed with a horrifying thought. What if he'd been dumped into space and the second he cut through the side of this box, he exposed himself to the vacuum of space?

Death would be much quicker than mere suffocation.

Get a grip on yourself, Finder.

The moment of fear retreated, swept away by a warm, comforting rush of common sense. He wasn't floating weightless in this box. Gravity still affected him. Therefore, cutting himself an air hole would do exactly that: let in air.

Vince flicked the cutter on with a press of his index finger against the faint indentation on its side.

A tiny red beam flared to life, stabbing through the blackness inside his box to light its interior with a fiery glow. It exposed what Vince had already concluded: he was in a box that could have doubled as a coffin. He ignored that, however, to press the tip of the laser cutter into the side of the box.

It wasn't a large cutter. It probably hadn't actually been intended to cut open things like this box. But as far as Vince was concerned, it was his only means of salvation.

The laser cutter hummed in his fingers, the red beam melting through the metal as he moved it in a tiny circle. The air in the box grew hot. Tiny beads of metal dripped down from the circle.

Beads of sweat formed on the back of Vince's neck, under his armpits. He blinked, his vision flickering and wavering. The laser beam was literally burning through the last of his oxygen.

He gritted his teeth again, forcing himself to take shallow breaths and hold them longer. His chest ached and burned. It took all his effort to keep moving the laser cutter in that tiny circle.

Come on, he thought. *Just a little hole. Come on!*

The laser beam cut through the last bit of metal just as darkness overwhelmed the Finder again. The laser beam abruptly shut off as his finger slid from the button. His hand dropped to the bottom of the box with a faint thump.

All was silent.

CHAPTER 49

Vince came to with a groan. His head was *killing* him. He was lying down on something hard, with only a tiny shaft of light piercing the darkness surrounding him. Disoriented, he tried to sit up—

—only to smack his head into something hard and solid.

Awareness returned then in a lazy wave. Right. He was trapped in a box.

Vince blinked once, twice, and then realized he could breathe. He inhaled, filling his lungs to bursting, and then slowly exhaled. Okay, the air was still a little stuffy, but he must have succeeded in cutting the air hole after all.

Turning his head sideways, his gaze immediately found the hole he'd cut. A tiny stream of light poured through it, providing faint illumination inside the box.

For a second, Vince stared at that faint light, struck by how even a tiny bit of light could chase away darkness. There was a metaphor there, somewhere, but he didn't have time to consider it.

He scrabbled around beside his thigh for the laser cutter again. He found it; his fingers closed around the small device in relief. He couldn't remember how long he could use it before the tiny power source had to be recharged, but he'd squeeze every bit of power out of it that he could.

Holding the laser cutter tightly, Vince studied the underside of his box's lid. From the inside, he couldn't quite see where the latches were. His eyebrows drew in to a deep frown. He might only get one shot at this.

Where to cut?

There could be as many as three latches on this thing—one on each end and one in the middle.

Vince paused, a hollow feeling flooding his chest. And that didn't even take into account the fact that he could be buried beneath more boxes. What good would cutting latches do if he couldn't get the stupid lid off?

His eyes found the tiny beam of light again, and an answering flicker of hope sprang to life, chasing the hollow feeling away. He'd cut his way to light. That told him that at least his box wasn't *completely* buried beneath a ton of other boxes.

Grimly, Vince spent a moment cutting himself another air hole beside the first one. The air grew stuffy and warm, but he didn't get lightheaded again. That was a good sign.

He pressed his face as close to the hot metal as he dared and breathed in fresher air. Then he reached down and held the laser cutter up to approximately the middle of the box's lid, where he hoped a latch might be. Start there, and maybe he'd get lucky.

Time stretched, minutes and seconds lasting an interminable length as Vince inched his way along the edge of the box. He willed his little laser cutter to keep cutting—the last thing he needed now was for it to run out of juice when he was so close to freedom.

So close.

"Keep going," he muttered. "Don't give up on me now."

Sweat beaded on his face, dripped down into his eyes. The Finder blinked the stinging away, gritted his teeth, and redoubled his efforts.

It was incredibly difficult to get leverage when you were trapped flat and couldn't even really raise yourself up on your elbows.

Vince did the best he could, pressing himself up against the roof of the box and *stretching* as far as he could to cut along the top edge. He stretched so far he risked dropping the cutter, or losing his grip on it entirely. If that happened, his only saving grace was the device's safety shut-off. The tiny laser cutter *should* switch off before it landed on his body.

Should being the operative word there.

Under normal circumstances, Vince would never dream of testing something like this, but…

Even for him, this wasn't exactly normal.

He sensed the extra give in the edge of the box right before he cut through what was probably the front latch. His laser cut jerked a little in his fingers as the resistance it had been meeting suddenly gave way.

Vince almost lost his grip on the little cutter, but hung on to it at the last second.

His finger slid off the power button and the red laser died away, plunging the box into darkness once more.

But not total darkness. The Finder's eyes adjusted quickly. Two narrow shafts of light streamed into the box from the air holes he'd cut, while at the top of the box, the barest hint of light glimmered along the edge.

Vince sucked in a deep breath, let it out in one grateful exhalation. He *was* close. Freedom wasn't that far away.

Dropping the laser cutter to his side, he splayed both hands against the lid and *shoved*.

It barely budged.

He shoved again, and this time he realized something was holding the lid down at both ends.

More latches. Great.

Vince let his head thump down against the bottom of the box. Okay. So he'd have to cut through the edges on both ends too. He'd known that was a distinct possibility.

The one above his head would prove a little tricky. He pressed his lips into a thin line. So far, he'd avoided outright burning himself. The skin of his hand was hot from where he'd held the laser cutter against increasingly molten metal, but the last thing he wanted to do was drop a bead of molten metal onto his face. Or his scalp.

As for the one at his feet…well, he had no idea how he was going to deal with that.

Not when he couldn't even *reach* his feet if his life depended on it.

A hoarse chuckle escaped Vince. Which, to be honest, it kind of did.

He brushed that thought aside. He'd deal with that when he got to it. Didn't have much choice but to try.

He huffed softly to himself. Help wasn't coming. Nobody knew he and Bella were even in trouble, let alone where they were.

Their only option was for him to escape this ersatz coffin by himself.

Taking a deep breath, Vince stared up at the edge of the box above his head. The fact that it was much shorter than the length of the box was a mercy. If worst came to worst and his cutter gave out before he finished, he *might* be able to shove the box open by sheer force.

Maybe.

Only one way to find out.

Closing his finger around his cutter, Vince took a breath and let it out slowly. Then, bracing himself, he raised the little laser cutter above his head and switched it on.

Once more, a faint red glow flooded the interior of the box. Vince narrowed his focus to that tiny laser beam. Scooting himself as far down toward the end of the box as he could, he stared up at the edge of the box as he dragged the laser cutter along it. Metal hissed and bubbled, tiny sparks flying.

A few of the tiny sparks landed on Vince's cheek and forehead, but he barely felt them. As long as he held the cutter steady, he'd be fine.

Keep going, he told it silently. *Keep cutting. You can do this.*

When he reached the corner of the box, he powered the cutter down and worked his arm back down to his side. He lay there for a few heartbeats, clutching the cutter with almost-numb fingers and saying a silent prayer of thanks to whoever might be listening (God? The universe?).

Two breaths later, Vince had to concede that attempting to cut the last edge of the box by his feet was currently impossible. If he'd had no skeleton, he might have been able to contort himself into some position that would enable him to move around, but as it was, being a full-grown, normal human being was a problem.

Another hoarse chuckle escaped him. Now he was just being ridiculous.

He'd just have to see if he could break out—and pray that there wasn't anything stacked on top of him.

Determination settling over him like a mantle, Vince flattened his hands against the box lid above him. He drew his knees up as far as they would go, until they were wedged tight against the lid. It was uncomfortable, and he had an inkling that this might hurt, but what was a little pain to the alternative?

Vince took another deep breath and then *pushed* with all his might. The box lid resisted at first—it seemed there *was* something on top of it.

The Finder just gritted his teeth and pushed harder.

Slowly, slowly, the pressure he exerted overcame the weight of whatever was stacked on top of his box. Above his head, the box lid began to bend backwards.

Vince heard a loud crash as something slid off the top of his box. The second that weight disappeared, he found himself wrenched upward as the lid gave a metallic groan and peeled backward. A rush of cool, fresh air fanned his sweaty face.

He was free.

CHAPTER 50

SNAGGING HIS CUTTER FROM THE BOTTOM OF his box with one hand, Vince lost no time in sitting up. He breathed deep lungfuls of cool, metal-scented air while he scanned his surroundings with alacrity.

Just in case a fist was headed his way.

He didn't have to do more than glance around to know he was alone.

From the looks of it, he was in the second row of a large number of shipping boxes stacked up in a cargo bay. Vince narrowed his eyes, taking in the dented, rusty-gray metal bulkheads. Hauling himself to a kneeling position, he peered down at the deck two meters below him. He was probably aboard a freighter, although he supposed there was a chance he was still somewhere a storage bay in Zone 4. (He doubted that, but it *was* possible.)

The boxes around him were a mishmash of plastic, metal, and cardboard in all shapes and sizes. They'd been stacked with an eye to order, and they bore names and labels with barcodes—none of which he could read from his current perch. They probably didn't matter either, but he'd look at a few of them anyway.

Just in case.

Laser cutter still clutched in one hand, Vince clambered out of his box and carefully balanced on the unbent end of the lid. The metal bowed under his weight, but it held steady long enough for him to drop two meters to the deck to avoid stepping on any of the other boxes. He landed in a half-crouch and stayed there, listening, his eyes tracking between the cargo bay door and a smaller hatch off to the right.

Nothing happened. The crash didn't seem to have alerted anyone.

That was a mixed bag, but it didn't matter. Vince hefted the laser cutter in one hand as he rose to his feet. If he had to cut his way out of here too, he'd do it in a heartbeat.

The owners could send him the bill later.

Right now, all that mattered was getting out and finding Bella.

Turning back to the array of boxes and containers stacked across the back half of the cargo bay, Vince surveyed them, searching for any other boxes that were human-sized. Anything that would indicate Bella was here.

"Bella?" His voice resounded off the metal bulkheads. "Bella? Can you hear me?" He paused. "If you can hear me, bang the side of your box."

He paused again, struck by a memory, and raised his voice even louder. "Better yet, scream!"

They'd learned by accident that when Bella screamed loud enough, she could hit a pitch that actually shattered glass.

Straining his ears, Vince listened for any sign of life. Anything that would tell him Bella was here.

He heard nothing.

His goatee bristled; he scrubbed a furious hand along his chin.

You didn't really expect that she'd be here, did you? asked a wry voice inside his head. *They wouldn't take a chance on putting the two of you together. Especially not when they think she's a normal gorgeous human.*

No. No, they wouldn't. Bella was someplace else.

He had to find her.

Vince sucked in a deep breath through his nose as a grim thought occurred to him. If they *had* put Bella in a box like they put him in, how in the galaxy was he going to find her?

She had an android body—it wasn't like any of the normal scanners would work.

He took another breath. His internal clock told him that it had been several hours since the episode at Saroyan Imports, but without his comlink, he currently had no way of verifying that. Bella could be gone by now. Jetting off through space somewhere, or hidden on another ship berthed in the Docking Bay, and he'd walk right past her.

Don't even go there. Vince shook his head, willing those thoughts away. He clenched his fists, resolve curling through him and strengthening him.

He was a Finder. Wherever they'd sent her, wherever they'd hidden her, he'd…well…*find* her.

No matter how long it took.

Even if he had to leave Zyga Space Station behind to do it.

He jolted with sudden realization. He'd better make sure he was still *on* Zyga Space Station.

Above the thundering of his heart, Vince paused again to listen, this time for the hum of a ship's engine. He hadn't been on a spaceship since he arrived on Zyga Space Station more than a decade before, but he remembered what it was like. The thrum of a ship's engines was louder than the space station, which had a quiet background purr in comparison.

Straining his ears, Vince listened. He heard no rumbling that sounded like a ship's engine.

Hope unfurled wings inside his chest, spurring him across the deck to the smaller entry hatch. If he was on a freighter, the freighter hadn't departed from its docking berth on the space station yet. He hadn't been out cold so long as to cause extreme complications, thank God.

Vine hit the rather ancient-looking doorpanel beside the cargo hatch with his fist, a little harder than strictly necessary. He held his breath, anticipating it being locked, but it was not. The door slid aside with a screech that begged for a little grease. He was through the hatch and dashing up the hexagonal corridor beyond before it finished opening.

The corridor ended in T-intersection that led off to port and starboard. Vince hurled himself around the corner to the right by instinct—

—and plowed headlong into a man coming the other direction.

"Whoa!"

They both tumbled to the worn, grimy deck. Vince picked himself back up in an instant; the other man was nearly as quick. He was a head shorter than Vince and much stockier, with light skin and a dark green mechanic's jumpsuit. A triangular white name patch read, 'Eddie.' He stared at Vince with astonished pale blue eyes.

"Whoa. Where did you come from?" The mechanic, Eddie, settled into a defensive stance. "You're not part of the crew and we ain't got any passengers."

Vince was so happy to see a fellow human being that he didn't let the wary unfriendliness the other man radiated faze him. "I was in a box. Back there." He jerked his thumb over his shoulder in the general direction of the cargo bay.

The other man stared at him over his fists. "What?" His eyes narrowed suspiciously. "Who *are* you?"

"Finder Vince Grable." Vince started to reach into the breast pocket of his brown leather jacket for his wallet. Thank the stars he still had it!

"Whoa, whoa." The shorter man brandished a fist under Vince's nose. "Keep those hands where I can see 'em."

"I'm going to show you my Finder license," Vince said patiently, despite the urgency thrumming through his veins with every beat of his heart. "I need to get off this ship. It's a matter of life and death."

He withdrew his wallet from his jacket and showed the ship's mechanic his license, complete with his name and a current pic.

Eddie didn't look impressed. "You need to see the captain, that's what."

The captain. Vince straightened, reigning in his impatience. That would work too. "Yes. Take me to your captain."

Eddie just stared at him uneasily, clearly thrown by the appearance of a stranger claiming to have been cooped up in the cargo bay.

Vince deepened his voice, adding a note of command he seldom used. "*Now.*"

The mechanic obeyed.

CHAPTER 51

E DDIE DIDN'T SPEAK WHILE HE LED VINCE through the freighter's corridors to a ladder that led to the upper deck. That was fine with Vince; with every footstep his sense of urgency increased. He was too anxious to take in more than the barest details of his surroundings.

The freighter was old—the rusty-gray metal bulkheads were evidence of that—and not well-maintained. The ladder creaked alarmingly under their feet. Vince wrinkled his nose. The air stank of old food and body odor, mixed with the inescapable metallic tinge that permeated everything in space unless you had a good airscrubber.

This was exactly the sort of crew that might take on an extra shipment or two without asking questions because they found themselves in need of some extra credits and weren't too choosy about where said credits originated from.

Along the way, he tucked his little laser cutter up his sleeve. Eddie hadn't noticed it, and Vince wasn't about to give up his only weapon. Just in case things went sideways.

Again.

Two meters from the ladder, Eddie barreled through a hatchway into a surprisingly roomy lounge compartment. "Captain Ellis!"

"What?" A heavyset man with graying hair and a scruffy beard looked up from his comlink. His dark eyes widened almost comically in his round, nut-brown face as he caught sight of Vince, before promptly narrowing in suspicion. "Who is this?"

He rose ponderously to his feet in an attempt to loom over Vince, but it was difficult to do seeing as how Vince stood half a head taller. "How did you get aboard my ship?"

Vince bit back a curt reply. He didn't have *time* for this. "I'm Finder Grable." He shoved his license under the captain's nose. "I was trapped in a box someone put in your cargo hold."

No need to outright accuse the man of being part and parcel to kidnapping. Yet.

"I need to use your comlink to call Station Authority. A woman's life is at stake. Please," he tacked on, when the captain only gaped at him.

The mention of Station Authority obviously alarmed the older man. His eyes darted sideways to his mechanic, and then around to the rest of his crew, who'd been lounging in chairs and on couches all around the compartment. These had now risen to their feet.

Vince ignored them to stare at the captain.

Captain Ellis blinked first. "Life or death, eh?" He puffed his chest out, glancing around at his crew. "You're trespassing. Oughta have you arrested."

"By all means," Vince inclined his head in a polite nod. "Call Station Authority." He narrowed his eyes, dropped his voice to a cold, low tone. "And then you'll be answering questions as to how a Finder came to be trapped inside a box in *your* cargo hold."

It was probably the wrong thing to say—he wasn't exactly in a position to make threats and he knew it—but it worked.

Something shifted Ellis' expression…and Vince knew he'd won. The captain didn't want to lose face in front of his crew, but he *also* didn't want any trouble from Station Authority.

And, short of killing Vince and shooting his body out of an airlock in deep space, there wasn't really any way to avoid that.

The Finder held out a hand, palm up. "Let me call Station Authority, and I'll make sure you don't get into too much trouble." He shrugged, his tone taking on a conciliatory note. "You were just hired to deliver a box someplace, right? Not your fault if the contents happen to be a live human being."

"No." Ellis grasped this as the life preserver that it was. "Not my fault if contents don't match up to shipping manifests."

Slowly, he reached out and dropped his comlink into Vince's palm. Behind him, his crew shifted uneasily.

"Thank you." A thrill of victory jolted through Vince, but it was quickly tempered by that terrible sense of urgency.

"Cap'n," one of the men began, but the captain held up a warning finger.

Vince had memorized the comm frequencies of the Station Authority switchboards in each Zone…just in case he ever needed them. This was one of those occasions.

He tapped in a number and held the comlink up to his ear.

A second later, he heard a cool female voice. "Zone 4 Station Authority, how may I help you?"

"This is Finder Vince Grable." He gave his license number. "I need to speak to Detective Commosky. It's urgent—life or death."

"One moment, please."

Five seconds later, Commosky's brusque voice demanded, "Grable? Is that you?"

Vince's forehead creased. The detective sounded irate. "Yes, I—"

Commosky didn't let him finish. "We had a report you'd been kidnapped. We've got people out looking for you."

Wait, *what*? A wave of dizziness swept over Vince. He almost put a hand out to brace himself on the nearest bulkhead, but stopped himself just in time. "What?"

"Your assistant reported you missing. What the hell is going on? Where are you? We'll send a transport pod for you, get this all sorted out."

"My assistant?" Vince felt like he was lagging four steps behind. "Bella's safe?"

Surprisingly, Commosky's voice turned a shade warmer. "She's fine, Grable. Been here at the precinct raising hell about *you*. Where *are* you?"

Vince blinked, and then the galaxy realigned itself. He let out a breath he hadn't realized he'd been holding. Bella was safe.

He didn't know how she'd done it, didn't know what had happened, but…she was safe.

He glanced at the captain. "I'm aboard the…" He raised a questioning eyebrow.

"*Mermaid's Kiss*, in Docking Bay 42E," Captain Ellis supplied reluctantly.

Vince relayed the information.

"Okay. We'll send somebody from the Level 6 Precinct to collect you." Commosky paused, cleared his throat gruffly. "Glad you're okay, Grable."

"Me too. And, Commosky?"

"Yeah?"

"I think I know who actually killed Dent Antwerp." Vince felt a knot of resolve harden in his chest. "And it wasn't his brother."

A pause greeted these words. Then Commosky said, "We'll talk when you get up here."

He ended the call and Vince handed the comlink back to the captain. "Thank you."

Captain Ellis jerked his head in nod.

"Station Authority will be here soon." Vince gave the man a stern look, before turning to include the entire crew in his sweeping gaze. "It'd be best for all of you if the box I cut myself out of is still in the cargo bay when they get here."

No one spoke, or even moved.

Vince transferred his gaze back to the captain and motioned to the hatch. "Captain."

"Finder." Captain Ellis let out a low growl of annoyance. "Come with me." He started forward, shaking his head roughly. "Best to handle this myself."

CHAPTER 52

THE *MERMAID'S KISS* TURNED OUT TO BE a medium-sized class-D freighter small enough to actually berth inside Zone 4's Docking Bay. Captain Ellis led Vince to the landing ramp and stomped down it with aggravated steps. Behind his bluster, however, Vince sensed real fear.

Clearly, the captain didn't want Station Authority prying too closely into his cargo. Maybe even his crew. Or both.

Ellis took up a grim position beside Vince at the bottom of the landing ramp. The massive corridor extending along the outer edge of Zone 4 was a hive of activity. Ships arrived and departed, and a constant stream of people moved cargo in and out.

Within moments, several shiny silver transporter pods glided to an abrupt halt outside of the freighter's docking berth, not far from the landing ramp. Vince didn't hold with all of Station Authority's policies, or the way they policed Zyga Station sometimes, but he had to admit there were occasions he was happy to see them.

This was one of those occasions.

Four Station Authority officers in blood-red uniforms with gray slacks and hats piled out of the transport pods and rapidly approached the *Mermaid's Kiss*.

Captain Ellis's space-worn face was impassive as he watched them, but out of the side of his mouth, he muttered, "This better not hurt my bottom line, Finder."

Vince glanced at him. "You might be a little choosier in who you do business with in the future, Captain."

The older man just pursed his lips together and glared.

Three of the Station Authority officers were strangers to Vince, but he recognized the man in the lead. Officer Ty Harris, from the Station Authority Precinct on Level 6. He was a tall, lanky man with light tan skin and curly blond hair that sometimes defied a regulation cut. Vince had met him three or four years earlier while working on a case that had originated in Zone 4 and ended up in the Core, and had liked him. As Station Authority officers went, Harris was more tolerable than most.

"Grable." Harris's face stretched in a smile. "Glad to see you. If Detective Commosky up on Level 1 is to be believed, you were on your way to disappearing."

"I was." Vince jerked a thumb over his shoulder. "Got crammed into a box that was fixing to be shipped off-station." He tipped his head toward the captain. "Ship's captain didn't know that, of course."

"Of course." Harris nodded gravely, assessing the captain with cool green eyes. "Kidnapping *is* illegal, after all. Defeats the purpose of making someone vanish if the crew's in on it."

Captain Ellis unbent enough to say, "True, that."

Vince fingered his goatee, which had started to bristle again. His sense of urgency, which had died down the moment he heard Bella was safe, flared to life again. "Officer Harris—"

Harris held up a finger and addressed the three officers who had accompanied him. One was a tall female, while the other two were male. "Devon, I want you to take the Captain's statement and then move on to the crew. Kendo, Gomez," the woman and the shorter man both straightened. "I want you to investigate the cargo hold."

He glanced askance at Vince. "You said you *cut* yourself out of a shipping container?"

"Yes."

"How?"

In answer, Vince produced his little laser cutter from its place up his sleeve.

Harris took one look at it and then threw back his head and laughed. "Never a dull moment when it comes to working with you, Grable." Still smiling, he turned back to Kendo and Gomez. "When you finish documenting everything, help Devon finish with the crew."

Captain Ellis drew himself up a little, but didn't say anything.

Harris glanced at Vince again. "You're sure this lot isn't involved?" He circled his finger in the air to encompass the entire freighter.

"Reasonably." Vince didn't look at Ellis. He didn't need to.

"All right." Harris turned back to the captain. "Captain Ellis, Station Authority thanks you for your cooperation. Provided my investigation turns up no evidence of wrongdoing—"

"Which it will not," Ellis said gruffly.

"—you'll be free to carry on your business within a day or so."

A muscle twitched in the captain's jaw, but he knew better than to argue. Instead, he ground out, "Thanks very much."

"Finder, with me." Harris turned on his heel and marched back to the first transporter pod. Vince wasted no time in following.

His head whirled, a hundred different questions spinning around in his mind, each one demanding to be answered.

The first question—the biggest and most important question—rose to the top of the pile.

How in the *galaxy* had Bella escaped?

A second question, of nearly equal burning importance, hurried in its wake. And how had she pulled it off without anyone realizing she wasn't strictly human?

CHAPTER 53

$\mathbf{V}$INCE MANAGED TO HOLD HIS TONGUE FOR the length of time it took to travel up to Level 1, though the effort made him feel like he was in serious danger of imploding. He couldn't imagine what Bella could have told Commosky, and he didn't want to ask too many questions. Better to let Commosky and the rest of Station Authority think he and Bella had worked out prior contingency plans than to sound absolutely gobsmacked.

The Finder bit down on the inside corner of his lip. Although, he'd done a fair job of *that* on the comlink. He'd just been so surprised to learn that *Bella* had escaped on her own and was trying to rescue him.

When they reached the Headquarters building, Vince was still so consumed by his thoughts that he barely noticed his surroundings as he followed Officer Harris through the lobby and security checkpoint (they passed this with no issues; Vince wasn't packing today) and up to the bullpen on the third floor where Detective Commosky and his team worked. The Finder's brain noted the faintly aquatic scent to the air and automatically scanned each room and hall for possible threats, but it wasn't conscious. His entire attention lay on Bella, trying to work out how she had possibly managed to escape Griffin's clutches unscathed.

His heart clenched. She *was* unscathed, right? Commosky hadn't mentioned anything about her being hurt.

Vince half-expected to be led back to a sterile interrogation room, but instead, Harris made a detour at the check-in desk and guided Vince toward the bullpen instead. A handful of Station Authority officers were lingering at their metal and synthglass desks, spread out through the large room, their attention fixed on—

Bella.

His assistant sat in a metal chair next to Commosky's desk, her legs crossed and one booted foot bouncing madly. As they'd recently discovered, being trapped in an android body didn't remove human tendencies like being jittery. Just because Bella *could* sit perfectly still without moving for hours didn't mean she *had* to. Her red blouse looked a little rumpled, and one knee of her black jeans was ripped, but she otherwise appeared to be all right.

Commosky occupied his desk chair, his expression one of a man who had received an unexpected gift but hadn't quite decided if it was a trap or not.

They both caught sight of Vince at the same moment. Bella reacted first.

"Boss!" She shot up out of her chair and practically ran across the bullpen. Flinging her arms around him, she hugged him—a little harder than perhaps she'd intended. "You're all right!"

Vince was hard-pressed to suppress a wince as she practically squeezed all the air out of him. His hands hung uselessly in the air for a second, until he awkwardly settled them on her back. It was at this moment that Vince realized it had been quite a while since someone hugged him.

It was…nice. Unexpected, but surprisingly welcome.

He caught the faint lift of Commosky's dark eyebrow. That look spoke volumes—clearly, Commosky was now wondering if perhaps something more was going on between Finder and Finder's assistant.

Vince cleared his throat. "I'm fine, Bella. Thank you."

Gently, he disengaged her arms and held her at arm's length, gripping her shoulders in his hands as he examined her. "Are *you* all right?" He shook his head, disbelievingly. "How in the galaxy did you escape?"

"That's what I'd like to know," Commosky said wryly, from his desk. He threw Bella a half-exasperated, half-impressed look. "She won't tell me." His lips pursed. "Not much for details, this one."

Bella shot him an answering look over her shoulder. "I told you I'd give you my statement once my boss was safe." She smiled sunnily at him. "So I don't have to keep telling the story."

Commosky's expression edged a little more toward irritated. "That's the point of a statement. We take it, and then compare it to your subsequent retelling of the story." His eyebrows drew together. "To make sure you're telling the truth."

Bella shifted to face him, propping on hand on her hip. "You think I'm lying about being kidnapped and nearly shipped off-station?"

"No." Commosky sat back in his chair, his face settling into neutral lines. "But that's not the point." He waved a stylus toward her. "There are a few things that don't add up."

That statement sent an ice-cold chill jolting through Vince. Any traces of fatigue or anything else fell away in the resulting rush of adrenaline. The last thing they needed was Commosky getting suspicious and poking his nose in Bella's life.

"You want my statement?" Bella made a dramatic show of stalking back over to his desk and seating herself once more. She sat ramrod straight and looked expectantly at Commosky. "I'm ready."

For his part, the detective pressed his lips into a thin line and rolled his eyes expressively toward the stars, as if to ask, *Why me?* Then he leveled a hard gaze at Bella. "And you couldn't have given me this an hour ago?"

"My boss hadn't been rescued yet," she said primly. "Now he has."

Vince watched, fascinated, as Commosky narrowed his eyes.

"What does that have to do with you giving your statement?"

"I can think straight." Bella flipped a lock of black hair over her shoulder, her heart-shaped face the picture of concerned innocence.

"Of course you can," Commosky growled. "More like you're trying to make sure you don't say anything you shouldn't." He pointed a stylus in the direction of the interrogation rooms. "Fine. We'll take your statement first."

Bella just shrugged and rose to her feet.

Commosky then swiveled in his chair and pointed the stylus at Vince. "You're next." One corner of his mouth turned down. "You can get the scoop from your assistant when we're finished."

"Fine by me." Vince dropped into the chair Bella had just vacated. "Gives me a chance to drink a cup of tea." He shook his head. "It's been a very long day, Detective."

"I can imagine." Commosky fixed him with a peculiar look, before pushing himself out of his chair. "All right, Miss Escovedo. With me." He glanced over his shoulder at his curious team. "Benito, get the Finder here a cup of tea." He glanced at Vince again. "Or three."

"Yes, Boss." A sallow-faced man with dark, mournful eyes and a neatly trimmed mustache rose to his feet.

Vince nodded his thanks and then leaned back in his chair to wait. His goatee bristled; he absently stroked his chin. He *was* dying to know how Bella got herself out of that jam, but…at the same time, the knowledge that she was safe and unharmed took the edge off that sense of urgency that had driven him since he woke up alone in that box.

Closing his eyes, Vince let the hustle and bustle of the bullpen wash over him. The ringing of comlinks, the low chatter of voices, footsteps, and more. He could wait a little longer to find out what had happened.

If he had to.

Which, apparently, he did.

He huffed a laugh to himself. At least it gave him time to put his thoughts in order and determine exactly how he was going to present everything to Commosky.

The truth wasn't always convenient—and that was especially true in this case.

CHAPTER 54

B Y THE TIME COMMOSKY RETURNED WITH BELLA in tow, Vince had nearly finished his second cup of tea. Even from across the bullpen, Vince could see the detective looked grim. Bella, by comparison, was positively serene. She followed Commosky meekly back to his desk, as though she was trying hard not to draw undue attention.

Vince had to press his lips into a thin line to suppress an amused snort. Good luck with that. Whether she knew it or not, Bella had drawn the attention of practically every male in sight.

He rose from the chair and offered it to his assistant as she drew near. Bella flashed him a small smile—they both knew it didn't matter whether she sat or stood, but appearance was everything.

"You don't look thrilled, Detective." Vince lifted an eyebrow at the shorter man. He couldn't resist adding, "This turn of events not to your liking?"

Commosky growled in the back of his throat. "You knew damn well I wasn't going to like it."

Vince just shrugged and leaned over to set his near-empty cup on the corner of the detective's glass-topped desk. "Can't change the truth, Detective."

Commosky ignored him. Instead, he addressed Bella. "Stay here until I'm finished with your boss." He tipped his head toward his team. "They'll be happy to get you anything you need."

Bella sketched him a salute.

The detective then glared at Vince. "With me, Finder."

Vince didn't speak. He merely followed Commosky in silence as the other man led the way to the same interrogation room they'd occupied that morning with Mrs. Antwerp. (Had it *really* only been just that morning? It felt like it had been weeks and weeks since he'd last been here.)

For a moment, the only sounds in the white-walled interrogation room were the scraping sound of chairs being dragged across the floor and the rustle of clothing as both men seated themselves on opposite sides of the table. Vince cast a quick glance around; nothing in here had changed. It was still just as cold and sterile as it had been that morning.

He glanced back at Commosky to find the detective watching him with hooded eyes. After a long moment that stretched ominously between them, Commosky finally shook his head and leaned back in his chair. "Leave it to you, Grable. Blow up my case and then complicate it further, all in the same day."

"Don't forget solving it." Vince spread his hands, his expression mild. "I was looking for the truth, Detective." He lifted his shoulders in the barest of shrugs. "Can't help it if that didn't coincide with what you were looking for."

"I wasn't—" Commosky began, before cutting himself off. Mouth twisting to one side, he regarded Vince with narrowed eyes. He drew in deep breath through his nose and then exhaled in a huff. "Believe it or not, Grable, I really do want the truth." One hand clenched into a fist. "I want the son of a black hole who beat

Dent to death." HIs fist released. "Even if it's not someone from the Ruby Gauntlet."

"Good." Vince gave the detective a frank look. "Because that's what you're going to get." He waved a dismissive hand. "The Ruby Gauntlet is a foe for another time, Detective. They're up to no good, I agree with you on that, but…"

"They're not behind Dent's murder."

Vince eyed the detective. Commosky's voice almost had a hollow sound behind it. He frowned slightly. "But you knew that already. Or," he amended, as something flashed through the other man's dark eyes, "you *suspected* it."

Commosky looked away for a second, a muscle in his jaw twitching, before he looked back at Vince. "Dent's death didn't exactly fit the pattern, no, but…" It was his turn to shrug. "Given what he was involved in, it was the most logical choice." He looked askance at Vince. "And regardless of all the holodramas, the simplest explanation tends to be the correct one."

"This *is* the simplest explanation." Vince smiled slightly, but there was no humor in it. "Once you know the facts."

"Yes. The facts." Commosky scowled, drumming his fingers restlessly on the edge of the table. "Your assistant gave me a crop of them, but there are some gaps. Care to fill them in?"

Vince inclined his head in a nod. "And then you can go arrest the son of a black hole and let my client go."

For the first time, a glint of humor shone in Commosky's expression. "Well, let's not get ahead of ourselves, Finder. Tell me your story first."

And what a story it was.

Vince sketched the scene with broad strokes before circling back to fill in the details. Bella had already mentioned Saroyan Imports; Commosky showed no reaction to the name. His eyes, however, grew narrower and narrower the longer Vince talked, until they were nearly slits.

At the end, the detective said, "You *do* realize how this sounds. Accusing one of Zone 4's major businesses of running a human trafficking ring."

"Don't forget ordering murders."

"No." Commosky regarded Vince thoughtfully. "How could I forget? That's the piece de resistance."

He was silent a moment, and then shook his head. "We'll have to prove it, of course. And that lot has money."

Vince thought of Mrs. Saroyan and the coldness in her dark eyes. "If those two were an animal, they'd be the kind that eats their young." It was his turn to shake his head. "I'm telling you, Commosky. Get enough evidence to convict Griffin and the Saroyans will let you have him to save their own skins."

"We've already got him in custody. Picked him up a couple of hours after your assistant called us." Commosky tipped his head toward the door behind him. "He's sitting in a holding cell right now."

Few things took Vince by surprise these days, but this did. He stared at Commosky in complete silence for a long moment. Finally, he allowed a slow grin to spread across his face. "You kept *that* close to your chest, Detective." He shook his head in admiration. "I'd have never guessed."

"You weren't supposed to." An answering smile tinged with satisfaction crossed Commosky's face. "I wanted you to tell me the truth, after all."

Vince raised an eyebrow. "When do I not?"

Commosky inhaled through his nostrils. "Don't get me started." He leaned back in his chair, and his expression suddenly lightened. "Never thought I'd see the day you got an assistant, Grable. Particular one as pretty and resourceful as Ms. Escovedo." He shook his head, a wry smile tilting his lips. "That must have been some 'help wanted' ad you put out."

"I didn't, actually. We..." Vince paused, considering how to put it without giving too much away. "...stumbled into each other."

It was his turn to shake his head. "She's turned out to be quite clever. I can't wait to hear how she pulled this off."

"It's quite the story." Commosky's wry smile grew marginally. "I'd tell you, but I think it'll make more sense coming from her."

That was probably an understatement. Vince didn't know whether to smile or frown. He settled for inclining his head in a nod.

A brief moment of silence settled over the two men, tinged with something that was almost-but-not-quite camaraderie.

But, Vince had a job to do.

"If you don't mind…" He leveled a cool look at Commosky. "I'd like to speak with my client." He held up a hand just as the detective opened his mouth. "And don't tell me visiting hours are over and that I need to come back tomorrow."

Commosky closed his mouth, smiled faintly, and then finally spoke. "Wouldn't dream of it." He eyed Vince a moment longer before shrugging as though he'd reached a decision. "Why not? You held up your end of the bargain."

Rising from his seat, the detective tipped his head toward the door. "Come with me."

CHAPTER 55

Holding cells were in a different part of Station Authority one floor up from the Homicide Department. Commosky personally led Vince back into the bullpen to collect Bella and then escorted them to the elevator and took them up Holding. The elevator ride was short and smooth, but Vince still felt anticipation prickle up and down his arms.

A security checkpoint was set up outside the door, manned by a short man with broad shoulders that stretched the seams of his crimson and gray uniform. He looked up from his computer display as they approached, his eyebrows furrowing into a frown as his gaze slid past Commosky to encompass Vince and Bella.

"You *do* know visiting hours are over, Detective."

"Special circumstances." Commosky jerked a thumb over his shoulder to indicate Vince. "He's a Finder. His client was my chief murder suspect up until this afternoon."

The shorter man's dark eyes widened a fraction. "The Antwerp case?"

Vince suppressed a smug smile. News traveled fast around here. Beside him, Bella stood perfectly still, looking around with interest.

The sergeant looked from Commosky to Vince and Bella, his gaze lingering on the latter, before he returned his attention to Commosky. "Cell 14. Ten minutes, Detective." He gave an apologetic shrug. "Rules are rules, even for Homicide."

"I understand." Commosky sounded downright pleasant. "Thanks, Sarge." He jerked his chin toward Vince. "This way."

The sergeant opened the secure door for them. It unlocked with an ominous thunk and emitted a hydraulic hiss as it slid aside. "Ten minutes," he said again.

Commosky waved in understanding and started down the gray metal hall. Vince and Bella followed.

Vince glanced around with interest. He'd never been in a Headquarters Precinct's holding cells before. They had a distinctly cleaner look than the ones he'd seen in the Zones' lower levels. Where most of this building was all shiny glass and metal and crisp white, the holding cells were constructed of slate gray metal. The air itself had a metallic tinge and smelled strongly of disinfectant.

Clearly, Station Authority didn't want anybody breaking in any more than they wanted somebody breaking out.

The faint hum of electricity overlaid the ever-present faint thrum of the Station's engine and life-support systems, the only sounds, save for their footfalls, which slapped gently against the metal deck. Vince appraisingly eyed the locked doors they passed. Either the occupants were all passed out asleep, or the doors had been soundproofed.

He'd bet on the latter.

A Headquarters precinct wouldn't want a bunch of malcontents they'd arrested getting rowdy and howling in their cells. It'd cause a disruption. Couldn't have that.

Vince glanced at the black letters etched into each door. Cell 6. Cell 10.

A moment later, Commosky stopped in front of a door that bore the marking Cell 14. He reached out and slid aside a panel at eye level to peer into the cell. Then he reached over to a doorpanel on the right side of the door and pressed a button three times in quick succession before pressing a button above it.

The entire door of the cell turned translucent, revealing a small cell only big enough for a bunk bed on one side and a tiny sink and toilet on the other. Vince didn't realize why Commosky had hit the first button a couple of times until his gaze fell on Corwin Antwerp, who was sitting bolt upright on the bottom bunk looking dazed and disoriented. Corwin was dressed in a bright orange jumpsuit with a number on the front pocket.

Vince's gaze narrowed. Clearly, that button triggered some sort of loud buzzer.

Corwin's exhausted, bewildered fell on the door and his dark eyes widened in shock—and fear. His hands gripped the edge of his bed as he warily slung his feet over the side.

Vince nodded to himself. So the translucency worked both ways. They could see him…and he could see them. Or at least Commosky. The detective was in front, blocking Corwin's view of Vince and Bella.

Commosky tapped the comm button on the door panel. "Sorry to wake you, Antwerp, but you've got visitors." He stepped aside, allowing the young man to see Vince and Bella.

Corwin locked eyes with Vince. It took him a split-second to recognize the Finder, but when he did, the look of relief on his face was so powerful that Vince almost had to clear his throat.

"You came." Corwin took two giant steps across the small cell. He halted right in front of the door, close enough that he almost smashed his nose into it. "I didn't think you were coming back."

"They wouldn't let me see you earlier." Vince shot a measured look at Commosky, who only shrugged, as if to say, *Not my fault. Protocol.*

Corwin's eyes widened further. "You've been here already?"

Vince studied the younger man for a brief moment, assessing his condition—physical and otherwise. He was acutely aware of time ticking away. He opened his mouth to speak, but Corwin beat him to it.

"Is my momma okay? They haven't hurt her, have they?"

"Your mother is fine." Vince held up a calming hand. "I've spoken to her several times today. She's fine."

There wasn't any point in telling Corwin what had happened, however. They didn't have time, for one, and, two...all it would do was upset him.

Corwin nodded, absorbing this, and then he visibly bit his lip. "It's not true, is it, Finder? My brother's not—he's not—" he cut himself off, unable to finish. His dark eyes were bleary, but full of a sudden hope.

Something twisted inside Vince's chest. He hated to be the one to finally crush that last glimmer of hope. He glanced at Commosky again, but the detective was studiously examining the cell door at the other end of the corridor.

"Corwin." Vince had to swallow before he could get the words out. "It's true. Dent is dead."

A muscle in Corwin's stubble-covered cheek twitched, and he bowed his head in grief, bracing himself against the door with one hand. He drew in a shaky breath, and then looked up. "I didn't do it." Tears swam in his eyes. "I swear I didn't do it, Finder. On my momma's life."

"I know you didn't."

"But can you prove it?" Agony chased grief over Corwin's face. "Because *he*," he jerked his chin toward Commosky, "says they've got proof it was me. And I didn't—Finder, I swear I—"

"We've got proof." Vince put a hand on the other side of the door where Corwin's hand rested. Seconds counted down inside his head. They didn't have time for him to tell Corwin the full story.

Not yet.

Corwin's entire body seemed to sag in relief, like he was a balloon and somebody had just let half the air out of him. "You—you do?"

"It's a long story." Vince shook his head. "Don't have time for it tonight. But we," he indicated all three of them (he might as well give Commosky a little credit), "wanted to tell you the good news."

"We have another suspect in custody," Commosky said, returning his attention to them. "And given what happened today, it looks like Station Authority will be releasing you in the morning, Mr. Antwerp."

Vince darted a sideways glance at the detective, dark amusement twisting in his chest. Commosky couldn't just come right out and say that they were going to let Corwin go?

Corwin was too tired for semantics. He rocked back on his feet, staring dazedly at the detective. "You...are?"

"Looks that way." Commosky motioned to Vince. "Thank the Finder." His gaze darted to Bella, who had yet to say a word. "And his assistant. They'll tell you the whole story tomorrow."

"Tomorrow." Corwin swayed again, before staggering back over to his bunk and sitting down heavily. He rested his head in his hands, too overcome to say anything else.

Bella edged a little closer to the door. "It's going to be okay, Corwin." She spoke quietly, but her melodic voice still carried. "We'll bring your mother with us tomorrow if you want."

He nodded wordlessly.

"Time's up," Commosky said, not unkindly. It was his turn to clear his throat. "Wanted you to be able to sleep tonight, Antwerp."

"Thank you," Corwin said in a muffled voice.

Vince raised an eyebrow at Commosky, who ignored him and leaned forward to turn off the comm speaker and make the cell door opaque again. The Finder frowned, weighing his options. He wanted to say something scathing, remind Commosky that the detective had basically locked up an innocent man, but he'd also agreed to keep that part of the investigation to himself.

And Commosky knew. Regardless of whether or not he'd ever admit he'd handled parts of this whole case poorly, he knew. And he knew that Vince knew he knew.

Vince nodded to himself. Justice was being served. That would have to suffice for now.

"Come on." Commosky started back down the corridor. "Time for you two to head home."

But they'd be back. Vince glanced over his shoulder at Corwin's cell door once more. Bella lingered at his elbow, her dark eyes wide and alert.

We'll be back in the morning, he promised Corwin silently. *You can count on that.*

He then turned back to Commosky who was halfway to the security door. "Commosky."

The detective stopped and looked at Vince over his shoulder, struck by the odd tone in the Finder's voice. "Yes?"

Vince struggled with himself for only a moment. Reaching into his pocket, he pulled out the little bag that held a lock of Dent's daughter's hair. "Would you check this against Dent Antwerp's DNA?"

Commosky didn't budge. "Why?" He jerked his chin toward the little plastic bag in Vince's palm as the Finder approached him. "What is it?"

"Probably proof that Dent fathered Mariella's child before he died."

One of Commosky's eyebrows lifted a little. "You were serious about wanting to tell the Antwerps about her?"

"If she's his kid, his family deserves to know." Vince shrugged. "She's an orphan, and the Purple Octopuses have enough orphaned kids to look after."

The detective's mouth firmed into a thin line, but he didn't disagree. It was hard to argue with the facts of life in the Core.

After a second, Commosky twitched his shoulders in a careless shrug. "Fine. I'll have the lab run it."

"Thank you."

Vince and Bella then fell in step behind the detective, leaving the cold, silent holding cell corridor behind.

CHAPTER 56

VINCE SHUT HIS OFFICE DOOR AND LOCKED it, running through his security measures with the speed borne of long practice. It was well after midnight and he was exhausted, but there would be no sleep yet. Not for a while.

Not until he knew the full story of what had happened today.

The office was silent, save for the faint strains of music he always left playing. His airscrubber was between cycles. The air, however, was blessedly clean. He sucked in a deep breath and gratefully exhaled. Bella's miracle cream worked, but it had less than a twelve hour lifespan.

Speaking of his assistant…

Vince turned to regard Bella, who had settled herself into her desk and was regarding him with calm expectation. The soft golden light from the glowpanels in the overhead made her glossy black hair glisten and played up the red in her scoop-neck blouse. *She* didn't look tired at all.

Of course she didn't. Androids didn't get tired. Or, rather, human minds trapped in android bodies.

The Finder arched a dark eyebrow at her. "Well?"

"It's killing you, isn't it?" Bella's calm expression morphed into one of amusement, colored with a little bit of awe. "I can't believe you made it this long." When Vince just continued to stare at her, she shrugged, a little self-consciously. "Well, I mean, I guess I *can* believe it." She shrugged again. "It's just…"

"I know." Vince brushed that aside with a flick of his fingers. "And it's not like you could just up and tell Commosky *exactly* what happened, now, is it?" His gaze turned knowing.

If androids could blush, he suspected Bella's cheeks would be flaming red. As it was, she only ducked her head. "Right."

"So…?" Vince waved a hand at her, indicating for her to start talking.

Instead, Bella nodded to the jade green credenza where the drink machine sat. "Why don't you make yourself a cup of tea first."

"*Bella.*"

"You need one. You'll feel better." She posted her hands on her hips, even though she was sitting down. "And it's not like another five minutes will kill you. You've waited this long already."

Vince wanted to tell her that wasn't the *point*, but…she had a point. A cup of tea *would* be nice, after everything. He scowled, narrowing his eyes at her, and then turned toward the drink machine.

What was five more minutes in the grand scheme of things? Commosky was still holding Corwin—his twenty-four hours wouldn't be up until the morning—and while they'd charged Griffin with kidnapping and attempted murder, Station Authority needed to gather more evidence before they could charge him for murdering Dent Antwerp. On the way back from Zone 4, Vince had called Corwin's mother and given her a brief, hopeful update to ease her mind.

The Finder's eyes narrowed further as he mindlessly brewed himself a cup of chamomile tea. They *would* find that evidence.

After the events of this afternoon, there wasn't a shadow of a doubt in his mind that Griffin was guilty.

Whether or not Commosky would be able to nail the Saroyans was another matter. And, a small voice inside his head reminded him, it wasn't his problem. He'd shed light on the issue—thanks to Dent Antwerp—and now Station Authority was responsible for investigating further.

He hoped this wouldn't be one of those occasions where allegations and evidence just faded into obscurity.

Vince barely felt the heat of his mug as his hand curled tightly around it. It wouldn't fade into obscurity. He refused to let that happen.

If he had to drop by Zone 4's Headquarters Precinct every few weeks from now until the day he died to make sure they weren't shirking their duty, then he would do that. It was—

"You okay there, Boss?"

Bella's melodic voice, tinged with concern, drew him back to reality.

Blinking, Vince turned to look at his assistant. She dropped her gaze to his hands, and he glanced down just in time to keep himself from sloshing hot tea all over himself.

Vince allowed himself a rueful shake of his head. "It's been a long day."

"Oh, I know." Bella tilted her head to one side. "Are you sure you wouldn't rather—"

"Bella…"

"Kidding!" She laughed, holding both hands up. "Just kidding." She waited for Vince to settle himself at his jade green desk and then leaned forward to prop her elbows up on the surface of her own matching desk. Her dark almond-shaped eyes were as bright as if she'd gotten twelve hours of beauty sleep. "Where should I start? How much do you remember?"

Vince didn't have to think. He knew *precisely* where their stories diverged. "Start with what happened after I passed out." He eyed her over the rim of his steaming mug of tea. "I know Griffin hit you with a tranquilizer, but obviously it didn't affect you."

Bella had the grace to look abashed. "Nope. Not in the slightest." She glanced down at her hands, which she'd folded on the desk. "It took me a second to figure out what had happened, actually."

Bella continued to stare at her fingers. "I didn't know what to do." She lifted one shoulder in a shrug. "You went down and I realized it would look *really* strange if I didn't pass out too."

Vince sipped his tea, listening in silence. He'd splurged and added a dollop of honey. The fragrant steam wafting up into his face had a calming effect all by itself.

"I told Detective Commosky that Griffin missed but I made him think he shot me." Bella quirked a small smile. "Griffin probably won't agree, but how else will he explain it?"

Vince imagined the expression on Commosky's face while an incarcerated Griffin tried to insist that he'd hit Bella with the same tranquilizer that he'd used to take down Vince himself. "Commosky won't buy it."

"Right. So…" If she'd been fully human, this would have been the point at which Bella took a deep breath. But, she wasn't, and so she sat completely still instead. "I pretended to collapse. You were out and I didn't know what else to do." She shook her head. "I didn't think I could fight him off."

"No." Vince could picture that scene too. "Griffin would have snapped you like a piece of plastic." The very thought made him clench his jaw.

"So I just laid there on the floor and listened. Griffin made three comlink calls—one to somebody named Morris, one to a man named Trey, and another to somebody named Flavia. He told Morris and Flavia he needed help and told Trey he had a couple more pieces of merchandise to add to their cargo."

Vince narrowed his eyes. Trey must have been responsible for getting him—or the box he was in—aboard the *Mermaid's Kiss*.

Here, Bella paused and glanced up at him. "I, ah, obviously lied to Commosky."

"Some might argue you only stretched the truth a little," Vince said mildly.

"No." Bella shook her head. "I lied. I told Commosky that I woke up after Griffin split us up and managed to escape and call Station Authority."

"How?"

She shrugged. "I said I swiped a comlink from Griffin and used it to call Station Authority, but that I lost the comlink in the process of finishing escaping." She spread her hands. "Obviously, I had my purse, but no comlink when I got to the Precinct."

That was clever. Vince nodded slowly, taking another sip of tea. "Although if it had been Griffin's comlink, that could have been very useful in helping prove he was involved." He started to take another sip, but stopped, the mug halfway to his lips. "You *said* you swiped Griffin's comlink?"

CHAPTER 57

BELLA NODDED SLOWLY, ALMOST RELUCTANTLY.

Vince stared at her, some of the fog clearing in his head. "If you didn't actually swipe it, then how did you contact Station Authority?"

"I'm getting to that." Bella reflexively tucked a lock of black hair behind her ear. "I wanted you to know what I told Commosky, in case he asks."

"He probably won't." Vince couldn't repress a smile. "He already assumed that you and I would be in collusion."

"With no proof?"

Vince waved a hand. "Just part of the long-standing trust between Finders and Station Authority Officers."

Bella cocked an eyebrow at the sarcasm dripping from that statement, but did not comment. Instead, she said, "It was all very logical, what I told Detective Commosky, and it's plausible." She shrugged. "He can't prove that I *didn't* escape that way—and Griffin can't exactly explain it either."

"He'd have to incriminate himself." Vince waved his hand again. "Either way, he's space dust." He nodded encouragingly for her to continue. "What *really* happened?"

"Well…" Bella shrugged again, a little bleakly. "I pretended to be unconscious. Griffin must have had people waiting, because it was only a couple of minutes before a couple of men joined him. They picked you up and Griffin picked me up and they carted us across the fake lobby to a transporter pod bay." She paused, her expression turning guilty. "I'm so sorry, Boss. They crammed you into this long cargo box and put you in the back of a pod and I couldn't—" she shook her head again. "I didn't know what to do."

"Bella." Vince set his mug down to lean toward her. "It's okay. Really. There wasn't anything else you could have done." He waited until she reluctantly met his eyes. "Besides, what you *did* accomplish was flat amazing." He shook his head in admiration. "You managed to escape. And then you contacted Station Authority and not only did you enable them to arrest Griffin, but you browbeat them into trying to find me."

Bella ducked her head shyly as Vince leaned forward.

"Those are incredible accomplishments, Miss Escovedo. By anyone's standards."

His assistant didn't look quite convinced, but she straightened up in her seat. "Thanks, Boss."

"So then what happened?"

"I figured they'd put us in the same transporter pod, but they didn't." Bella hunched her shoulders in distress. "They stuffed me into another pod, and by the time I realized what had happened, it was too late. We were already in motion."

Vince stared at her. "They just put you into a transport pod?" He waved a hand in her general direction. "As is? Out in the open?"

"Out in the open," Bella said grimly. "Like I'd just passed out from partying too hard and needed help getting home." Her guilt disappeared, to be replaced by stern anger. She tossed her head. "I guess they figured they could get me aboard a ship without needing to hide."

"That's…" Vince searched for the right word. Despicable? Terrifying? "…brazen."

"I know." It was Bella's turn to shake her head. "Anyway, I pretended to be unconscious for a while, and the guy they sent with me must have really thought I was down for the count, because he didn't pay much attention to me at all."

Vince gave Bella a smile that was gentle around the edges. "Never thought the fact that you don't do things like breathe anymore would come in handy, did you?"

This startled a laugh out of Bella. "No." Her gaze dropped briefly to her hands again as her expression turned somber. "No, I didn't." She shook her head, smiling, but her smile held a bittersweet tinge. "He didn't even check to see if I *was* breathing. None of them did." Her head snapped up, a little too fast. "I could have *died* from an allergic reaction to that tranquilizer dart and they wouldn't have even known. Well," she amended. "If I was still human, that is."

"Geniuses, they are not." Vince raised his mug in an ironic salute. He was still itching to know how she'd managed to get a hold of Station Authority, but it was her story and it was obvious there would be no rushing her.

"Anyway…" Bella shrugged, a little self-consciously. "I waited until the transport pod had to stop at an intersection and I—" she paused, then ducked her head. "I, ah, slugged the guy in the face. I *think* I broke his nose." She held up her right hand and closed it into a fist. "Turns out, I pack quite a punch. Who knew, right?"

Vince burst out laughing. "You slugged him?"

"Yep. Like I said, I think I broke his nose. He started bleeding and cussing and I tried to open the door so I could get out, but it was locked."

That made sense. Vince nodded. "Didn't want you escaping if you woke up suddenly."

"I guess." Bella shrugged. "I panicked a little, but—" she broke off, shaking her head. "I could still *think*. It's not the same as before." She looked at Vince, her eyes wide and clear.

Eyes that *looked* human, because of the human mind inside looking out.

"It's like my brain is still sending out panic signals, but this body doesn't react in quite the same way." Bella held out her hands and looked at them. "My panic subroutine isn't quite the same."

It was Vince's turn to shake his head. "And to think some people want to leave their bodies behind."

"They're crazy," Bella said flatly.

Vince cleared his throat; they'd gotten off-track. "What did you do?" He nodded to her. "When you discovered the doors were locked."

"Well…" Bella had the grace to look abashed. "Like I said, I panicked a little. And I was afraid the guy was going to hit me once he got over his nose. So…" she shrugged again, a trifle embarrassed. "I kicked him in the, ah, crown jewels."

Vince's eyebrows shot up, even as a part of him winced in sympathy. "That was…quick thinking."

"Well…it worked."

"I would imagine so."

Bella flicked a lock of hair over her shoulder. "That gave me enough time to access the navpanel and unlock the doors. I was afraid, for a second, that they'd have installed some fancy new tech that enables only certain people to unlock the doors, but they didn't."

Now *that* was a terrifying thought. Vince sucked in a breath and held it for a second, imagining. Bad enough that somebody could be kidnapped and locked in a transport pod, but a lock system that couldn't be opened even if you managed to overpower or outsmart your kidnapper?

"Anyway, I opened the doors and jumped." Bella cast a rueful glance down at herself. "Ripped the knees on my pants and skinned my knee, but…" she shrugged. "I made it out and called Station Authority."

Vince had noticed that. He wanted to ask if Bella had damaged her knee badly, but he also wanted to know the rest of the story. He set his mug down on his desk again and leaned forward. "How did you call Station Authority, if you didn't actually swipe someone's comlink?"

Bella went perfectly still. Statue still. She held that pose for twelve seconds (Vince counted), before she glanced away. "It's going to sound crazy, Boss."

Vince raised an eyebrow at her. "Any crazier than your story already does?"

She looked back at him, her own eyebrows knitting into a frown. "I…I… didn't realize it until recently, but it turns out I have a—" she hesitated, and then closed her eyes and forced herself to finish. "I have a comlink inside my head."

CHAPTER 58

A …COMLINK…INSIDE HER *HEAD*? VINCE STARED AT HER for a second, and then sat back in his chair. He let the comfortable material conform to his body while he digested this.

In the background, his airscrubber kicked on, disrupting the silence.

"Well?" Bella demanded, opening her eyes. She sounded half-impatient, half-nervous.

"Believe it or not, Bella, it's not the craziest thing I've ever heard." Vince quirked a small smile. "It's not even the craziest thing about you. In fact…" he nodded slowly, "makes a strange kind of sense. Dr. Frog and his crew *were* trying to create a body for people that allows them to 'transcend the normal human experience.'" He made sarcastic air quotes with his fingers. "Stands to reason they'd make a few tech upgrades in the process."

Bella practically wilted with relief, her shoulders slumping dramatically. "Okay. Great." She tilted her head to one side. "I'm sorry I didn't tell you about it earlier, but I wasn't sure how."

Vince gave her a stern look. "It's not that complicated." He waved a hand. "In the future, just tell me, 'Boss, I can do such and such.'"

"Okay."

Silence fell over them for a moment, and then interest sparked to life. Vince leaned forward, staring unabashedly at Bella's head. "How does it work?"

"I don't know exactly. I was thinking about calling you the other day and this…app…opened up in my vision." Bella waved to her face. "I actually tried calling you from that, but ended it before you answered." She made an apologetic face.

Vince vaguely recalled that incident. It wasn't unusual to get calls from unknown comm. frequencies of people who didn't leave messages. At the time, he hadn't thought anything of it.

He motioned for Bella to continue.

"Anyway, I called the Headquarters Precinct and eventually got a hold of Detective Commosky." Bella made a face. "I don't think whoever I spoke to at first actually *believed* me, but…" she shrugged modestly. "I said enough to get them to transfer me to him. Once that happened…" she spread her hands. "The rest was easy."

Vince was nodding, his brow creased in concentration. "Neither Griffin nor Commosky will ever be able to prove that you *didn't* call from a burner comlink."

Bella gave another modest shrug. "That's what I was thinking. Although…" she grimaced slightly, "It could be a problem if I ever have to call Station Authority again."

"Not really." Vince waved a hand. "Frequencies get reassigned all the time."

His assistant looked askance at him. "Yeah, but the odds of me getting the same exact frequency as a supposed burner comlink used by a human trafficking ring?"

"I see your point." It was Vince's turn to shrug. "Stranger things have happened, though." He frowned thoughtfully, reaching for his tea and taking a sip. It had cooled considerably. "If you can make comm calls from inside your head, however, I'd be willing to be you could run your calls through a proxy."

Bella was silent for a moment, digesting this. Then she tipped her head in a nod of acknowledgement. "I'll have to experiment."

Silence fell over them again, and then Bella straightened. Briskly, she said, "There isn't much more to tell after that. I told Commosky as much of the story as I dared and he sent men out after Griffin. And to find you." Her pretty mouth twisted into a grimace. "Just between you and me, Boss, I'm glad you escaped on your own. I don't think they'd have found you in time."

That same thought had been running through Vince's mind. He offered Bella a wry smile. "Ditto. I'm glad *you* escaped. If you hadn't…" he trailed off, unwilling to put his dark speculations as to where his assistant would be into actual words.

Instead, he cleared his throat and straightened in his chair. "What I mean to say is, I'm proud of you, Bella. You adapted in the face of a stressful, dangerous situation and you overcame it." He smiled at her. "You even got Station Authority to send out a rescue team for me."

"Well…" Bella shrugged. "I couldn't just let you disappear now. You're the best boss I've ever had." She waved a hand, indicating the office. "And I've just gotten the hang of this job."

"You can say that again." Vince raised his mug to her in a salute.

Bella beamed at him as he drained the last of his now-cold tea. She waited until he set the mug back down on his desk to ask, "What do you think will happen to the Saroyans?"

The Saroyans. The very thought of them left a bad taste in Vince's mouth. He shook his head, his mouth twisting into a frown again. "Depends."

"On what Griffin confesses?"

Vince nodded. "Commosky will have him for Dent Antwerp's murder. And I'm sure that will extend to framing Corwin. Commosky might even be able to use Nasard Mutual's visit to Mrs. Antwerp to poke around the Ruby Gauntlet further. But whether or not Station Authority can use this to stop the Saroyans from shipping people off-station?" He held his hands out. "That's an entirely different ball of ugly."

"Surely they'll stop." Bella leaned forward, her entire android body radiating righteous indignation. "Surely they'll see that if they keep going somebody's going to stop them." She dramatically smacked a hand into her fist. "*We'll* be there to stop them."

Vince had to press his lips into a thin line to keep from smiling at her enthusiasm. "We might be." When Bella just stared at him, he gave her a prosaic shrug. "We don't get paid unless somebody hires us, remember?"

"This could be a pro bono case." Bella shot from her chair and began to pace the confines of the office. "Boss, please tell me you're not going to just let these…" she waved a vague hand, as though searching for a word that was strong enough, "…*scumbags* get away with ruining people's lives like this, are you?"

"Bella—"

"Because you can't. *We* can't just let it go." Her eyes met his, those dark, almond-shaped mechanical eyes that Vince could *swear* were actually human. Bella waved both hands in the air this time. "We can't just let them be bought and sold like this without at least *trying*—"

"We're not."

"—to help. Wait. What?" Bella stared at him. "We're not? But you just said—"

"I said we *might* be." When Bella opened her mouth, the Finder held up a hand to forestall her. "Believe it or not, Bella, Station Authority as a whole *does* take a stand against things like this." He shook his head. "The Oswari Family may get away with a lot, but if something comes out in the open like this, there *are* good men and women inside Station Authority who do their best to bring the perpetrators to justice."

His eyes glinted as he held her gaze. "Regardless of whether or not Griffin confesses, enough was revealed today that people *will* be investigating."

"And if they don't?" Bella lifted her chin, a challenge written all over her heart-shaped face.

Vince paused, considering. This wasn't a promise he could make lightly. These weren't just careless words to pacify indignation at the injustice that had appeared, like somebody had shone a spotlight into a dark crevice of Zyga Space Station and illuminated a mass of filthy, writhing, crawling insects.

No, if he made Bella a promise—made *himself* a promise—his assistant would hold him to it until her internal power source finally gave out. Or the end of time.

Whichever came first.

"If they don't," he said slowly, "then you and I will make our own investigation."

"And we'll put an end to it," Bella said firmly. "If Station Authority fails."

Their gazes locked. Vince nodded solemnly. "Yes."

He felt the weight of that promise seep into the very molecules of clean air filling his office. It settled over him like a mantle—a promise made to the universe, it seemed.

There were many areas in which Vince didn't trust Station Authority one whit. Up until the past couple of days, this had been one of them. But now…now their reputation was on the line.

But if they failed…Vince nodded slowly to himself. If they failed, he and Bella would pick up where they left off.

He couldn't right most of the wrongs aboard Zyga Station. There were too many and he didn't have the authority to do much.

But this? His eyes narrowed in cold certainty. *This*, he could do.

If he had to.

CHAPTER 59

THE LOBBY OF ZONE 4'S STATION AUTHORITY Headquarters was surprisingly busy for nine AM in the morning. A constant stream of people moved back and forth across the pale marble floor, lit by the golden sunlight being piped from the globe-like chandelier in the ceiling. Vince and Bella sat on a beige couch in the waiting area off to one side of the lobby with Mrs. Antwerp, who clutched her gold-fringed shawl around her thin shoulders with the air of a woman who almost couldn't believe what was about to happen.

Vince didn't blame her. The past two days felt surreal for *him*; he could only imagine how Mrs. Antwerp felt. He glanced at Bella, who was looking around with keen interest, and then looked back at Mrs. Antwerp.

He still didn't know if she was officially a grandmother or not yet.

Vince had been hoping to hear from Detective Commosky before now, but he knew it was a slim hope. It would be a while longer before they had results. Also, in his professional opinion as someone who dealt in the results of human behavior, he'd calculated that the odds of Mrs. Antwerp not wanting her grandchild were extremely slim. Almost certainly, she'd take the child.

But…there *was* that tiny percentage that he was wrong.

Either way, there was no need to get anybody's hopes up prematurely. Vince shifted slightly in his seat, which was surprisingly comfortable for a couch in a Station Authority precinct. There would be plenty of time for celebration later once Commosky got him results.

"They're running late," Bella said after a moment. She kept her voice low against the faint chatter of conversations and bustle filling the lobby."

"It's like going to the doctor." Vince snorted slightly. "You show up when they tell you to and then you wait."

Mrs. Antwerp made a soft hum of agreement. Her worn face held less anxiety today than it had the day before, but her fingers still twisted nervously in her lap. She wouldn't believe Corwin was really in the clear until she saw him with her own two eyes.

Vince didn't blame her for that.

He spent the next few minutes watching the goings and comings in the lobby, but his attention darted to the elevator every time the doors opened. After nearly ten minutes of this, he finally spotted a familiar figure.

His eyebrows rose in surprise. Make that *two* familiar figures. Detective Commosky was personally escorting Corwin out.

Before Vince could say anything to let the others know, Mrs. Antwerp caught sight of her son. She was on her feet in an instant and heading across the marbled lobby floor as though drawn to her son by a tractor beam.

"Momma!" Corwin broke away from Commosky to meet his mother halfway. Mrs. Antwerp flung her arms around her son as Corwin hugged her back, practically picking her up off the floor. The young man still looked exhausted and grieved, but not hopeless.

"Oh, Corwin." Mrs. Antwerp framed her son's face in both her hands before looking him over as though she expected to find him covered in wounds. "Are you all right? You're not hurt, are you?"

"No, Momma, I'm fine." Corwin placed his hands over the top of his mother's. "I should be asking *you* that." He looked from her to Vince, who had followed Mrs. Antwerp at a more leisurely pace with Bella. "Did anybody come—"

His mother interrupted him. "Everything will be all right." Her lips quivered, and then she braved a smile. "Finder Grable and Station Authority are helping us work it all out."

Vince nodded to Commosky. "Detective. Thank you."

"Least we could do." One corner of Commosky's mouth curled upward in a wry smile. He watched the Antwerps for a few seconds before turning to Vince. "About that request you had…"

Vince lifted a questioning eyebrow, but inside he went very still.

"The answer is yes." Commosky held his gaze, before giving a firm nod. There was a light in his swarthy face that hadn't been there earlier. "They're a match."

The Finder let out a slow breath, before inclining his head. "Thank you."

Commosky nodded in acknowledgement and then turned to rest a hand on Corwin's shoulder. "Sorry to interrupt," he said, "but I just want to remind Corwin here not to leave Zyga Space Station for any reason. We'll need your testimony."

"I understand." Corwin nodded, his expression filled with dazed relief.

"And, Mrs. Antwerp?" Commosky addressed the slight woman. "We will be in touch regarding this Nasard Mutual business." He held one hand out palm-up. "It's an ongoing investigation, and it may be some time before we get it all wrapped up. But we will." He nodded once for emphasis.

"Thank you, Detective." Mrs. Antwerp offered him a thin, but grateful smile.

With one more slightly awkward nod, Commosky departed.

Vince watched the short, broad-shouldered detective stride back to the elevator with the air of a man escaping a rather uncomfortable situation. He glanced at Bella, who smiled. She'd been watching the Antwerps' reunion with satisfaction.

Vince let Corwin and his mother talk for another few minutes, but when they showed no signs of slowing down, he intervened. Stepping over to them, he gained their attention and jerked a thumb over his shoulder in the direction of the door. "What do you say we get out of here?"

Corwin and Mrs. Antwerp exchanged glances and then they both followed Vince and Bella across the pale marble floor. As they passed through the double doors and made their way down the marble steps to the broad boulevard that ran in front of the Headquarters Precinct, Corwin glanced up at the starry expanse of space visible through the synthglass ceiling stretching above the entire length of Level 1.

"I was afraid I'd never see this again." Corwin shuddered, and his mother wrapped her arm around his waist and hugged him.

After a second, he disentangled himself and turned to Vince. He extended a hand, his dark eyes shining with gratitude. "Finder Grable. I—" he shook his head. "I don't know what to say, other than thank you." He took a breath and blew it out, but couldn't seem to find any other words.

"You're welcome." Vince waved his thanks away. He glanced from Corwin to his mother and back. "We do need to talk."

"Yes. Yes, of course." Corwin nodded eagerly. "I can't wait to hear this story." He froze, as though he'd been struck by a bolt of electricity. "Mr. Pho! I need to call him. And my classes!" His hand flew to his forehead. "Oh, stars. They're all going to think I'm a—"

"No," Mrs. Antwerp said firmly, tightening her grip on his arm. "They are not. Your name is clear." She looked at Vince as she said this.

The Finder nodded. "About as clear as it can be, at the moment. They have another suspect in custody, and they've released Corwin, obviously."

"Good." Mrs. Antwerp released a breath. "Good." She nodded once, rather decisively, and then looked at Vince and Bella. "We'll go to our apartment." Her face split in a relieved smile. "Have some tea yes?"

Vince found himself smiling back at her. "That sounds wonderful."

CHAPTER 60

Half an hour later, Vince took a sip of his now-cool tea to wet his throat. He, Bella, and the Antwerps sat crowded around the small dark brown table in their tiny kitchen with its pearl-gray bulkheads and green vines pattern curling around near the overhead. Mrs. Antwerp had insisted that Vince hold off on his story until they were all properly fortified, which gave her a chance to fuss over her son.

Bella accepted a cup of water, saying she wasn't much of a tea or coffee drinker, but she only touched it occasionally. Not that either Corwin or his mother noticed. They were too caught up in the whiplash of the past two days' events.

Vince laid out most of the story, but he brought Corwin and his mother in to describe their parts where needed. Bella also made periodic interjections. When he heard about the incident with the man who had accosted his mother and her friend, Corwin's dark face grew bloodless. Mrs. Antwerp squeezed his hand in silent comfort.

When Vince reached the part of the story regarding Dent's attempt to track down Mariella, he inwardly tensed. This was the hard part. Predictably, by the end of the story, both Corwin and his mother looked confused.

"But, why? Why would he risk it?" Mrs. Antwerp shook her head, sitting back in her chair and spreading her hands. "Was he in love with this girl?" She glanced at Corwin, her dark eyebrows drawn into a frown. "He never showed much interest in women before. Always too busy with his games."

"He loved her." Bella leaned forward to rest her elbows on the table. Her voice was gentle as she looked across the table at Mrs. Antwerp. "He might not have been very good about showing it, but he loved her." She glanced from Mrs. Antwerp to her son. "Just like he loved you."

Bright tears flooded Mrs. Antwerp's eyes; she looked down into her cup of tea to hide them.

For his part, Corwin clenched his jaw, as though the words had hurt him. Vince could understand that. Truth often was painful.

Speaking of which… Vince took a deep breath and straightened in his chair. "You've heard the whole story now." He looked from Corwin to his mother. "Except for one part."

They both tensed, somehow managed to look both wide-eyed and wary.

Vince took another breath, giving himself a precious few seconds to gather the right words. "Mariella," he said carefully, "left behind a baby girl when she disappeared. This group down in the Core has been taking care of her, but if she has any family left, they'd like for her to go to them." He paused. "To you."

Corwin was the first to realize what this meant; his eyes widened in an expression of dawning realization.

"Dent was her father." Vince held up a hand to forestall comment from Corwin as the younger man opened his mouth. His eyes bored into Corwin, willing him to be patient and listen. "I gave a sample of her hair to Detective Commosky and he confirmed she's a genetic match to your brother." He smiled wryly. "I don't believe he has any reason to lie to me about it."

Mrs. Antwerp swallowed heavily, one hand flattening over her chest. "I have a—a granddaughter?"

"You do." Vince's smile widened. "She's beautiful. Needs a little more to eat, but they're doing the best they can to keep her fed."

Mrs. Antwerp's black eyes filled with a mix of disbelief, grief, and longing, but Corwin didn't look convinced. "And this…" he waved a hand, "Purple Octopus group is just going to give her up?" He snapped his fingers. "Just like that?"

"They want her to have her family," Bella said gently. "They know about you. Dent told them."

"And then there's my reputation." Vince raised his mug in a half-salute. "They might live in the Core, but that doesn't mean they can't do a little investigation of their own."

Mrs. Antwerp looked at Corwin, reaching out a hand to place it over his, which he'd balled into a fist on the table. "Your brother has a child."

"And of course he's gone and left her all alone too." Raw grief threaded every word. Corwin bowed his head, but he opened his hand beneath his mother's and curled his fingers around her smaller digits.

Vince and Bella traded glances. "It sounds like he was trying," Vince said. "He was trying to be different, for Mariella, and for their daughter. He just…" He trailed off, shrugging wordlessly.

Couldn't change soon enough to make a difference for Mariella.

Couldn't win against the Saroyans and their hired muscle. He'd tried, though. He'd tried.

Silence fell over the kitchen.

It was broken by an incredulous, happy, tinkling laugh. "I have a granddaughter," Mrs. Antwerp said, her voice full of dazed wonder. She sat back in her chair, shaking her head in amazement. "How—how old is she?"

"Couple of months."

Corwin shook his head too. "Can't believe she's still—you know." He made a vague gesture with one hand. "I wouldn't have thought an abandoned baby would survive in the Core."

"Some don't. A lot of bad things happen in the Core." A muscle in Vince's jaw twitched as a few memories welled up in his mind. Memories he'd tried to forget. He stuffed them back into a dark corner of his mind. "But Mariella was part of this Purple Octopus group, and they were trying to take better care of each other. Make a difference in a place where nobody else cares."

Across the table, Mrs. Antwerp hazarded a darting glance at her son and then looked down at her half-drunk mug of tea, biting her lip. Her expression went distant, and Vince knew she was waging an internal debate.

It wasn't much of a debate.

A second later, the older woman looked up, her expression one of fierce determination. "They want us to have her? My granddaughter?"

Vince exchanged a glance with Bella, who was trying to suppress a giddy smile. "Yes," he said, looking back at Mrs. Antwerp. "They would like you to take her and raise her…love her." He shrugged. "Family is important to them. Mostly because they don't have any."

"Momma…" Corwin began, but his mother held up a hand.

"Don't you dare tell me this isn't the right thing to do." Her voice was gentle, but firm.

"I'm not! I wouldn't—" Corwin held up both hands. "That's not what I—" he broke off, swallowed, and tried again. "All I was gonna say is that if we don't have enough money to go through all the red tape, I'll pick up extra shifts at Mr. Pho's. Or I'll get another job someplace else."

"You are *not* dropping out of school to do all this." His mother leveled him with a fierce look.

"I won't, I just…" Corwin shrugged, a little helplessly. "I know these things take money, and we don't have much." He squared his shoulders. "Dent might have put us through hell, but that little girl didn't do anything wrong. If she's his daughter, that makes her my niece, and I can't live my life knowing we just left her down there." He waved a hand through the air in the general direction of the Core.

Vince felt something warm in his chest. He'd run into some folks in his time aboard Zyga Space Station who would have taken one look at this situation and said tough luck, it wasn't their mess to take care of. "That's admirable of you."

"It's the right thing to do," Mrs. Antwerp said softly, her eyes shining as she looked at her son. "And I'm proud of you, Corwin." She sniffed and dabbed at her eyes. "So proud of you."

Bella leaned forward. "It won't be as expensive as you think." She smiled encouragingly. "The Purple Octopuses don't have any official affiliation with any of Zyga Station's authorities, so…" she shrugged. "There's not much of a paper trail on this child."

"Oh, stars." Corwin sank back in his chair, rubbing a hand over his face. "I didn't even think of that." Dropping his hand, he looked at his mother. "No paperwork. That means no birth certificate, no citizen ID, nothing."

Mrs. Antwerp's eyes widened in realization, but then she lifted her chin. "We will manage. She has come to us for a reason." She turned one hand palm up. "Everything will work out."

"I know some people who can help." Vince offered Corwin a reassuring nod. "This isn't as uncommon as you might think."

"And then there's your fee to consider." Corwin met Vince's gaze. He was still slightly bleary-eyed from fatigue, but the mind looking out from those eyes was sharp. "It might take me a while, but I'll pay it."

Vince held up a hand. "That won't be as much as you're expecting either."

"I don't want chari—" Corwin began, but Vince cut him off. "Don't worry. It's not."

Corwin subsided, and in the sudden silence that fell over the kitchen again, Mrs. Antwerp pushed her chair back and rose to her feet. "When can we go get my granddaughter?"

A slow smile spread across Vince's face. His feeling that she might react like this was justified. The maternal instincts in this woman were strong.

He reached into the breast pocket of his brown leather jacket for his comlink. A new comlink, since the odds were mighty slim that he'd ever get back the one Griffin had confiscated at the Saroyans' behest. "Let me make a call."

CHAPTER 61

VINCE HAD TO HAND IT TO THE Purple Octopuses—for being a ghost group hidden away in the depths of the Core, they had responded quickly to his request to meet. Yes, they would turn the little girl over to Mrs. Antwerp. No, they wouldn't leave the lower levels of the Core. Yes, they would meet Vince partway.

Partway turned out to be Level 16-A.

Vince could live with that. Mrs. Antwerp and Corwin would be relatively safe there. They wouldn't stick out too much. Any farther down, however, and it would be blindingly obvious that they did not belong in that part of the Core.

He expected Corwin and his mother to blanch a little and they did—Level 16-A was farther down in the Core than either one of them had ever been before. But, they were determined to help retrieve Dent's daughter.

Determination, Vince had learned over the years, counted for a lot more than most people realized.

Now, four hours later, the Finder, the Antwerps, and Bella stood in a dingy elevator headed down to Level 16-A. Vince glanced sideways at his assistant, who looked calm and professional. Bella had insisted on coming along, asserting that she didn't want to miss such a momentous occasion as a little girl being united with her family. She'd never been down this far into the Core either, but the only sign she was nervous was the way her gaze kept darting around the inside of the elevator cab, as though expecting some danger to pop out of nowhere.

As the elevator doors creaked open on Level 16-A, Mrs. Antwerp drew closer to her son. They were already arm-in-arm; she tightened her grip. For his part, Corwin angled himself to keep his body between his mother and the elevator doors.

Vince braced himself for the smell that always hit him down here—unwashed bodies with that ever-present metallic tinge that permeated the entire space station—and stepped forward. A few worn-looking people in worn clothing in shades of dingy brown, gray, and green stood huddled to one side of the elevator, as though attempting to make themselves invisible while they waited for an elevator cab.

The Finder didn't recognize a one of them. Not the Purple Octopuses.

The rest of the corridor leading deeper into Level 16-A was empty and dimly lit. More than half of the glowpanels in the overhead were dark.

Corwin moved out of the elevator cab behind Vince, drawing his mother along. He shook his head. "Doesn't look like Maintenance has been down here in a while."

His mother only looked around with wide eyes.

"It's sad, really," Bella said in a quiet voice. She brought up the rear with light footsteps.

Vince led the way down the corridor, which was lined with closed hatches, just like every other Level in the Core's lower regions. The metal deck was grimy, but still relatively trash free.

Corwin pitched his voice lower. "Doesn't anybody care what happens down here? If things are broken this far down, won't that eventually have an effect on the rest of the Core?" He glanced all the way around them. "And eventually the rest of Zyga Space Station itself?"

"You'd think so," said a new voice from a hatch that had just opened a few meters down the corridor. "But nobody in charge seems to be thinking long-term these days."

Zaslo appeared in the hatchway, casually resting a bare muscled arm against the hatchframe. The expression on his dark face, however, was anything but casual as he watched Vince and the others approach. He scrutinized Corwin and Mrs. Antwerp, unmoving.

Vince wondered exactly what the head of the Purple Octopuses was looking for (although he was impressed the young man had come up here himself), but he didn't ask any questions. Finders liked questions—questions were the bread and butter of their business, after all—but there were times no questions should be asked.

This was one of those occasions.

Zaslo would say what was on his mind, or he wouldn't. Either way, there was no point in irritating him. Vince wanted the transfer of the little girl to go as smoothly as possible.

Just as he and the others came level with the hatch, Zaslo pushed off the hatchframe and straightened. "You're related to Dent, that's for sure." He shook his head, making ends of his dreadlocks dance. "No mistaking the family resemblance."

"Did you think we wouldn't bring Dent's family?" Bella asked, her eyes on Zaslo.

Vince glanced sharply at her, but his assistant's voice was full of genuine curiosity.

Zaslo eyed her, before his gaze transferred to Vince. He jerked his chin toward Bella, almost accusatorially "Who's this?"

"My assistant." Vince eyed Bella as well, who just shrugged. "Insisted on coming to help."

"Harder to hide a big group." Zaslo made a sound in the back of his throat, but he turned and disappeared through the hatch. "Get in here."

Vince motioned for Bella to go first, followed by the Antwerps. He brought up the rear. As soon as he'd cleared the hatch, someone shut it behind him. A glance sideways told him it was Tank. He nodded in recognition, but the taller man just gave him a hard look.

One quick glance around told Vince all he needed to know about their surroundings. They were in a small, dingy living compartment much like the one in which he'd first met the Purple Octopuses. A few beat-up pieces of furniture had been pushed up against the dingy white bulkheads: a couch, two ratty-looking recliners in brown and gray, and a couple of small jade green plastic end tables that reminded Vince of his own furniture. A tiny kitchenette stood in one corner, and in the other corner, a short hall led off to one side, lined with closed doors.

Zuzu stood in the shadows of this hall, cradling a tiny bundle wrapped in a worn blanket. Her copper cheek was pressed to the top of the baby's curly dark head, her brown eyes wary. She'd traded her green sweater for an equally faded purple sweater.

Mrs. Antwerp spotted them both immediately. Her eyes widened as she looked at the baby. She crossed the battered gray rug to the pair as though drawn by a tractor beam, but stopped half a meter away.

Her gaze darted from the baby to Zuzu, and then she held out her arms. "May I?"

Zuzu glanced at Zaslo, as though to confirm this was indeed the plan. The leader of the Purple Octopuses gave her a wordless nod and Zuzu carefully transferred the baby into Mrs. Antwerp's arms.

Dent's mother looked down at his child—her granddaughter—and the baby looked back up at her with wide, dark eyes. She was wary, but not frightened.

An expression of such hope and love blossomed on Mrs. Antwerp's face that Vince had to clear his throat and look away. His gaze met Zaslo's, and something passed between the two men. An acknowledgment of sorts, for promises fulfilled.

Zaslo looked away and Vince glanced at Bella, who was watching grandmother and granddaughter, her hands clasped to her chest and a wide, happy smile stretching her face. If she'd still been capable of producing tears, he was sure they would have been dripping down her cheeks.

Zuzu hovered at Mrs. Antwerp's elbow, seemingly torn between relief that the Purple Octopuses now had one less tiny mouth to feed and concern about letting the baby go.

Mrs. Antwerp cradled the baby in one arm and gently stroked her downy cheek with her free hand before running her fingers through the baby's dark curls. "Beautiful," she murmured softly. "You are such a beautiful little one."

The baby curled her tiny hand around her grandmother's finger, looking up at her with wide eyes.

"And so strong." Mrs. Antwerp's gentle smile filled with maternal pride. "You've survived, even though your momma—" Her breath hitched in her throat; she only smiled sadly and shook her head.

"We'll take good care of her." Corwin's voice broke the sudden silence. He was watching Zuzu watch his mother and the baby. When Zuzu's startled gaze snapped to his, he smiled encouragingly. "Don't worry."

Zuzu lifted a challenging eyebrow, as if to say she wasn't worried, but she otherwise made no reply.

Zaslo turned back to Vince, bare arms still crossed over his purple vest. "Not that it matters," he said, in a tone that implied it wasn't his problem anymore, "but you got ID for her?"

"Yes." Vince nodded to Mrs. Antwerp. "We'll take her to the Hospital Wing and have her checked over, and then they'll fill out the remaining paperwork."

Zaslo merely nodded in response, but the keen flash of interest in his dark eyes told Vince the leader of the Purple Octopuses wasn't as disinterested as he tried to appear. The Finder filed that away for future reference and approached Mrs. Antwerp.

"We need to go now." He kept his voice soft and low, so as not to frighten the baby. Although, to be honest, given where she lived, that might not even be a concern.

Mrs. Antwerp nodded and turned to Zuzu. "Does she have anything else? Maybe a favorite toy?"

In answer, Zuzu leaned over and reached into the baby's blankets to extract what looked like a bracelet made of colorful chunky plastic beads. "This." She placed it in the baby's hands and stepped back, biting her lip. "It was her mother's."

"I see." Mrs. Antwerp's face filled with compassion again as she looked down at the baby. That gentle, beautiful smile flooded her face again. "It's a gift from your momma, baby girl. A pretty bracelet to chew on."

The baby cooed in response, waving her tiny dark arms.

Mrs. Antwerp bit her lip before she asked her next question. She looked at Zuzu, an apology in her dark eyes. "I know this is probably a stupid question, but does she have a preference for a certain formula or anything?"

Vince expected bitterness from the younger woman, but her answering smile was surprisingly sunny. It was like a flash of bright, cheerful light in an otherwise dim corridor.

"The baby? Have a preference?" Zuzu shook her head, still smiling. "She's not picky. She's a sweet little thing. She always drinks whatever we can get for her." She stretched out a hand and passed it over the top of the baby's curly head.

"Okay." Mrs. Antwerp nodded, a little relieved. She turned toward Vince, cradling the baby as though she was the most precious thing on Zyga Space Station.

She might be right, at that, Vince thought suddenly. He couldn't say he'd ever had a burning desire to have children of his own—and there were days in his line of work when he doubted he'd live long enough—but even he knew children were the future of any society.

There was something poetic about literally holding the future in your hands.

Vince resisted the urge to shake his head at himself. *Get a grip, Finder. Don't go all smooshy now.* That was best left to those moments when he was in his office by himself, trying to remind himself why he did what he did

"Thank you," Mrs. Antwerp said, turning to regard Zaslo, Zuzu, and Tank one last time as she and the others reached the door.

"Take care of her," Zuzu said, a warning in her voice.

"They will." Zaslo's calm assurance was unexpected. He inclined his head toward Corwin. "Dent had his problems, but he always talked about how much he loved his little brother. He was proud of you."

Corwin's stoic expression wavered; for a second, it looked like he might cry. But in the end, he only nodded jerkily in response.

Tank opened the door, and Vince was the first to exit. He wasn't about to take any chances down here, even if he was *mostly* sure everything would be fine. Corwin exited behind him, silently stepping aside in the corridor to make room for his mother. Bella brought up the rear. She bestowed a solemn smile on the Purple Octopuses, and then the hatch slid shut, leaving them alone in the corridor.

Vince gestured down the corridor, which was still empty. "Back to the elevator."

CHAPTER 62

THE SMELL DRIFTING DOWN THE BOULEVARD CORRIDOR sidewalk from Pho's Noodle Shop was incredible. Garlic, soy sauce, and half a dozen other scents that all blended together into one fantastic aroma. Vince quickened his pace, his stomach growling loud enough that he wondered if the tiny woman who brushed past him going the other way had heard it. This was becoming a habit.

Pushing open the door, he stepped into the noodle shop's foyer and blinked as his eyes adjusted to the dim light. Beyond the hostess—a different young lady today—he saw that the restaurant's shiny black lacquered tables were only sparsely populated. He was in that odd spot in the middle of the afternoon—too late to be considered lunch, but too early for the dinner rush.

But, oh, he was hungry. Breakfast had been a small, rushed affair before he departed his apartment to make the trek to Zone 4 so he could assist Mrs. Antwerp with collecting Corwin from the Level 1 Precinct, and in the midst of explaining things and arranging for the Antwerps to get Dent's daughter, thoughts of food had been far from his mind.

That was not the case now.

One corner of the Finder's mouth lifted in a smile. The Antwerp case was finished, so now he'd moved on to less pressing things.

He and Bella had escorted the Antwerps to Zone 4's Hospital Wing, where they'd presented the results of the paternity test Vince had asked Commosky to run along with the paperwork Vince had gotten that granted the Mrs. Antwerp temporary emergency custody of her granddaughter. There were a few more hoops she would have to jump through before she could get permanent custody, but Vince was confident it wouldn't be a problem.

He'd told Mrs. Antwerp to call him if she ran into any snags. He knew people. Plus, Dent's murder case was shaping up to be if not high-profile, then at least medium-profile. That might help grease the legal wheels to turn a little faster.

Not that Zyga Space Station's legal departments wouldn't take Mrs. Antwerp seriously, but they sometimes moved much slower than it seemed logical that they should.

"One?" the hostess asked with a smile. She was tall and slender, with a cheerful face and dark hair tied up in two ponytails on either side of her head.

"Yes."

"Table or booth?"

"Booth."

"Follow me, please."

Vince fell into step behind the hostess as she threaded her way through the maze of tables. She stopped at a booth not far from the one he'd occupied the day Corwin slid into the other side of his booth. After taking his drink order and his food order (Vince hadn't needed to look at the menu; he was splurging again), she disappeared into the dim shadows between tables.

Vince settled into the slick purple seat, stretching his feet out beneath the table. His stomach growled loudly again. Part of him wished Bella had come with him; it would have been nice to have a little company on an occasion where they *weren't* in danger of getting kidnapped.

He smiled slightly at the thought. On the other hand, he'd had a hard enough time convincing Bella to actually go home after everything that had happened. It was probably for the best.

Especially since she couldn't really eat anything anyway.

Vince leaned his head back against the back of the booth, a sudden wave of weariness settling over his body. Besides, if he was honest with himself, he could use a little time to himself.

A dark figure emerged from the shadows between the tables. Vince had a split-second's warning before Mr. Pho himself slid into the seat across the table from him.

"Finder Grable." Mr. Pho inclined his head in a solemn nod, the light from the round golden lamp hanging above the table glinting off the silver in his black hair.

"Mr. Pho."

"It is good to see you this side of the Great Divide, Finder." Mr. Pho's wrinkled cheeks folded in a genuine smile as he motioned across the black lacquered table at Vince. "At this rate, you'll be one of my best regulars."

This drew a low laugh from Vince. "I wish." He shook his head slightly. "I'm merely taking advantage of still being in Zone 4."

"You enjoy your dinner yesterday?"

Vince didn't have the heart to tell Mr. Pho that he hadn't actually gotten to eat any of the food he'd ordered the day before. Instead, he merely smiled slightly and inclined his head in a gracious nod. "I wish I lived closer."

"You could always move here." A sly smile spread across Mr. Pho's face, the kind of smile that said he knew he was being funny.

"I could." Vince paused a moment to consider that. His office *had* occupied its current location for the better part of a decade, but his clients were from all over the space station and the bulk of them found him via referrals from friends or a ComNet search.

Moving was…not outside the realm of possibility.

He tucked that thought away for future reference and smiled. "I'd have to switch to a less expensive dish, though."

Mr. Pho just laughed.

Vince's waitress arrived with his tea just then, and the Finder gave her a nod of thanks as she set a small teapot in the center of the table before adding a teacup and saucer. "Your food will be out shortly," she said, though her gaze flicked to her boss's figure occupying the other side of the booth.

"Thank you."

Mr. Pho waited until the waitress had gone and Vince had poured himself a cup of green tea. Only once Vince had inhaled the steamy light fragrance wafting up from the cup and taken his first tentative sip did the noodle shop owner speak. "I wanted to thank you for helping Corwin."

"You're welcome."

"And…" the older man hesitated. "I also wanted to assure you that I had nothing to do with—with the events that transpired after you left my restaurant yesterday." He met Vince's gaze across the table, his eyes wide and earnest. "I have seen the news reports. I understood what many do not."

"Never believed you were involved." Vince took another tentative sip of his hot tea before he smiled at Mr. Pho over the rim of the teacup. "I'm becoming one of your best regulars, after all."

The sudden tension that had seeped into the darkness around the table to throw an invisible net over them suddenly diffused as though the lamp above the table had just gotten brighter. Mr. Pho visibly lightened. A few of the lines faded from his face and his shoulders straightened.

"No, no," he said, a hint of relieved laughter in his voice. "A good restaurateur never jeopardizes his regulars."

"They've been watching your place for a while." Vince set his teacup back down, barely clinking it against the saucer. "Just in case anyone was able to trace Dent Antwerp back to them."

A shadow fell over Mr. Pho's face again. "It is a terrible thing." He dropped his gaze to the lacquered surface of the table. "I am grateful my shop has mostly kept out of the news." He tried for a smile, but didn't quite manage it. "I am not sure how well the old adage about no publicity being bad publicity holds up when it comes to things like murder."

He spread his hands. "Many of my customers are like family. How can I risk a temporary swell of curious new customers if my regulars no longer feel safe here?"

Vince nodded sympathetically. "That's tough." A thought struck him; he raised an eyebrow at Mr. Pho. "*Have* you had new customers as a result of this? It's barely been three days."

"Too early to tell." Mr. Pho lifted one shoulder in a noncommittal shrug. "A few. And thankfully none of my regulars seem to have stopped coming."

"That's good."

Mr. Pho only harrumphed.

Vince started to say something else, but at that moment, his waitress materialized out of the darkness between the rows of tables carrying a laden tray. She set his food down with quick, gracious movements, gave him a little half-bow, and disappeared as silently as she had come.

Mr. Pho made to get up. "I will leave you to your meal now, Finder."

"Mr. Pho."

The noodle shop owner stopped, looking at Vince across the table.

Vince met his gaze across the table and held it. "If you know more about Saroyan Imports and their side business, now is the time to share it."

CHAPTER 63

Vince leaned forward a little, his expression turning earnest as Mr. Pho drew in a breath and shook his head. "I mean it. The court might not be able to charge the Saroyans yet, but they'll take Griffin down. And I know for a fact that Station Authority has opened an investigation into them."

He could see from the way the older man's face closed off that his words fell on deaf ears. Despite that, Mr. Pho gave him a surprisingly gentle smile tinged with a hopelessness that made something in the Finder's chest hurt.

"It is not the first time Station Authority has investigated things like this." Mr. Pho shook his head once, gravely. "It will not be the last. They will investigate, and in the end they will do nothing."

He shrugged prosaically and slid out of the booth. "Just like always."

The ache in Vince's chest grew worse. Steam wafted up enticingly from the food on his plate, but he ignored it, his attention fixed on the noodle shop owner.

"Things can change, Mr. Pho. Just because nothing has happened up to this point doesn't mean there's no hope."

The older man stared at him for a handful of seconds, before he shook his head. "The Families—" He cut himself off, his gaze darting fearfully around the dimly-lit interior of his restaurant. Dropping his voice to a harsh whisper, he said, "The Families have too strong a hold. You and me?" He shrugged helplessly. "What can we do except stay out of their way?"

Vince stared at the noodle shop owner. It was as if the golden lamplight had pushed back a few layers, shining through to the man within. He could almost see the defeat and hopelessness practically etched into Mr. Pho's wrinkled skin.

No.

Something deep inside him raised its head. *No.* Fierce certainty sprang to life, forming a resolute bulwark inside him.

The future of Zyga Space Station and its citizens was not etched in stone.

"No," Vince said aloud. "That's exactly what they want us to think. That we can't change anything."

He had a second to take in Mr. Pho's startled expression before he shook his head, spreading his hands. "They want us to think that we're powerless. But we're not." He continued to shake his head. "Not if enough of us stand up. Not if we shine a light into the dark crevices where they've been hiding all these years."

Mr. Pho stood frozen, but a spark of interest had kindled in his dark eyes.

"The Families are just made up of people. Ordinary, fallible people." Vince smiled wryly. "They've got a lot of money and power, sure, but they're still people. Nobody's above the law forever." He gestured to their surroundings. "It doesn't have to be this way forever."

Mr. Pho stood frozen, as though contemplating what that looked like. Then a sudden bark of laughter from the other side of the dim restaurant snapped him back to himself. He drew in a long, slightly shaky breath. "You paint a picture of a world I would like to inhabit, Finder."

It was his turn to shake his head. "I think you will find it is a difficult battle getting there."

Vince's smile grew warmer. "Aren't all the important things in life?"

Mr. Pho inclined his head in silent acknowledgment of this. "I wish you the best of luck, Finder." He paused. "We both know you will need it." He gestured courteously to Vince's food. "Thank you for your time. Please enjoy your meal."

As the restaurant owner disappeared into the shadows, Vince turned his attention to his food. It was perhaps a little colder than he would have preferred, but the conversation they'd just had was worth it.

Fighting corruption on Zyga Station wouldn't happen overnight. It might not even happen in the next couple of years. But…

Vince thoughtfully chewed a delicious bite of beef and expertly sautéed onion. They had to start somewhere.

And it had to start with someone.

He smiled grimly. Lucky for him, he already had a head start in this department.

Anyway, wasn't that part of his job? Helping people ultimately Find better tomorrows?

If he could find the root of Zyga Space Station's problems and help root it out, life would be better for everyone. He could do that. Bella would help him, and he could rely on Brill for information when needed.

And there *were* good men and women in Station Authority. Sergeant Rychek and Detective Commosky, just to name a few. He wasn't completely alone in this fight.

Vince's smile widened; he raised his teacup in a silent toast to the universe. They could change Zyga Space Station. One case at a time.

For now, that would be enough.

ACKNOWLEDGMENTS

Writing may be a solitary endeavor, but it doesn't happen in a vacuum. I am so blessed to have family and friends to cheer me on.

For my husband, Tim. Thanks so much for always encouraging me to keep pursuing the dreams and talents the Lord has given me. Thanks for putting up with a wife who regularly writes down what the voices in her head say. ::grin::

For my children—thanks for keeping things to a (mostly) dull roar.

For my mom and siblings—thanks for your encouragement and support.

A big thanks to Connie Trapp, for being a fantastic beta reader. Your insight over the years is much appreciated.

Thank you also to Kim Burns and Heather Stearns for being excited readers, great friends, and great listening ears when I need to talk about writing.

A very special thank you to all of the people who supported the Kickstarter I ran for *Overload*. Thank you, Tim Leary, Susannah Figueroa, Kimberly Burns, Daniel Bailey, Matthew Wollmann, Susan Jones, Julia A. Paskey, Dean Wesley Smith, T.F. Torrey,

Wayne Kramer, Cathy Smith, Rob Vagle, D.M. Pruden, Pauline Baird Jones, Johanna Rothman, and James Palmer.

Y'all are amazing and I am so grateful.

Thanks also to Lori Christie, Sarah Reschar, Chelsea Stevens, Hannah Hatton, Sarah Gharib, Emily Bare, Kristie Sullivan, Felicia Bridge, Meta Clark, and many, many others for your encouragement and support.

Coming soon!

Finder Book 5

BLOWBACK

THE LIGHTS DIED IN FINDER VINCE GRABLE'S small office right in the middle of a conversation he was having with an increasingly hysterical middle-aged woman about a missing family heirloom. Conversations like this weren't unusual. Vince's job was to find missing people and things and he was pretty good at it.

The power cutting out on Zyga Space Station, on the other hand? *That* was unusual.

Seated in his comfortable desk chair behind his jade green desk, Vince froze, wide-eyed, in the sudden blackness. His personal office airscrubber died mid-cycle, leaving an awful silence in its wake.

His client, Mrs. Kawana, cut herself off mid-sentence.

At her desk two meters away, Vince's dark-haired assistant Bella Escovedo also froze, but unlike Vince, Bella could see in the dark. Being a human mind stuck in an android body had its upsides.

For one heart-stopping moment, Vince felt gravity lose its hold on him. He was weightless; his slightly stocky, average-height body no longer confined to his chair. He swallowed. The sound seemed too loud in his suddenly tomb-like office.

The dark silence was complete, pressing in around him like some giant living being attempting to swallow him whole. The only difference was that the crushing vacuum of open space hadn't killed him.

Vince took a breath that still smelled faintly of Bella's floral perfume and strained his ears, trying to determine if even the ever-present thrum of the space station's engines had ceased. In the more than ten years he'd lived aboard Zyga Space Station, he had never ever experienced a power disruption.

Just then, the Station's emergency backup system kicked in and gravity reasserted its hold. Vince's rear end thumped back into his chair. The furniture in his office made muffled thuds as everything fell a centimeter or two to the floor. Something ceramic made an awful cracking sound and the scene of fresh aloe vera filled the office.

At the same time, tiny red emergency lights flared to life along the edges of the beige carpet covering the deck. They cast an eerie red glow over everything, lending a perspective to his office Vince could honestly say he'd never seen before. At the same time, the two massive holoscreens he'd hung on opposite walls to keep his small office from seeming claustrophobic switched back on, displaying an emergency message Vince had never seen before.

He glanced to his right at the large glass window that separated his office from the enclosed boulevard outside. Lines of red lights appeared along either side of the boulevard. Dark shadows made the lights blip in and out as the pedestrians who had been traveling along the boulevard scattered in a panic. It looked like the power had gone out in most—if not all—of Level 7.

Still clutching his comlink to his ear, the Finder then glanced over at Bella. His assistant stared back at him, her almond-shaped eyes wide with shock. Half of her ivory, heart-shaped face was splashed red, and the other half lay in shadow. It was an odd effect;

it looked like half of her black hair and blunt-cut bangs had disappeared.

In her dark eyes, however, he saw reflected the same question running through his mind: what in the galaxy had happened?

Vince planted his feet flat on the deck and prepared to launch himself to his feet, but at that moment his client got over her shock and started shrieking hysterically into his ear. Wincing, Vince yanked his comlink away from his ear and held it out in front of him. The red glow from the emergency lights looked strange against the darkness of his skin. Dimly, he wondered if the red light made his black goatee and curly, close-shorn black hair look as strange as Bella's.

He didn't have time to think about that now, though. He finally stood up, unconsciously holding onto the edge of his desk as though he expected the grav generator to go on the fritz again.

Although, really, he thought in bemusement, *the desk isn't likely to help me much. It's not like it's bolted to the deck.*

His shock passed, and Vince started processing everything. Mrs. Kawana was still shrieking hysterically. She lived on Level 8 in Zone 2, so this power outage, whatever it was, was affecting at least two of Zyga Space Station's five spoke-like Zones.

That…was not good. Particularly since Zone 2 housed the Station's agricultural department.

"Mrs. Kawana, please." Vince kept his deep voice as calming as he could. "Breathe. Just breathe. It's going to be okay."

It took a moment before the woman could speak coherently—and not in an ear-shattering pitch. "What is going on? Why is the power out?"

"Are the emergency lights on where you are?"

Instead of reassuring his client, this only set her off again. "Of *course* the emergency lights are on! They're *supposed* to be on when something like this happens! But why is this happening? What is going on?" She barely seemed to be even drawing breath.

A soft snicker drew Vince's attention sideways, just in time to see Bella clap a hand over her mouth. Her long fingernails glinted reddish-silver in the emergency lights. She raised expressive eyebrows at Vince as though to say, *Is she for real?*

Vince rolled his eyes. Mrs. Kawana's stream of borderline hysterical comments and questions continued. He opened his mouth, preparing to find a good spot to cut in and take control of the conversation again, but at that moment the glow panels in the overhead flickered back to life.

Blinking in the sudden wash of warm golden light, Vince focused his attention on the deck beneath his feet. Even through the beige carpet, he thought he felt the faint vibration that signaled the Station's engines were functioning properly.

It could have been his imagination. He wasn't completely sure you could even *feel* that vibration out in the Zones, away from the Core, the center of the space station.

Mrs. Kawana drew in a sharp, sudden breath—and Vince knew the power was back on in Zone 2 as well. Crisis averted.

At least temporarily.

"The power—it's back!" she cried exuberantly. "I—"

"Mrs. Kawana," Vince cut across her. "I'm glad you're all right. Thank you for all the information you've given me. I will keep you posted on my investigation. Now, if you'll excuse me, I have other clients to attend to."

The Finder barely gave her time to stutter some sort of acquiescence before he ended the transmission. He then dropped his comlink on the jade green surface of his desk and turned to his assistant.

Bella sat at her desk, one hand still flattened on its matching green surface as though she thought she could somehow hold it down by sheer force. She looked as unnerved as Vince felt.

If she'd still been human, he was sure she'd be breathing heavily, one hand pressed to her chest. But Bella wasn't strictly human anymore, and so little things like unconscious physiological responses no longer applied to her.

"What was that?" she asked, her voice higher-pitched than usual.

Vince suppressed a wince. Okay, make that *most* unconscious physiological responses. He'd once seen Bella literally shatter glass with her voice; they didn't need a repeat.

Bella shook her head, the movement making her long, shiny black hair glint under the light from the glowpanel. "I've lived here my entire life and I've never seen the Station lose power before."

"Never?" Vince stared at her, his mind working furiously. He'd only been here a little over a decade. "Ever?"

"No." Bella shook her head again, a little too enthusiastically. For somebody who'd been transported into an android shell against her will, she had handled the transition fairly well, but there were still moments when her lack of full control showed. "Not in my lifetime."

Well, that was interesting. Vince blew out a considering breath, his client and her missing heirloom temporarily forgotten. "Then you know the media will be all over this."

He kept abreast of Zyga Station News, but he didn't often watch the news feed. The official narrative was helpful, but there were many times he needed information from people in parts of Zyga Space Station the media would never cover.

Rubbing his goatee, which was bristling, Vince wondered what category this power outage would fall under. He turned to one of the holoscreens mounted on the wall to his left.

Only one way to find out.

ABOUT THE AUTHOR

E. R. Paskey fell in love with mysteries and science fiction and all their possibilities at a young age. She is the author of twelve books, including the *Finder* series and a Christian space opera series, *The Guardians*. She currently lives in Southern Indiana with her husband and their five children.

You can find her website at: erpaskey.com.